THE WOMAN WHO WOULDN'T DIE

Also by Colin Cotterill

The Dr. Siri Series
The Coroner's Lunch
Thirty-Three Teeth
Disco for the Departed
Anarchy and Old Dogs
Curse of the Pogo Stick
The Merry Misogynist
Love Songs from a Shallow Grave
Slash and Burn

The Jimm Juree Series
Killed at the Whim of a Hat

THE WOMAN WHO WOULDN'T DIE

COLIN COTTERILL

First published in Great Britain in 2013 by
Quercus
55 Baker Street
7th Floor, South Block
London W1U 8EW

Published in the United States in 2013 by
Soho Press, Inc.
853 Broadway
New York, NY 10003

Library of Congress Cataloging-in-Publication Data

Cotterill, Colin.
The woman who wouldn't die / by Colin Cotterill.
p. cm.
ISBN 978-1-61695-206-8 (alk. paper)
eISBN: 978-1-61695-207-5
1. Paiboun, Siri, Doctor (Fictitious character)—Fiction.
2. Coroners—Fiction. 3. Clairvoyants—Fiction. 4. Laos—Fiction.
5. Mystery fiction. I. Title.
PR6053.O778W66 2013
823'.914—dc23 2012038332

Interior design by Ellipsis Digital Limited, Glasgow

Printed in the United States of America

10 9 8 7 6 5 4 3 2 1

Thanks to Polly, Steve, Robert, Scott, Kiang, Ali, Denny, Mac, Jim, Jane, Clair Voyant and Liz. And to my readers, Bambina, David, Kay, Lizzie, Dad, Michaela, Brother John, Tony, Leila, Kye, Rachel and Tang.

Contents

1

The Used-To-Be Woman

Madame Keui was flesh and blood, or so they claimed, although nobody could remember touching that re-warmed flesh, nor seeing her bleed; not even when a second bullet passed through her. Even so, to all intents and purposes, she was alive in October of 1978 when this story takes place. They'd see her walk along the ridge to collect her groceries or ride her bicycle off into the forest. Some in the village had even heard her speak. She had become Vietnamese, they said. Her Lao was thick with it like too-large lumps of mutton in a broth. She no longer talked directly to the villagers, but strangers from afar came to seek her out. They'd go to her house, a fine wooden structure with expensive Chinese furniture; couples and elderly people and families with children. They'd sit with her in the living area visible from the quiet dirt street. And when they left, those strangers would seem elated as if a heavy rock had been removed from their souls. But when the villagers stopped them to ask what had happened there, they were silent. It was as if they'd forgotten they were ever with her.

And perhaps that was why they called her Keui: Madame Used-To-Be. Because whenever they talked about the beautiful old woman it was in the past tense. 'There used to be a woman who spoke with many voices.' 'There used to be a woman who seemed to get younger as the months passed.' 'There used to be a woman whose house gave off a warm yellow glow even when there was no hurricane lamp oil to be had at the market.' And even though they might have passed her on the street that morning, at the evening meal they'd still say, 'There used to be a woman in our village who . . .'

And perhaps that was because two months earlier they'd carried her body to the pyre and watched the flames engulf her.

2

The Ninjas From Housing

They lurked in the shadows of the late evening. They'd waited out three nights of diamante skies, the streets lit by a billion stars. And, at last, a bank of clouds had rolled in and given them this brief cover. There were five of them, each dressed in navy blue, which was as near as damn it to black. And in the starless navy blue of the Vientiane night they would have been invisible were it not for the battery-powered torches each carried. The beams negated all the preparations of dressing darkly and applying charred cork to their faces. But in the suburbs east of the That Luang monument there was as yet no street lighting and there were any number of potholes in which to step. At eleven p.m. most of the householders were asleep and dreaming of better times. For any times were better than these. Only one or two windows gave off an eerie khaki glow from lamps deep inside and one by one these were extinguished as the men passed. Torch beams as loud as klaxons. Everyone in East That Luang knew something was about to go down and they all knew better than to come to their windows to watch.

Still a block away from their objective, the leader crouched on one knee and signalled for his men to turn off their lamps. They were immediately plunged into the impenetrable black belly of a giant naga. None of them dared move for fear that the earth all around them might have subsided. Yet, not wanting to be considered cowardly, none of them turned his torch back on. So there they remained. Petrified by the darkness.

'Give your eyes a few minutes, lads,' the leader said in a whisper that seemed to ricochet back and forth through the concrete of the new suburb.

Those few minutes crawled past but still the men's eyes had not become accustomed to the dark. Even so, their leader stood. They heard the rattle of the large bunch of keys on his belt. They knew it was time to continue the advance on house number 22B742. Butterflies flapped inside them. This would be a moment from which careers were honed. Medals were given for less.

They kept close in single file behind the leader who seemed to have a nose for darkness. Up ahead, their target emerged from the night. The house glowed brazenly. Candles flickered in the two front windows and . . . could that be the scent of a tune? Yes. Music. Some decadent Western rubbish. The comrades inside were asking for trouble. Begging for it. They'd get what they deserved this night. The front yard was visible now in the candle glow and the men could see one another's beady eyes. The leader pointed.

'You and you, around the back,' he whispered. 'Don't let any escape. We take every last man, woman and child.'

The two men ran to the side alley with a crouching gait not unlike that of Groucho Marx. But their flank advance was stymied by the fact that the side gate was locked, or blocked, or perhaps it was just a fence that looked like a gate and was too high to climb. They looked back for advice from their leader but he couldn't see them in the shadows. Believing the rearguard to be in place, he led the rest of his team up the garden path to the front porch. He was no lover of these room-ridden, occidental-style accommodations. Give him open spaces any day. He reached the door. He had a duplicate key, of course, for number 22B742 but it served no purpose. The door was ajar. He swallowed a gasp and pushed against the heavy teak. The door opened far too obligingly on oiled hinges and if not for a sudden lunge to stop its swing it would have crashed into the hallway wall.

The flutter of candlelight shimmied from open doorways to the left and right, and up ahead a room he knew from previous visits to be the kitchen was shining brightly. That was the source of the decadent music. And that, he knew, was where the transients would be gathered. They'd attempt to flee through the back door and into the trap he had laid. From his side pack he produced a Russian Lubitel 166. Not the most compact piece of equipment but efficient and easy enough to reload. There would be no mistakes this time. He would have them all.

Meanwhile, the two men sent to the back had retraced their steps and were now attempting to round the building on the east side. This too was a problem because they were met by a dog, an ugly, mean-spirited dog who stood and snarled. Drool dripped from its fangs. The men stopped in their tracks. They had reached the rear kitchen window through which a bright light shone on to their uncomfortable situation. Fortunately the dog was chained and beneath the window was a motorcycle. By climbing on to its seat they were able to both avoid the dog and see inside the house. Just as their heads appeared at the mosquito screen, the leader and his two men burst into the kitchen.

'Freeze!' shouted the leader and there was a flash, then another from his camera. 'Don't anybody . . .'

But there were no transients in the kitchen, just a solitary old man. He was standing naked in a large zinc bathtub. He was up to his shins in bubbly water and held a particularly impressive loofah. Far from being shocked or embarrassed, the old man laughed, turned away from the men, and loofahed his backside with enthusiasm.

'Search him,' shouted the leader. There was no rush to do so. 'Search all the rooms, the closets, the cupboards, the crawl space beneath the roof.'

His head turned in response to some slight movement through the window screen where he saw the faces of the two men who should have been watching the garden.

'What are you doing there?' he shouted.

One of the men waved. The other said, 'There's a dog.'

'Idiots,' said the leader.

'Now that's the kind of sight I'd have gladly sacrificed my left arm – all right, perhaps my gardener's left arm – to see,' said Comrade Civilai. In his two years since stepping down from the Lao politburo he had sold his soul to the kitchen. The post-politico Civilai outweighed the bald, skinny central committee member (who had maintained his trim weight by disagreeing with almost every decision the politburo made) by some six kilos.

'Preferably from the point-of-view of Siri,' he added. 'I can't say I have any great desire to know what the little doctor looks like in the buff.'

His comment was greeted with a round of laughter. As was now the custom, the group had met at Madame Daeng's noodle shop after closing time on Wednesday evening. It was the rare appointment all of them made the effort to keep and was often the only opportunity they had to catch up on one another's news. Recently there had been absences. Civilai off chairing cooperative meetings in the provinces. Inspector Phosy burning the midnight beeswax poring over some crime or other. And Dr Siri Paiboun, now into the third week of retirement from his post of national and only coroner, off getting, as he put it, 'cleansed'. He'd been invited to attend fourteen sessions of 'debriefing and reaffirmation of political stance' seminars. These were purportedly compulsory for senior government officials heading into retirement. To keep everyone happy he'd haggled the number down to three. The official running the seminars had had enough of him after the first session and didn't invite him back after the second. Siri was thus officially disencumbered of Party obligations.

'Exactly where did you hide everyone?' Nurse Dtui asked. Her baby, Malee, was gurgling happily on her lap.

'Huh. Hi . . . hi . . . hiding people. That's a good joke,' grinned Mr Geung.

'And it's information that will only be released on a need-to-know basis,' said Siri.

'So much for the one-for-all, all-for-one policy,' said Civilai. 'I thought we shared everything.'

He raised his glass of rice whisky which was joined in the air by four more. Mr Geung and baby Malee had yet to develop the habit.

'To sharing,' he said.

'Good luck,' said Madame Daeng.

'Good luck,' repeated them all.

They downed their drinks and Daeng set about refilling the glasses.

'It's true, older brother,' Siri agreed. 'We do share everything. And this knowledge will also be broadcast. But not just yet. As it stands, disclosing the location would cause a conflict of interest to one of our number.'

'Meaning me,' said Inspector Phosy, surreptitiously holding Nurse Dtui's hand beneath the table, an uncommon gesture between a man and his wife in those parts. It was a habit he had picked up from Siri and Daeng who displayed their affection openly.

'And meaning you've done something illegal ... again,' he added.

'I'm shocked and stunned,' said Siri. 'But if that were indeed the case, you should be grateful I'm keeping my mouth shut. Though tell me, how serious a crime could a frail old man commit?'

This comment was met with a chorus of groans for they all knew that Dr Siri and the law were old adversaries. And, technically, they were all breaking the regulations just by being there that night. All told, assuming a two-year-old counted as a whole person, there were seven of them present. Any meeting of a non-familial group consisting of more than five members was obliged to be accompanied by a certificate of assembly which could be obtained after a long wait at the department of Meetings and Appointments. This was one of the many red ribbons wound around the population of socialist Laos. If the group hadn't carried the weight it did they would surely have been reported by one of the neighbourhood spies, perhaps a member of the youth movement. But carry some weight it did. Siri and Civilai had accumulated over eighty years of membership of the Communist party between them. Madame Daeng was also owed a great deal by the old men in power. She had been in Vientiane only one year. In that time she had pursued and wed Dr Siri, established the most popular noodle shop in the capital, and helped to solve a number of mysteries that had baffled many. The sixty-seven-year-old had skills far more reaching than the perfect combining of spices and herbs. Hers was a secret past that few in the capital knew of.

Also in the restaurant was Mr Geung, a proud flag-bearer for the ranks of Down's syndrome. Until recently he had worked as the most able morgue assistant. But, upon Siri's retirement, and the official closure of that establishment, Mr Geung had been bound for the red tag bag room – the hospital laundry where all the unspeakable body parts and waste were separated from the linens. In a daring last-minute rescue, Siri had brought Mr Geung to Daeng's shop where he served noodles and made delicious coffee with a full three centimetres of condensed milk in each glass.

Inspector Phosy, as he had done many times before, pretended not to have heard of Dr Siri and his illegal activities. In a country without a constitution or a body of laws, the term 'illegal' was debatable anyway. He had to admit he could thank this group for some of the fluffiest feathers in his cap. Their victories in the field of crime suppression had propelled him to the rank of

Senior Head of Crime Division – Political Branch. This was a promotion accompanied by a monthly rise in salary of 400 *kip* – about a dollar fifty – a metal filing cabinet and his own garden rake.

His wife, Nurse Dtui, also left in limbo by the closure of the Mahosot Hospital morgue, had finally been transferred to the old Lido Hotel which now housed the National School of Nursing. She was teaching basic physiology and Russian language. The former because she had seen and handled more internal organs than anyone else on the staff. The latter because, until her untimely pregnancy, she had been on her way to the Eastern bloc to become qualified in a field in which she already excelled – forensic pathology. With Malee rocking back and forth in a small hammock at the front of the classroom, she would attempt to explain Russian grammar to young hill-tribe girls who barely understood Lao.

'Just to put our minds at ease, little brother,' said Civilai, 'you haven't done away with them all, have you? Sacrificed them so the Housing Department wouldn't get its greasy hands on them?'

'They're all alive and well,' said Siri.

'All eleven of them,' said Daeng.

'Eleven? Ah, I knew it.' Civilai nodded his head. 'You've been putting together a football team. Secretly training them at your house.'

'Just providing a home for the homeless,' said Siri. 'Taking in waifs and strays.'

'I've warned you about this,' said Inspector Phosy. 'How many times have I warned you? Our Party can handle it. There's a policy to–'

'There's a policy to clear people off the streets by whatever means is available.' Siri raised his voice. 'Cram them into crowded little rooms with no services just to make the place look neater. The temples are full of such people. I have a perfectly good house over there in That Luang provided by the committee. It has running water and electricity – once they've worked out how to connect it. What's so wrong with allowing my fellow human beings to share in my good fortune?'

'The fact that you don't live there, for one,' said Phosy. 'You live here above the shop. The truth is you shouldn't even have been allocated an official residence.'

'I'm a senior Party member,' said Siri.

He stood and put his hand on his heart. Madame Daeng and Civilai laughed and followed suit. Civilai began to hum 'La Marseillaise'.

'I am a seasoned field surgeon having survived some five hundred campaigns,' said Siri. 'I was educated in France and I speak three languages.'

'Four if you include double-Dutch,' said Civilai.

Siri ignored him. 'I am an advisor to prime ministers and presidents – a man loved and admired by the masses. I deserve my house and, damn it, I should be allowed to decide what I do with it. If I so wish to cover it in ice cream and lick it, that is my prerogative.'

Mr Geung clapped loudly.

'They'll find them you know,' said Phosy. 'You can't get away with hiding eleven people in this day and age.'

'I bet you I can,' Siri said.

3

The Man With a Star on His Forehead

'Ah, Siri,' said Judge Haeng. With his pimples and watery eyes and green safari shirt, the prematurely middle-aged man looked more like a frog at a desk than the head of the Public Prosecution Department. He stood and offered his hand to the white-haired doctor but, as always, avoided staring into his deep green eyes. He'd had nightmares about those eyes sucking him inside that cantankerous old head full of horrible things. Siri gave a cursory shake to the outstretched hand because he knew this show of politeness came as a result not of love for his fellow man but of blackmail. The doctor was a collector of news, you see. He had the goods on a number of senior officials gleaned from eve-of-battle confessions, records of embarrassing medical procedures, and access to official government files written in French, which few in the ruling Pathet Lao could read. He had come across information that, should it fall into the wrong hands, might signal the end of the judge's very comfortable lifestyle. It might even lead to a spell of re-education in a distant province from which many did not return.

Judge Haeng was the type of man who would happily arrange for an accident to befall a blackmailer. But Siri was the cordon bleu of blackmailers. All his news was stored in a number of 'Open in the event of my untimely death' metal deposit boxes in Laos and overseas, a fact that all his victims were made aware of from the outset. A fact that was a total fabrication. They were under his mattress. Apart from his wife, nobody else knew this tasty information. But Siri used this weapon not for evil or for financial gain, but for good. There was nothing like a little incentive to keep a government official on the straight and narrow.

'I . . . er . . . read your complaint,' said Haeng. 'I haven't yet submitted it to the Ministry of the Interior.'

'Well, what are you waiting for?' Siri asked. 'You've had it three days.'

'I know. I know and I'm sorry. I just . . . Why don't you take a seat?'

Siri remained standing.

'I was just wondering whether you might reconsider,' said the judge.

'What's to reconsider? I'm taking a bath in the comfort of my own house when suddenly this army of nincompoops led by a midget comes charging in. And Shorty flashes his camera at my private parts, no less. I half expect to find my image pinned to every telegraph pole across the city.'

'Siri, Comrade Koomki is just short of stature. If he were legally a midget he wouldn't have been given the role of Head of Housing Allocations.'

Siri raised his bushy eyebrows and shook his head. What was going on in the mind of this Soviet-trained bureaucrat?

'Judge,' he said, 'I don't care whether he's legally a midget or not. What I care about is that he invaded my house and my privacy. He deserves to lose his job. I'm entitled to make an official complaint.'

'It could be . . . embarrassing.'

'The redder the faces the better.'

'I don't know. I suppose I could be inclined to submit it . . .'

'Good.'

'I could be inclined to submit it . . . if you could see your way to lending your country a hand just one more time.'

'What?'

'Lending a hand.'

'A man has only so many hands, Judge. Would you accept a finger?'

'Now, Siri, there's no need for that attitude. Until his final breath, a good socialist will always have enough oxygen to give resuscitation to a drowning comrade. No matter how choppy the sea. I'm well aware of the services you have selflessly performed for our nation. But I know too how much you enjoy the occasional junket. These little trips around the country at the expense of the committee.'

'I'm retired.'

'A perfect time to see the sights. A few days in a scenic guest house. One or two cold beers and good food. You could take Madame Daeng along. Call it a second honeymoon.'

Siri hesitated.

'Where to?'

'Sanyaburi. The boat races at Pak Lai.'

'The races were last month.'

'Down here they were. It's up to the cadre in charge in each province when the workers would most benefit from a few days of joy and recreation. Luang Prabang doesn't have theirs until November.'

'I don't know. On my last junket I was caught in the middle of a massacre. The one before that I was tortured and left for dead. Joy and recreation seem to have escaped me somehow.'

'This will be different, Siri. A couple of hours of work then you're free to stay as long as you like to enjoy the countryside. You can take the two-tier ferry up there and hop on one coming back.'

'What's the catch?'

'You're always such a sceptic. Why should there be a catch? You'd merely be there as a . . . what shall we call it? An observer. This would really be easier if you'd take a seat.'

Siri remained standing.

'An observer of what?'

'Something quite ridiculous, to be honest. Even so, I wouldn't doubt it's right up your alley.'

'What alley might that be?'

'Oh, you know. Ghosts and the like.'

'Why should I be hanging around in any alleyways with ghosts?'

'Come on, Siri. There are those who believe you like to dabble in the supernatural.'

'Nonsense.'

'That's what I tell them. He's a man of science, I say. There is no place for superstition in the mind of a medical man. But you know what this place is like for rumours. Even the Minister of Justice seems to think you might enjoy this ghost hunt.'

Siri sat. The rickety wooden chair creaked beneath him. He considered standing again.

'And whose ghost might I be hunting?'

'The brother of the Minister of Agriculture.'

'Really? And who exactly is the Minister of Agriculture this month?'

It was a response that would normally have caused Haeng to reprimand the doctor for his lack of respect for the longevity of government appointments. But, with so much resting on the success or failure of the current farming cooperative programme, the role of minister in charge of such a mess was something of a revolving door.

'General Popkorn,' said Haeng.

Siri sighed. He knew them all. Natural commanders in the field of battle and clueless behind a desk.

'Go on,' he said.

'His brother was presumed killed in a covert military operation. They never retrieved the body. The general's wife is Vietnamese and she believes there's disquiet amongst the ancestors because her brother-in-law is unsettled and that's causing problems in the family. Personally I think the family problems are caused by the fact she's a nasty cow but don't quote me on that. She believes the brother wants to come home and be afforded his just rites.'

'Where was he presumed to have died?'

'Hmm. That's not such an easy one to answer. He was operating under cover, mostly organizing guerrilla attacks on royalist-held bases. The last dispatch they got from him was from Luang Prabang in June 1969. There were suggestions he might have been discovered and killed there. But there was no mention of him in royalist reports.'

'If he was under cover they wouldn't have known who he was. I doubt he'd have been carrying his citizen identification card.'

'That's true.'

'Then he could have died anywhere.'

'Also true.'

'Then how on earth are they going to return his body if they don't know where it is?'

'The minister's wife – and feel free to laugh at this – has hired a witch.'

'Does she come with a broomstick?'

'What?'

'Never mind.'

Civilai was perhaps the only person in Laos who got all of Siri's funny lines. Haeng got none of them. Not even the ones that were culturally inclusive.

'Tell me about the witch,' said Siri.

'The locals call her Madame Keui – the used-to-be woman. She's what they call a *ba dong*,' said Haeng. 'She claims to be able to locate the bodies of soldiers killed in battle. They say she's good. Give her an object that belonged to the departed one and she'll draw you a map to where his remains are. It's all nonsense of course but the minister obviously has no control over his wife and she's insistent. She dragged her husband off for a meeting with the witch last weekend. The old woman did some mumbo-jumbo incense burning gobbledegook, performed a couple of magic party tricks and hey presto, they're both sucked in. According to the witch the body's a few kilometres upriver from Pak Lai.'

'That's two hundred kilometres from Luang Prabang.'

'He escaped by boat, she says. Succumbed to his injuries before he could get to a qualified medic. It's not clear where he got off the boat. A lot of the river round there is deep in jungle. No settlements. It appears that's where the mystic radio waves ran into some interference.' He laughed at his own cleverness. 'That's why the witch needs to go there and take a look for herself.'

'Good grief. You're sending me on holiday with a witch?'

'You don't need to have any direct dealings with her. Just wait around. On the off chance she turns up with a body, you do the examination.'

'Why is it that people hand me bones and expect me to know whether the skeleton was a paid-up member of the local trade union?'

'I've made it easy for you, Siri. Major Ly, that's the name of the brother, had been injured in a grenade explosion a year before he disappeared. He'd had work done in Hanoi to put his chin back together. There's a screw in his jaw. The doctor was Cuban. He kept records and an X-ray. I'll have them for you before you go.'

'You seem confident I'll agree to all this.'

'Ah, Siri. You're a curious man. Retirement doesn't suit you at all. You love mysteries like this.'

'I don't know. I'll see what Madame Daeng says.'

'That's the spirit. A good soldier–'

'Right. I've had my socialist maxim for the day already. When's the supposed departure?'

'Thursday. I know you'll do the right thing.'

Siri stood and considered his next action carefully. Then he reached into his shoulder bag and produced an envelope which he handed to the judge.

'What's this?' asked Haeng.

'It's a letter from some judge asking the US consulate if he can have a condominium overlooking the Pacific in exchange for the odd secret.'

'I . . .'

'It's the original. I didn't make any copies. I'd hurry up and burn it if I were you.'

Siri rode his bicycle home along Fahngoum Road. Ugly the dog trotted behind him. It was a remarkably fine day. There was a cool breeze off the Mekhong and the sky was, at last, the colour of the airport: Wattay blue. It still seemed to be the only paint colour available in the city. The small maggot blooms along the roadside were a wash of colours but smelt like vomit. To his right, every other shop and restaurant he passed was padlocked and shuttered. The river road had been a happier place when the Americans ruled the roost. Beer and girls and loud music that lurched across the river and collided with loud music from Thailand. Now, on the Lao side, the cicada male voice choir was the loudest sound you could expect. Vientiane was a green city. That isn't to say a Western-type city with sporadic outbreaks of controlled vegetation, but a forest of a city with big sprawling trees along the roadways and patches of jungle that would one day give themselves up to development – but not without a fight. The plants ruled and, thanks to them, the city breathed. The street was paved but covered in mud and there were no cleaners to dig down to the concrete. Siri's tyres left slalom grooves. His was the only transport on the road.

He caught a brown flash of movement low on the bank of the river. At first he thought it was an animal.

A wild cat. But as he squinted against the bright sun Siri could see that it was a man. Naked. Indian. He seemed to be tracking the squeaky bicycle like a jungle predator. Hopping from bush to bush. Crazy Rajid had apparently arrived at the belief that if he were undressed he would be invisible. If anyone spotted him he could merely freeze in position certain that he had blended into the surroundings. He was Vientiane's own street person. Mad as a sack of rats. Unpredictable. Uncommunicative. Yet with a frozen pond of skills Siri had only just broken the surface of. He waved at the loping vagabond. Crazy Rajid froze in position. Siri looked around as if wondering where he'd gone. Rajid's face broke into a vast white smile.

Siri laughed. It had been a fun day. He'd left the judge gaping like a mortar wound to the chest. He hadn't really expected a 'thank you'. Giving him back his letter had been a difficult decision to make. By holding on to it, the doctor could have kept the man chained indefinitely. The official would continue to be polite and efficient and respectful to his elder. But, to be honest, where was the fun in that? Since their first meeting in 1975, the year the Communists took over the country, the year Siri was railroaded into a job he didn't want, Judge Haeng had been a wonderful nemesis. Incompetent but wielding great power. Awash with misguided self-confidence. Slippery as a freshly peeled mango. Judge Haeng had been the face of the Party. Siri couldn't break the Party, but my word he could break the face. That's why he'd released the judge from his spell. He wanted the battle to continue.

And what joy this new mission offered. A witch, no less. A woman who could trace the dead. He'd heard of them, the *ba dong*. There were many in Vietnam. There had been incredible stories. A rescue team directed by map to a remote mountainous crop and to within a metre of a shallow grave. Nothing visible above the surface. This was the world that Siri was inadequately a part of. In spite of his own common sense and his medical training, he was well aware that he hosted the spirit of a thousand-year-old shaman. His scientist self had immediately fallen into a fit of denial. He'd argued himself silly that possession was biologically impossible. He'd attributed his visions to dreams, to drunken hallucinations, to heatstroke. But after some time, when the spirits began to make direct communication, supernature and nature collided unmistakably. He was left with no alternative argument. There was, without a shadow of a doubt, a spirit world. And once his stubborn streak had let go of his prejudices, they came. In ones and twos at first, leaving clues. Making efforts to establish a two-way link. He saw them. He heard them too, albeit in a tinny second-hand form through his own mind. He even felt the icy blades of the malevolent few who wanted his resident shaman annihilated. And the more he believed, the more he saw. In their hundreds on the old battlefields. In their tens of thousands in Cambodia. And it came to the point where they were as much a part of his landscape as his wife Daeng, and his friends, and everything else he had come to see as normal.

But there was a blockage. He didn't know where the main pipeline to the afterlife was clogged or how to clear it, but he still could not conduct any two-way conversations with his visitors. It was as if he were on one bank of the Mekhong and they were over there on the Thai side. They're waving and shouting but he can't hear. And so they resort to pantomime. Charades for the hard-of-channelling. Most of the time he didn't get it. He had no idea what they were trying to tell him. When a murder case was resolved by more scientific means he would look back over his dreams and his encounters and slap his ever-bruised forehead. 'So that's what they meant.' It was like looking at the filled-in crossword on the solutions page of *Le Figaro*.

He was tired of guessing. He needed a tutor. He believed that, like the sciences, the super-sciences could be learned from an expert. He'd met one such seer: Auntie Bpoo the transvestite fortune-teller. One had to look beyond her sumo build and her penchant for the type of clothing one might see in Pigalle late in the evening. He-she had the direct line. There was no question. He-she could have taught Siri everything. But he-she, and she preferred to be referred to as she, was a most exasperatingly certifiable human being. Siri had recently hounded her for tutorials but she had been occupied to the point of unavailability by 'the do'.

Fortune-tellers, if they're worth anything at all, should be able to see everything. Auntie Bpoo had seen her own demise. She knew the date and the time and she had been planning a Phasing Away party in memoriam of herself. For the past month she'd been preparing for the evening – for, luckily, she would be dying at approximately nine p.m. – by handwriting invitations and working on a menu. And, naturally, there was the costume. A girl had to go out on a high fashion note. Siri had begged – not something he did willingly – for some insights, but she had dismissed him with fortune cookie comments such as, 'Under a full moon all is clear.' He wanted to strangle her but he knew she'd see it coming. She would be phasing away, with or without his help, at nine p.m. on the fourth Tuesday in October, which wasn't a full moon night at all.

But here was an even better chance. A ghost whisperer. A witch. More likely a sorceress or a spirit medium, but with enough of a track record to win over a cynical Lao general. A few days away together on the Mekhong. Enough time to probe her mind. Perhaps Madame Keui, the used-to-be woman, would be the medium to take his hand and lead him through the teak doors to the beyond.

'He'll be sleeping with you next,' said Daeng.

She was on her bamboo recliner in front of the shop shelling peas. She had 'the smile'. It was a different smile to the one that greeted her husband in their bed every morning and welcomed the customers to the restaurant. This one came to her unnaturally, care of the opium she took to fight off the ravages of rheumatism. Siri had attempted to guide her to less addictive pain relief but, having seen the misery in her eyes, he no longer begrudged her. He shared the sigh of relief when the demons let go of her joints for a few hours.

'No danger of that,' said Siri climbing down from the one-speed Chinese Pigeon. 'Ugly is an outside dog. He stands watch at the door then accompanies me to the next appointment. If I were accosted along the way he would bite off the leg of the attacker. If I were stabbed in my sleep he would shrug and leave it all up to the police. He's never been inside a building. Doesn't trust 'em.'

'He told you all that?'

'We dogs have an innate understanding. How was lunch?'

'Crowded. I'm not sure what we'll do with all this money I'm making.'

'Madame Daeng, you charge so little and add so many exotic but expensive ingredients, we average one *kip* profit on each bowl of noodles. In another five years we'll be able to buy a teapot.'

'People have to eat.'

'That's the UN's job. Feeding the hungry. We are a business. They're all hooked now. It's time to cash in on the addiction and double the price. Start raking in those *kip*. Put in a pool. Drive German cars.'

'You've been listening to Thai radio again.'

'They all have spin driers over there, Daeng.'

'We could always sell your Triumph. A lot of Soviet advisors come by to look at it.'

'They will not touch my motorcycle. It's a classic, as are you. Could you see me signing you over to a Soviet advisor and watch him ride you off into the distance?'

'You never use it.'

'I do. I shall. It's there for emergencies. This flightless Pigeon is just my back-up. Exercise. It helps me be a cog that runs in time to this city's clock. When we need speed we'll have my Triumph.'

'We can't afford the petrol.'

'That is exactly why you need to double the price of your noodles. It's time for us New Socialist Mankind to embrace old Capitalist thoughts. I know. Let's fire Mr Geung. He uses up far too much of our profits. He even has the nerve to eat free. That's the ticket. Retrenchment. Where is he?'

'Out the back,' she laughed. 'Naming the chickens.'

'Again? How are we supposed to chop their heads off and pluck 'em if they have personalities?'

'He likes them.'

'That's it. He's got to go.'

Siri, attempting to wipe the grin off his face, marched through the restaurant and into the small back yard. Mr Geung was squatting on the ground cuddling a chicken.

'Geung!'

'Yes, C . . . Comrade Doctor?'

'What are you doing with that chicken?'

'Talking.'

'Mr Geung. You do know tomorrow that chicken is going to be redistributed into the stomachs of a lot of hungry people?'

'I . . . kn . . . know.'

'And?'

Geung looked up at the one small cloud that travelled slowly over the yard.

'Her life is . . . is . . . is not so long like ours,' he said. 'I give her a name and a . . . a cuddle and she'll have ssssomething nice to remember from this life to . . . to . . . to take to the next.'

He had a tear in his eye. Siri sat on the dirt beside his friend. The concept of dignity was beyond Mr Geung but that was exactly what he was bestowing upon these temporary visitors. Mr Geung was giving the chickens status. Siri squeezed his hand.

'What's this one called?' he asked.

'Lenin.'

'All right. You win. I won't fire you.'

'Thank you.'

Geung still hadn't turned away from the cloud.

'Is there something interesting up there?'

'An old man.'

Siri looked up, half expecting to see a basket hanging from the cloud with a man in it.

'Where?'

'In the market. This ar ... ar ... afternoon. A *farang*.'

'Probably Soviet, Geung.'

'No. *Farang*.'

The Lao had divided the sparse Western community into two categories. On the one hand were the Soviets, which included every eastern European national. These were foreigners ill-suited to hot climates who were surprisingly easy to detect from their scent. On the other hand were the *farang* which incorporated everyone else with white skin. And they weren't always the sweetest either.

'He smelled like ointment,' said Geung.

'You got close enough to smell him?'

'Yes. Yes ... no. The market lady tol ... told me. I was far. And he spoke French. The market lady can unnnnderstand French.'

'And was there something special about this *farang*?' Siri asked.

'Yes.'

The cloud continued to fascinate.

'And are you going to tell me?' Siri asked.

'He's got ... got a star. On his hhhead. Here.'

He pointed to his forehead above his right eye.

'A tattoo?' Siri asked, even though he considered his own question ridiculous.

'No. A scar. He ... I saw it when he passed me. Not so easy to see. Bbbut I could see.'

'So you went to talk to the market lady.'

'Yes.'

'And she told you about the French.'

'Yes. And about Comrade Madame Daeng.'

Siri looked away from the cloud and into Geung's eyes.

'What about her?'

'That's why th . . . the . . . the Frenchman was in the market. He was asking where was Comrade Madame Daeng from the sssssouth.'

'It's a common name, Geung.'

'He wanted my Comrade Madame Daeng.'

'How do you know?'

'I know. Her ol . . . ol . . . old name, Keopakam. That's what he said. And it's not good news, Comrade Doctor. Nnnot good at all.'

There were as many Daengs in Laos as there were tea leaves in China. As there were spin driers in Thailand. But Siri was a believer in fate and instinct. If Geung had sensed something, there had to be a negative current that passed into him from the Frenchman. Judge Haeng's offer of a few days away, specifically mentioning Daeng, had to fit somehow into this karmic jigsaw puzzle. Siri had learned to his detriment that ignoring the fates was a terrible mistake.

'Fancy a holiday?' he asked his wife.

Daeng was sweaty and pink in the evening noodle rush. She leaned into the steam from the broth pot to swat away a persistent beetle.

'OK. Madrid,' she said.

'I wasn't actually offering you a choice of location.'

He held out the bowls as she gently scooped the noodles into the broth. Mr Geung took them from Siri and scurried off between the tables. It was as crowded as Paris St Germain in the rush hour but with no soundtrack. Great noodles left no room for conversation.

'So, where?' Daeng asked.

'How do you fancy Pak Lai?'

'Pak Lai, Sanyaburi?'

'The same.'

'What's there to do?'

'Boat races, beer, views, elephants, holding hands on a slow ferry upriver.'

'When?'

'Thursday.'

'All right.'

'Really?'

'Yes. We'll have to take Geung.'

'We will?'

'Of course. If we close the shop he'll be bored and miserable. And we invariably need back-up.'

'Why would we need back-up on a romantic cruise up the Mekhong?'

'Because we wouldn't be going if you hadn't been handed some impossible task that will toss us higgledy-piggledy into the slow-burning furnaces of the devils.'

'That was very poetic.'

'Bowls.'

'What?'

'Hold up the bowls.'

'Sorry.'

At the end of the early evening noodle shift Siri and Daeng partook of their late evening constitutional with Ugly trotting along behind. Siri was always aware of his wife's condition but Daeng invariably insisted they take their sundown stroll. They admired the shimmering reflections of Thai street lights that reached across the river like beggars. They passed the locked confectioners where they paused and pretended to buy strawberry ice-cream cones. Then, as if by chance, they walked two circuits of the French embassy compound which took up an entire block. The couple's instincts had different origins. Daeng's the gut feeling of a fighter. Siri's the subliminal screams and yelps from the beyond. But between them they were confident by the second lap that they had not been followed. They stopped beside the metal side gate on Rue Gallieni and Siri banged three times. For effect, he pretended to be tying his bootlaces as they waited. Daeng reminded him he was wearing sandals but he told her that from a spy blimp they'd not be able to see that clearly. The gate creaked open a slice and the couple slid inside the empty embassy.

France and Laos, you see, were having a ladies' tiff. It was the ultimate *porte-monnaie* slap fest. The French embassy in Vientiane had apparently been urging the upper classes to leave the country. Visas had been as easy to come by as tropical ulcers. In France, a Lao government in exile was being encouraged – if not openly supported – by the anti-communists. To the Pathet Lao administration this was starting to look a lot like the tacit support of a *coup d'état*. All the staff at the Vientiane embassy, including diplomats, had been banned from travelling further than three kilometres from the embassy compound. The French retaliated by restricting the Lao staff of their embassy in Paris to a three kilometre perimeter. This troubled the Lao more than the French as three kilometres from the Vientiane embassy was little more than rice fields, whereas the ban left the Lao diplomats as prisoners in the extortionately expensive inner suburbs of Paris. The Pathet Lao refused to accept any new diplomatic postings so the French closed their embassy and took their tricolour home. Thus the embassy compound, the zero kilometre mark for all road distances from Vientiane, became a ghost town.

Monsieur Seksan, the embassy caretaker, beamed and shook the hands of his visitors. He was a solid Lao with a fine paunch nurtured over thirty years of employment with the French civil service in Paris. He'd arrived in Europe aged two and naturally didn't have too many memories of his homeland, fond or otherwise. He'd spoken Lao at home with his nurse but was raised and educated a Frenchman. Despite claiming a first-class degree in law and having French citizenship, the man had been overlooked for promotion so many times he'd come to believe that nothing short of plastic surgery would put him on the diplomatic fast track. At first, when the foreign service had called him aside and offered him a posting at the embassy in Vientiane, he'd had ambassadorial flutterings. When he found out all the French embassy staff had been recalled in protest and that he'd be bouncing around like a single pea in a pod, he was not amused. In fact, he was pissed off.

Dr Siri was an acquaintance of Monsieur Seksan's father. They'd studied at the temple together. The young man had made contact as soon as he'd arrived in his alien homeland. His Lao was raw and his knowledge of Laos was fundamental, but Siri had welcomed the boy warmly. They drank together often. And in Siri, Monsieur Seksan found a man he could trust and he told him all his frustrations. So, it was only to be expected that when Siri sought refuge for Lao citizens who were being persecuted by the socialist doctrinaires, Seksan said he would be delighted to help. They'd arrived late one night, eleven of them. They were no trouble and had even brought their own instant noodles. In fact Seksan enjoyed the company. One of the refugees, a young lady recently returned from a failed venture in Thailand, had become particularly close. The embassy compound had turned into a village and Seksan was the headman. He had a real Lao family and was, day by day, strand by strand, discovering his roots.

'How's the team?' Siri asked.

'They're keeping me sane,' said Seksan.

He gave a respectful *nop* to Daeng who patted his cheek in response.

Technically, Siri's eleven refugees could have had a residence each in the sprawling compound. There were some twenty buildings including staff cottages and administration offices. In many of them the furniture was shrouded in dust covers dotted with mouse and lizard droppings like huge lumps of chocolate-chip vanilla ice cream. But the team preferred to bunk together in the visitors' dormitory rooms, a bungalow which had at one time housed the French horses. Mrs Fah's children, Mee and Nounou, were the first to spot Uncle Siri and Auntie Daeng. They sounded the alarm with their screams. Their mother followed with her two nieces recently returned from an unsuccessful spell across the river working as karaoke hostesses. Both Gongjai and Tong were adamant that the Japanese craze would never catch on. The blind beggar, Pao, and his granddaughter, Lia, were there as was Comrade Noo the ostracized Thai forest monk. Uncle Inthanet, a man of Siri's age, had not yet appeared but he'd found himself a girlfriend half his age and they spent a good deal of their time 'discussing' behind a closed door. Then there was the latest inmate, a tall, skinny middle-aged woman who could not remember her name. She had been walking aimlessly around the town for a week before Daeng confronted her and asked her where she was going. She could not remember that either. She carried no identification so Siri had taken her in and was waiting for the fog to clear.

After a round of cheek sniffs and handshakes and present giving, Siri and Daeng sat with Monsieur Seksan at a large wooden table in the chef's residence. A solid teak door at the far side of the room with several broken padlocks lying beside it opened on to a staircase which in turn led down to the cellar. The sign, *Passage Interdit*, had been ripped in half. Siri, Daeng and Monsieur Seksan were sampling the ambassador's personal 1958 Latour Pauillac. Siri found it rather amusing. Daeng said it was piss weak. Seksan could only laugh.

'What exactly do you plan to do when the embassy staff return and find the cellar empty?' Siri asked.

'Blame you bastards,' said the caretaker with a chuckle. 'Here I was, sitting down having my *petit déjeuner* one day when a gang of soldiers marched in and cleaned out the cellar. I'll show them the powder burns on my upturned palms where I tried to protest. "Take me but spare the wine of my ambassador," I had shouted. But to no avail.'

'We'd better set about clearing that cellar before the bastards get here,' said Siri.

'*Avec plaisir*,' said Seksan.

Perhaps unwisely, Siri had decided not to tell his wife anything he knew, or thought he knew, about the Frenchman at the market. He wanted to introduce the subject gently and observe her reaction. After all, there might have been nothing sinister about the visit at all. What if he was an old boyfriend who wanted to get in touch? Nothing wrong with that, he thought, although his teeth may have clenched at the idea.

'So, there aren't that many French tourists around town for you to look after,' he said.

'One or two might sneak in,' said Seksan. 'But we soon sniff them out and send them packing.'

'Oh, some survive,' said Siri. 'In fact our restaurant's maître d' spied one at the market today.'

'Geung didn't tell me that,' said Daeng.

'You work the poor man so hard I'm surprised he has a chance to speak at all,' said Siri. 'He told me during his down time while I was applying balm to the lash marks on his back. He'd seen a man about your age, he said. Tall. Good looking.'

'We're obviously starved of entertainment if the sight of a Frenchman at the market is the highlight of the day,' said Daeng.

'Ah, but Geung wasn't so impressed with his nationality as he was with the star over the man's right eye.'

There it was. Slight but you could make it out if you knew what you were looking for. Daeng had what they called in the West a poker face. Unless you studied that face the way Siri had every morning as he lay beside her, memorizing her tics and twitches when she spoke, you would never have noticed it. A shadow passed over her at pace and in under a second it was gone. But in that fraction of time, his wife had clearly travelled three hundred kilometres and thirty years.

'A star? What, you mean like a tattoo?' asked Seksan.

'No. Geung said it was more like a scar. I've seen a number of smallpox scars that resemble stars. I think that's what impressed Mr Geung.'

'What made him believe the man was French?' Daeng asked.

'Some of the market women told him,' said Siri. 'Why?'

'I might know him,' she said.

Siri felt a pang of jealousy as he watched the blood fill in his wife's cheeks.

'Perhaps he's come looking for you,' said Seksan.

'Perhaps,' said Daeng.

'I wonder if we can get in touch with him somehow?' Siri asked.

'I wonder,' said Daeng.

'Well,' said Seksan, 'we have nothing to do with the visas they hand out in France. In the days when there were people here to read them, the Lao embassy in Paris used to wire a list of the names of successful applicants and the projects they'd been invited to consult on. They'd get the odd tourist here but the visa process in Paris took so long it left everyone feeling Laos didn't want them. Which, in fact, is true. The Lao have put up a lot of red tape to make life hard for French entrepreneurs and opportunists to get in. The casual visitor would have fallen at the first hurdle.'

'So my friend at the market . . . ?' said Daeng.

'Would have come in some official capacity or paid baksheesh to sneak in.'

'Who handles consular matters for the French now the embassy's closed?' Daeng asked.

'The Germans.'

'Do you know anyone at the German embassy?' Siri asked.

'Everyone,' said Seksan. 'They're big party animals. When they found out I spoke German, they–'

'You speak German, too?' Siri asked.

'I have an ear.'

'I have two ears, but . . . Well, technically I have one and a half, but my language bank was full after Vietnamese.'

'The Germans?' said Daeng with some urgency.

'They're all as depressed to be here as I was,' said Seksan. 'I consoled them with a few bottles of Beaujolais.'

'So if we wanted to get hold of our mysterious Frenchman's visa details . . . ?' Siri asked.

Seksan smiled, reached for the telephone and dialled. After a baffling gabble of German language he put down the phone and said, 'We'll need another glass.'

Twenty minutes later, Stephan Bartels, the First Secretary of the Federal Republic of Germany's embassy, was banging on the side gate. He arrived with a large grey envelope and a bottle of Korn Schnapps for later. He was so frightfully handsome Siri edged closer to his wife. Seksan went through some sort of German greeting ritual and, in no time, a glass of white appeared in front of the visitor. Stephan gave them a brief introduction to himself through Seksan. He spoke fluent Spanish, he said, for which he'd expected a posting to South America. And he was fluent in English, and quite competent in Kiswahili which they agreed was as useful in Laos as a can opener in a coconut grove. This was why they were speaking through an interpreter.

Stephan opened the envelope in front of him and produced a fax. He explained the complicated process of obtaining a visa for Laos with the embassy in Paris closed. The applicant had to travel to another country which had an active embassy and apply from there; in this case the applicant had travelled to Thailand. But, due to strained relations between Laos and Thailand, the Lao embassy in Bangkok was not currently offering consular services. The French embassy in Thailand had to apply directly to the Ministry of Foreign Affairs in Vientiane if one of its citizens wished to travel to Laos. A copy of the application would be sent from there to the German embassy. Siri and Daeng were getting bored.

'So, is his photograph on the fax?' Daeng asked as she reached for the file.

'Sort of,' said Seksan. 'They have a Russian fax machine at the ministry. It makes all the photographs look like Jesse Owens. You'd certainly never forget this character if you saw him walking down the street.'

Daeng stared at the picture trying to see through the smudge of ink. It was true. He looked like the character on the Darkie toothpaste tube. You wouldn't recognize your own mother in a MoFA fax.

'According to the application, his name is Hervé Barnard and he's a consultant on the Swedish roads project down in Takek,' said Seksan. 'Judging by the date of the first contact he'd been waiting in Bangkok for his visa for almost a month. He's French, born in Marseille. Age sixty-six. Engineer. Single. Any of this ring a bell, Madame Daeng?'

She was still staring at the photograph.

'Where's the original application?' she asked.

'At the French embassy in Bangkok, I'd imagine.'

'Would they do a better job of faxing it here?'

'No doubt. I'll call them in the morning if I can get a line out.'

'Meanwhile, do you have any contacts at the Swedish roads project?' Siri asked.

'We might need another glass,' said Seksan.

In half an hour the SweRoad director, Lars Stiegsson was banging on the side gate. By then the white burgundy had given way to schnapps and the mood was light. The group had been joined by an exhausted Comrade Inthanet and his girlfriend, Bébé, and Seksan's young lady, Mrs Fah's niece, Tong. They cheered at Stiegsson's arrival. He was a wiry character with a shock of white hair. He carried a bottle of akvavit and an envelope. They all looked on in amazement as Seksan welcomed him and engaged in a long question-and-answer session in Swedish.

'I presume there are one or two languages you don't speak,' said Siri to Seksan as they were arranging the newcomer a seat and a glass.

'I never really had an ear for Cantonese,' said Seksan, suggesting that everything else was a piece of cake.

'So what about our visiting Frenchman?' Daeng asked.

To their delight, Stiegsson spoke reasonable Lao and he answered them directly.

'I've never heard of him,' he said. 'We haven't had any new consultants of any nationality for months.'

He opened his envelope and pulled out a letter.

'And I have some disturbing news for you. This letter was handed to me by my Lao counterpart at the Public Works Department. It is purportedly from me asking for the ministry to expedite the visa application of the same Hervé Barnard. There was a CV and job description attached. My Lao colleague told me yesterday that everything had been taken care of. The wheels of the system roll slowly here. I didn't write this letter. This is not my signature. Your friend Mr Barnard is an imposter.'

Siri and Daeng staggered along the river road arm in arm, each holding the other up. Ugly trotted along behind.

'So, what's the missing part of your story, my husband?' she asked.

'Why should there be anything missing?' he replied.

'You would make a terrible secret agent, Dr Siri. I can tell when you're holding something back from me just as I can tell when you find me irresistible but forget to inform me.'

'You know I always find you irresistible.'

'I need constant reminders.'

'I shall make a point of doing so.'

'And?'

'What?'

'He asked for me, didn't he?'

Once more, Siri was astounded at his wife's instincts.

'Yes,' he said. 'Should I be worried?'

'About being alone in the dark with me?'

'About Barnard.'

'Of course not.'

'But you think you know who he is.'

She was silent for a long time.

'I hope not,' she said.

'Were you lovers?'

Daeng stopped walking and swung around clumsily to face Siri.

'Why on earth would you say that?'

'I'm psychic.'

'You are not. You just carry spirits around. You're a . . . a suitcase.'

'I am certainly not a suitcase, madam. I have innate gifts. And I'm right, aren't I?'

'Do you really want this to be the moment that I

confess to the tens of thousands of men I've had in my bed?'

'No, only this one.'

'Why?'

'Because he's unsettled you. I've never seen you ruffled before.'

'Nonsense.'

She took his arm and they continued to stagger.

'Then why did you try so hard to get visa information on him?' Siri asked.

'A girl my age doesn't get too many men asking for her. I was flattered. I wanted to check him out.'

'Do you want to tell me the story?'

'I can. I mean, I will, Siri. But you need to give me some time to organize it. It's an important story.'

'Then don't tell it. Write it.'

'What?'

'Really. Consider it the first instalment of your memoires. The Women's Union has been on at you since you arrived to start documenting those years. And we're always complaining that there's nothing to read in our language. You and I should start the presses rolling.'

'I've never written anything longer than a shopping list.'

'It's exactly the same but with a few verbs and adjectives thrown in. We can work on it together until you feel confident.'

'I don't–'

The pop-pop-pop of a Lambretta emerged from the silence behind them. There was a shout. Something like, 'Hey, you!' Siri and Daeng staggered on.

'I do believe we're about to be arrested by the People's militia,' said Daeng.

'Well, you will keep me out late.'

'Should I handle it?'

'No. Allow me.'

The pop-pop got closer and the shouting more aggressive. Siri and Daeng laughed and wheeled around to face their pursuers. Two skinny young men with the scent of the northern hills still on them skidded their motor scooter in front of the couple. They were draped in washed-out Lao People's Revolutionary Army uniforms like scarecrows. Their armbands said they were security police. They had their weapons at the ready: the driver an ancient rifle, the pillion rider a night stick. It seemed they hadn't long graduated from the course in how to terrorize citizens out after curfew. They were still yelling obscenities, drowning each other out. Pillion slapped the truncheon against his own palm, most certainly causing himself pain. Perhaps they were used to violators trembling with fear before them but they certainly weren't sure how to react to two smiling old folk.

Siri disengaged himself from his wife and stepped up to the boys. The driver bravely raised his rifle. Siri reached forward and pushed the barrel to one side. All the time he glared at the young policeman. A Siri glare could be a powerful thing.

'Listen,' he said calmly. 'Stop shouting, the pair of you, and look at this face.'

His confidence disoriented the boys. A nervous silence fell over them.

'Have you not seen this face before?' Siri asked.

'I . . .' began the driver.

'Think carefully before you answer,' said Siri. 'Think about this year's national games. Think about the covered stand with the ribbons. Think about the VIP box where the politburo members and their wives sat.'

'I didn't go,' said the driver.

'Perhaps you're missing the point then,' said Siri, taking one more intrusive step into their insecure space. 'The point is, do you think I would be walking the streets after curfew if my face wasn't in every newspaper? If my voice wasn't broadcast on public radio day after day?'

'I . . .' began the driver.

'I'm sure to a boy of your age . . . what are you, thirteen, fourteen?'

'Twenty-eight.'

'Right. To your generation all grey-haired old men look alike . . .'

'Comrade, it's not—' began the pillion.

'. . . which I can forgive,' said Siri. 'But use some common sense. Did we flee in panic at the sound of your little motorcycle? Am I quivering here before you?'

'No, Comrade.'

'And what does that tell you?'

'That you're . . . somebody?'

'Good. I won't embarrass you by asking what my name and my position are. But, next time you see my wife and me strolling beside the river after dark, show a little respect. I won't report this. You can go now.'

There was a pause. Thailand seemed to be watching with bated breath.

'Did you hear me?' Siri asked.

'Yes, sir,' said the driver. 'I'm sorry.'

'We're sorry,' said the pillion.

The driver engaged and revved up his scooter with enough gusto to send it through to the next time zone and the boys were gone in a cloud of exhaust smoke. Siri and Daeng watched them go before taking one another's arms and resuming their promenade.

'You'll notice I didn't lie this time,' said Siri.

'I'm impressed. I find honesty in a man very erotic.'

As if by magic, their pace quickened.

4

How To Kill a Frenchman

I was two months short of my fourteenth birthday when I killed my first Frenchman.

'Do you think it's all right to start like that?'
'It's your story. Start any way you like.'
'I don't want to sound racist.'
'You could qualify it.'

I was two months short of my fourteenth birthday when I killed my first Frenchman.

At the time it didn't matter that he was French, or European, or even a man for that matter. I killed him because he was evil. Because I had no choice. It was several more years before I developed a penchant for killing men just because they were French.

'That might be considered just a tad . . .'
'I'll cut it out later.'

There were those who said I'd been driven to it by the Fates. I was born in December 1911, slap in the middle of the Chinese revolution. My grandfather named me Daeng to mark the event. Daeng is usually a nickname but he told everyone his grand-daughter of the revolution would be known to everyone as Red. *The bamboo hut in which I first opened my eyes was in a minority Lao Teung village in Savanaketh Province. Ours was a district famous for a three year uprising against French taxes. Very few of our men lived to boast of their bravery. My father had been one of the unlucky ones.*

I was born into a country called Laos that had already spent a quarter of a century as a jewel in the French colonial crown – a crown that included the three provinces of Vietnam, Cambodia, and us. We were a small, particularly dull jewel. Our French lords described us as The least urgent souls on earth with a thousand obstacles and superstitions to interfere with the accomplishment of work. *Their profits from Laos never amounted to more than one per cent of their total revenue from Indochina. We were a terrible disappointment. In fact we weren't even a country before the French came along, just a hotchpotch of diffuse tribes stirred together to make the paperwork easier. As I grew up in my mother's house it seemed like the most natural thing in the world that the pale-skinned, easily sunburned gods should be our masters and mistresses. Like the deaths of newborn babies from preventable diseases and the enslavement of our healthy men, that was just the way of it. It was our penance for being a country too stupid to administer itself. Too lazy to work. Too indifferent to rebel. How fortunate we were that the masters recognized our inadequacies early. They shipped in Vietnamese labourers to build, farmers to work our land, and administrators to keep us in our place. None of the clerks or the section heads at our regional government office spoke Lao. Vietnamese and French were the languages of administration.*

Of course, to learn French it would have helped to have gone to school. There was one down in the town. But it was exclusively for the children of the gods and the sons of the wealthy Vietnamese. So, we Lao of little ability struggled as best we could, picked up words here and there and kept our fingers crossed that we didn't get ill. There was a small regional hospital but that too was reserved for the service of the French and Vietnamese. Growing up in my small Lao Teung village, this was my normal.

'Siri. I wasn't expecting to see you again so soon,' said Seksan. 'Madame Daeng not with you?'

'Her head's giving her some trouble. In fact she can't find it.'

Seksan laughed. He had an infectious giggle.

'I'm afraid we hit the bottles a little too hard last night,' he said, opening the embassy gate to let his friend in. 'In fact, I'm surprised to see you up so early. What can I do for you?'

'I was wondering whether I could take a quick peek at the embassy's top secret files.'

Seksan laughed again but noticed that Siri wasn't smiling.

'You're serious.'

'Yes.'

'You're asking me whether I'd allow an ex-member of the Lao Issara, a sworn enemy of the French colonists, who proceeded to wage war against my adopted country for twenty years, to thumb through the embassy's secret files?'

'Yes.'

'You do realize there are several legal and diplomatic arguments as to why I probably shouldn't allow it?'

'Well,' said Siri. 'If they'd made you ambassador I'd listen to those arguments. But they gave you a broom and a toilet brush and told you to keep the place clean. Right now this is just a sprawling compound of quaint little buildings with no diplomatic status at all. I'm betting the staff didn't bother to take anything with them because they're expecting us to beg them to come back any time soon. I mean, if they left the wine . . .'

Seksan smiled at him.

'There's a store building full of files,' he said.

'There you go.'

'I have orders to set light to it if the compound is taken over.'

'If they're prepared to burn them, they can't be worth that much, can they now? Give me an hour.'

'I might come and have a look for myself.'

In its heyday, the two-tier *C'est La Vie* had plied between Vientiane and Luang Prabang during the high-river months, taking joyful French families and off-duty squaddies on an exotic Mekhong River cruise, a highlight of their time in Indochina. Until the river started to attract snipers, the *C'est La Vie*, now renamed *King Burom*, did the same trip with Americans, who, you may recall, were technically not in Laos at all. They would hire the good old *King* and escort their 'girlfriends' and crates of bourbon on romantic overnight cruises. Take photographs of one another's backsides and throw up over the side. Good for the fish, they said. But now the old girl had lost that international romance. There were so many layers of paint on her she'd become amorphous. Under the Party moniker of *Voyage of Harmony*, she chugged up and down the river picking up chickens in rattan cages and trussed pigs and burlap sacks of dried manure. And every now and then she'd take a passenger, the few whose laissez-passers were in order. And then there'd be someone for the old river pilot to converse with on the eighteen-hour journey from the new capital to the old.

Rather than sit cross-legged on the splintery deck, Siri, Daeng and Mr Geung had brought their own folding chairs. They'd even been thoughtful enough to bring along a fourth for Comrade Civilai. He was on his way to Luang Prabang on one of his many post-retirement functions. He'd refused the helicopter ride, arguing that his haemorrhoids acted up at altitude. Instead he would leave a day early and enjoy a leisurely cruise with his best friends. He liked to grumble about the assignments they gave him here and there yet, to be honest, that feeling of being needed was a drug. But, of late, this cooperative bunkum was getting him down. He'd sit for hours in meetings with sensible farmers trying to convince them that socialism would make them all equally wealthy. And he'd wait for that old-timer to put up his hand and ask, 'And will the system share the poverty just as fairly?' Civilai wanted to shout 'Yes.' The floods and the droughts would distribute misery evenly to all the co-op members. And the politburo would sit back and scratch its head and come up with a new system for next year.

Civilai's enthusiasm for the doctrine he believed in had won hearts in those early years. He was a communicator. He was a faithful party member. And then he got old and one day over breakfast – it was eggs lightly fried in soy sauce with a sprinkling of grated onion, he remembered quite clearly – he'd looked up from his plate and said to his wife, 'It isn't working.'

Peasants didn't want to wait a year or two for group rewards. They wanted profits now, or at least enough to feed the family tomorrow. They'd do whatever it took to succeed. There wasn't one system that would keep everybody happy. You needed a mix. But as soon as he started to advocate eclecticism his future in the politburo began its downward slide. It reached a hell that he was lucky to have escaped from with his head on his neck. So now, here he was heading off into rural villages that had survived quite nicely for hundreds of years without once hearing of this Karl Marx fellow, and reading to the elders from the manual. He didn't ask for questions at the end of his talks. They gave him a drink, asked after his family and waved him off. Nothing ventured. Nothing gained.

'You don't sound that enthusiastic,' said Siri. They were passing the elephant hills of Ban Chang. Civilai sat between Siri and Daeng on his deckchair slurping coconut water directly from the shell.

'It's doomed,' he said. 'We're all doomed. The end of the world is nigh.'

'Well,' said Daeng. 'I must say they couldn't have chosen a better diplomat to enthuse the masses.'

'Doomed,' said Civilai.

Siri and Civilai had a lot in common. They had both studied in France and returned to fight the revolution against the oppressors. They had both joined the Pathet Lao and lived in harsh conditions in the fields of battle. And now they shared another badge of courage. Both were missing their left earlobe. Siri's had been bitten off in a fistfight. Civilai had recently made the mistake of putting his ear in the path of a speeding bullet. The doctor believed it was a deliberate act on the part of the politician, who envied Siri's deformity of valour. But the old men were once again a matching set.

'Are you going to have time to stop over in Pak Lai on your way upriver?' Daeng asked.

'No. They want me there at the weekend. But if you're still around on Monday I'll abandon ship and celebrate the end of the world with you.'

'How sweet of you,' Daeng laughed.

'I'd rather hoped I might meet your witch on board,' said Civilai.

'Not a good sailor, evidently,' said Siri. 'The Ministry of Agriculture flew her up in a helicopter yesterday.'

'She didn't have her broomstick?'

Madame Daeng looked baffled.

'Just the two of us, older brother,' said Siri. 'Just the two of us.'

Mr Geung joined them on the upper deck clutching a whole cleavage of coconuts.

'More,' he said and sat on the deck with his sharp machete lobotomizing them one by one. Ugly chewed on a half shell that was his alone. Siri had entrusted the dog to the care of Mr Bhiku David Tickoo, the father of Crazy Rajid and the head cook at the Happy Dine Indian restaurant. Crazy Rajid spent his mute days wandering the streets of Vientiane or bathing naked in the river but many nights he would sleep behind the restaurant. Siri'd had a little business to discuss with him the night before their departure and he took the opportunity to chain the dog to the restaurant's back fence. After a plate of beef curry, Ugly seemed perfectly content to spend a few days there. When Siri and Daeng arrived at the ferry that morning, Ugly had been there waiting for them, tail wagging, a big smile on his deformed face. How he knew about the ferry trip nobody could say.

'And what news of your handsome paramour, Madame Daeng?' Civilai asked.

'I'm starting to wish I hadn't told you about him,' said Daeng. 'Nobody else knows.'

'You had no choice,' said Civilai. 'I am a man of influence. I can open doors. My minions at the ministries of Foreign Affairs and Interior are hunting out his arrival documents as we speak. Any chance he's just here to shake hands with old foe? Love across the Atlantic? World peace?'

'We can hope,' said Siri. 'Goodness knows the French spread so much goodwill and happiness while they were here.'

'Nuts?' said Geung.

As our working men had been disposed of horribly and publicly to end the rebellion, our village soon started to break up. My mother and sister and I travelled to Pakse in the south where Ma and me found laundry work. I was eleven. My sister, Gulap, was sixteen but she couldn't help us. She was a victim of what I later learned was called cerebral palsy. At the time they called her a spastic. She could neither speak nor walk but she was easily the most beautiful girl I'd ever seen. She smiled continuously. An irresistible smile. I was a daisy to Gulap's rose. I talked to her all the time. I told her stories. I know she understood me.

Our laundry was behind a large auberge. *We did the wash for the guest house and took in laundry from the resident foreigners around the town. It was there that I learned to read and write and cook. I was a curious girl and I was always pestering people to teach me something I didn't know. I was tired of being an ignoramus. Gulap would spend her days smiling at the world from a chair beneath the Buddha tree in the back yard. I always believed there was a magic word you could say to her and the mistake that distorted my sister would be rectified. I began by learning my own language and tried every word on her. When that didn't work I decided it had to be a foreign magic word. I started to collect French from the guests in the* auberge. *Every day I'd gather half a dozen new words, run back to our room and attempt to free my sister from her demon.*

And that was how I met Claude. He was a doctor from Paris. He was kind and patient and so unlike the other French men. I hardly noticed how unpleasant he looked: fat and ginger-haired, his teeth stained grey from wine and cigarettes. None of that mattered because Claude offered to save Gulap. The doctor travelled with a Vietnamese, a shifty man with a paunch and hair greased flat to his skull. They would come to stay at our auberge *every twenty days or so. They'd stay two nights. The Vietnamese spoke Lao. He told me that Claude would treat my sister free of charge because he liked me. When I told this to my mother she was so happy she cried all over the newly ironed pillow cases. We dreamed of the day that Gulap would be able to talk to us. Tell us how she felt.*

Dr Claude kept his word. He treated her twice. When his work at the hospital was over, he and the Vietnamese carried Gulap to our room and for half an hour or so they did whatever it took to remove the evil spirit from my sister's soul. They didn't let me see, of course. It was dangerous for somebody unqualified to be present, they told me. I even believed I was seeing an improvement in my sister. She was trying so hard to speak. She became so excited the second time she saw Dr Claude arrive. She clapped her curled hands and . . .

'I can't do this. All it does is remind me of how stupid I was.'

'You were thirteen.'

'Surely common sense comes long before that.'

'Some people never get it. Write!'

. . . and seemed so excited.

Dr Claude and the Vietnamese hadn't come for two months. I was anxious that they might not return. I asked at the auberge *when the doctor was due back. The owner told me she knew nothing of a doctor. 'Dr Claude and the tall Vietnamese,' I said. 'Claude?' she laughed. 'Claude is no more a doctor than I am a cabaret singer. Those two deal in bathroom attachments. They're travelling salesmen, young Daeng.'*

My sister, Gulap, the most beautiful girl I'd ever seen, died giving birth. My mother had considered terminating the pregnancy but they wouldn't let us in the hospital. Only the village shaman with potions you wouldn't give a rabid dog, and midwives with rusty knives were available for people like us. So my mother put her trust in nature. And nature let her down. With medicine and the hands of a surgeon, Gulap might have survived. But she was in the hands of fate and it took my sister and her baby from us.

*

The *Voyage of Harmony* reached Pak Lai exactly eleven hours after leaving Vientiane. It didn't feel that long. Siri had always marvelled at the timelessness of river travel. For hours they hadn't seen anything the early French explorers wouldn't have experienced a hundred years before. All right, perhaps they wouldn't have seen so many 333 Beer bottles floating nearer the towns or Che Guevara T-shirts on fishermen. No odd TOA paint cans lined up for shooting practice. But, basically, the cruise could have been before history. Before the ridiculousness of war. Before the greed of generals and the land lust of politicians. This river had defied it all and survived. Still her willowed banks bowed to the passing pirogues. Still the grey terns surfed the cool current above the water.

The pilot switched off his engine some hundred metres before the modest bamboo dock and waited for it to lure the boat home against the gentle current. There was barely a creak as the ferry kissed the old tyres that hung from the posts. Siri and Daeng had never been to Sanyaburi. It was a province that had often found itself changing nationality in the political lotteries. Civilai argued that the place was a victim of its spelling. On French and American maps there were no fewer than seventeen attempts at its transcription. More worryingly, there were three different versions on Lao maps. He argued that if it were easier to spell, a country might be more inclined to hang on to it. It was currently one of two Lao provinces with real estate on the west bank of the Mekhong, but that could change at any time. The players still sat around the board.

Siri, Daeng and Mr Geung were met at the dock by a smiling man in a grey safari suit and plastic flip-flops. He had a shaved head that rose gently to a cone like the sharp end of a coconut. Two twiggy men in football shorts and once-white singlets stood behind him. He had a booming voice.

'Comrades. Comrades,' he said. 'Welcome to Sanyaburi.'

Ugly was the first to step ashore and the man kicked at the dog and missed. His flip-flop flipped and flopped into the river but he ignored it. Siri saw him as the type who would only wear flip-flops on formal occasions. He kicked off the other sandal, stepped across the gangplank and shook the hands of Siri and Daeng with great enthusiasm. He took one look at Geung and ignored him completely.

'I'm the inspector of river traffic, the imports tariffs collection director general and I also have the honour of being the governor of this great province. My name is Siri Vignaket,' he said.

Dr Siri was immediately resentful to have this man share his name.

'It's nice to be here,' said Daeng who knew her Siri wouldn't be saying anything. 'This is Dr Siri Paiboun. My name is Daeng; I'm his wife.'

'No need to tell me that,' said Siri II. 'I can see you're a bit over the hill to be his mistress.'

His laugh shook leaves from the trees and frightened birds from the branches. Some people take days, even weeks to make a bad impression. Governor Siri had managed to alienate everyone in under three minutes. A remarkable feat.

'Can't have too many Siris, that's what I say,' bellowed the governor. 'Right, old man?'

Daeng squeezed her husband's hand. The sound of a titter could be heard from the other passenger on the boat who hadn't bothered to get up from his seat and introduce himself.

'His hearing's all right, is it?' asked Siri II. 'Never mind. I've brought my men. They'll carry your luggage up to the Peace Hotel. That's where you'll be staying. Top floor all to yourselves. Good view of the river. Double bed but I doubt you'll be making full use of that.'

Again the laugh. Again the trembling trees.

'This is all we have,' said Daeng with admirable restraint.

In his clenched fist, Siri held a canvas BOAC airline bag he'd once won in a tombola. It contained his travelling mortuary kit and a few clothes. His was a wash-and-re-wear philosophy. Daeng had her small backpack over one shoulder and three light deckchairs at her feet.

'Travel light, do you?' said the governor.

'Weren't you ever in the military?' Daeng asked.

'Me? Hell no. Mug's game.'

'How could you avoid it?'

'By using this old fella,' he said, tapping his index finger against his forehead and leaving the visitors in doubt as to whether he'd avoided military service by using his head or his finger.

'I was very proud of you,' said Daeng.

They sat on the edge of the double bed in the Peace Hotel penthouse suite. At least that was how the landlady had described it. It was indeed the entire top floor of a three-storey building but there was masonry evidence to suggest they'd intended to turn it into four separate rooms but had run out of money. The bedhead leaned against the north wall. There was a brisk twenty metre walk to the wardrobe at the south. A heavy wooden coffee table with a hot thermos of tea and a full-sized chair occupied the west wall and four doorways opened on to the balcony to the east. Only one of them had a door attached.

'I wanted to . . .'

'I know you did,' said Daeng. 'But we're on holiday. No point in starting a vacation under lock and key.'

'He's . . .'

'I know he is. Let's take a look at the view.'

They walked out through the second doorway.

'At least it won't get stuffy,' said Siri.

'And there is a mosquito net.'

The view made up for almost everything. It was splendid. The weather continued to be ideal. From their eyrie they could see the tail end of Civilai's ferry chugging its way around the bend upriver. Pak Lai was nicely laid out. There was something English about its large village green. You'd expect cricketers to walk out on to it after tea. Of course they'd need machetes rather than cricket bats as the grass had been left to its own devices for too long. The two unemployed porters were in the grounds below thrashing at the overgrown weeds with ancient scythes. A woman across the river propelled her coracle with an old frying pan. The dogs of Pak Lai had obviously been waiting for the coming of the alpha messiah because a dozen of them were following Ugly, up to their elbows in the river, rooting for crabs.

'We should bring Geung up,' said Daeng. 'He'd enjoy the view.'

The landlady had taken one look at Mr Geung and suggested he'd probably be more comfortable on the bunk in the back of the chicken coup. Siri told her that, as tempting as that sounded, his assistant would rough it in one of the guest house rooms.

'It's the boat races,' she'd said. She was a large woman whose eyebrows were very close to her hairline. In moments of surprise they merged.

'And that means what?' Siri had asked.

'All the rooms will be full,' she'd said. 'There'll be a crowd down from Sanyaburi municipality. People from Vientiane. The races have been cancelled the last three years. There's a lot of interest.'

'Then it's just as well we arrived before them,' said Siri. 'And as a show of good spirit, Mr Geung will give up his chronological right to the bunk in the chicken house.'

So, now, Mr Geung had a room to himself in the guest house. Beside the bed he'd put his Thai plastic chicken alarm clock that awoke him with a 'cock-a-doodle-doo' and his framed photograph of his beloved, Tukda, the prettiest Down Syndrome canteen worker at Mahosot Hospital. Everything was poised for an enjoyable few days. All they were missing was the witch. According to Siri the governor, she had refused first option on the Peace penthouse in preference for a private room at the old French colonial building at the back. Apparently, she wanted a room with a door. There was no accounting for taste.

Siri and Daeng were on their deckchairs with an early evening cocktail. Thai brandy and more Thai brandy without ice, courtesy of the horrible governor. The sky to the west was crimson but the sunset was wasted way back behind the jungle and the hills. But, when it arrived, they knew they'd have front seats for the moonrise. And that, as everyone knew, was the time when spirit energy was at its most potent.

'Any sightings?' Daeng asked.

'Anybody specific in mind?'

'I suppose I was wondering about the minister's brother, Ly,' said Daeng. 'I mean, if his body really is here and his spirit's in limbo, I imagine he'd be getting, you know, worked up.'

'It sounds like he's already found his own direct line through the witch. He wouldn't waste his time banging his head against my locked front door when he's got an ever-open spirit-flap to her.'

'So you're not getting any vibrations?'

'You know, Daeng, it's not so much an energy – more like visions. I see them all the time. It's just another dimension laid on top of this one like cartoon cells. You draw Daffy Duck on one layer and superimpose it on to another. I see both dimensions.'

'How can you tell them apart?'

'The living and the dead?'

'Yes.'

'The living are better dressers. The dead have this permanent "too long in the washing machine" look. Their colours are all washed out. Their lines are a little smudged.'

'I don't know why I'm always putting myself up for this, the hairs are already standing up on the back of my neck. But . . . can you see them now?'

Siri gazed across the river.

'Yes.'

'Shit.'

'It's not that scary, Daeng. Most of them are just lying around waiting. You know how you try to make a booking through Aeroflot and they ask you to come back to the office again and again to see how your application has progressed? Well, it's like that. Most of them seem resigned to the fact that they're on their way to the next incarnation, or the promised land or hell, whichever travel agent they've booked with.'

Daeng poured them two fresh glasses.

'So how do you think it works?' she asked.

'What?'

'Religion.'

Siri laughed.

'That's a bit heavy for six p.m. after just the one glass, don't you think?'

'I've asked you before when you were halfway down a bottle but you always make a joke of it.'

'Why is it important?'

'Oh, you know. If something happens to me I'd like to be prepared.'

'You're in your sixties. If you haven't settled on a tour company yet you probably never will. You'll be travelling solo. And, besides, I won't let anything happen to you.'

'Oh, Sir Siri. My hero. But tell me anyway.'

'There isn't one answer, Daeng. I know from experience that the spirits of the dead often hang around. This knowledge is a heavy weight to bear. It makes you want to have your brain laundered. I'm nothing special so it's quite obvious that legions of similarly haunted people throughout history have borne this weight too. So, throughout time, I'm convinced all these confused spirit-seers got so freaked out they needed to find a way to explain it to themselves. Form logical parameters to make sense of it.

'Like you, I grew up in a remote animist village. But then I went to school in a Buddhist temple. I underwent a strict Catholic education in France. I was perfectly content to accept the grand Shee Yee of the Otherworld and the Lord B, and Jesus and his mother as my spiritual icons as long as I didn't have to spend too long on my knees. I would have settled for a committee. I just wanted order. But once I started to see my own ghosts I understood what these religions were all about. They were clubs set up by people like me to stop themselves going mad. You know what I really think happens? You die. You wait for your number. There's a bit of time to take care of unfinished business. And you pass on. And, as you don't come back, nobody actually knows what you pass on to. But that description has never been acceptable. People wanted an ending. They didn't want to vanish into thin air. So these great religious gurus made some endings up. The more comfortable and happy your ending, the more members signed up and paid their fees. And it's what the masses wanted. They ate it up. And the kings and emperors started to add rules and regulations to subjugate the commoners and keep 'em in line. And so they invented hell and told you if you coveted your neighbour's mule you wouldn't even get into the clubhouse at the end of it all.'

Siri took a sip of his brandy and smiled towards the river.

'Nice,' said Daeng. 'The "You Just Die" philosophy of

religion. I doubt you'd fill many seats on the holy day. But I suppose that's fitting for a coroner. Except you know they don't just die. I thought you'd seen the Otherworld?'

'I did. But you would have noticed I wasn't dead at the time. I was just in a trance. And as far as I can work out, the only spirits I see are the ones with unfinished business. But, I can't know that for sure. I had no idea what I was seeing and no control over what happened there. I have this gift-cum-curse and I don't even know how to switch it on and off.'

'Is that why we're here? An audience with the witch medium?'

'No . . . Perhaps. I'm so close, Daeng. I feel it. I know I can communicate with these spirits. It shouldn't be that hard. You see that fellow over there on the rock?'

'No.'

'Of course you can't. He's dead. But I should be able to call him over, sit him down here on the spare chair and ask him where he thinks he's going. Ask him how he lost his arms.'

'You think the witch can teach you to do that?'

'It's because of her and the word of a dead soldier that we're all here. They do it all the time in Vietnam. They see the departed and ask them where the body is. If they can communicate, so can I. I'm sure it's a question of confidence. Half the victory is in believing in yourself. You can't tell me that faith hasn't driven you through life.'

*

I was almost fourteen when I next saw Dr Claude and the Vietnamese. The bathroom fittings business was obviously doing well because they'd gone upmarket and were staying at the hotel in the centre of town. And they were travelling in a nice car. I'd delivered some laundry to the front desk and I saw them huddled at a small table. If they recognized me they didn't react. I walked out and stood behind the outdoor barber stand opposite. My legs were like tofu. I couldn't have gone back to the auberge *if I'd wanted to. And I didn't want to. I wanted to see where these devils were headed.*

They could have walked but I suppose they wanted everyone to see their nice car. They drove it about two hundred yards and parked on the river bank not far from an open-air bistro. It was the type with hostesses in sexy clothes. The type the men liked; too young and just stupid enough. I'd sprinted to catch up with the car and I was out of breath when I threw myself under a hedge near where they parked the car. I watched them eat from there. I watched them drink. I watched them fondle. I'm not sure I had it in my mind to kill those two men. I don't remember what was going through my brain. Perhaps I merely wanted them to feel what my mother and I had felt every day since we'd lost Gulap. And I had to do it then, that night, because I was afraid I'd never have the opportunity again.

It was getting late. Claude and his whore left the table and she propped him up as they walked along the river bank. He was drunk as a prince. The car was parked on a slight bluff with a scenic view of the Mekhong. They got in and there was some hanky-panky in the front seat. I'd learned all about hanky-panky at our auberge. *The car rocked a little. Then there was nothing. Five minutes later the young lady of the night stepped out of the car and staggered back to the bistro. I came out of my hiding place and looked through the rear window. The moon lit up the river with a cheesy yellow glow. I could see the silhouette of Claude's head. It didn't move. I wondered if she'd killed him for me. But probably not. He was asleep. I'd heard all about men falling asleep at the wrong times as well. Too drunk to do his seedy business he'd decided to sleep it off.*

I didn't know anything about cars. Had never been in one. But I'd seen wheels before. I knew if you gave a handcart a good enough shove you could get it to move. I'd never heard of a handbrake and it wasn't until several years later when I was learning to drive that it occurred to me that the spirits had left it off especially for me that night on the Mekhong. And even now I wonder whether I imagined what a laugh it would be if the car should roll all the way to the river and Dr Claude emerged angry and wet from the water. Or whether I hoped he'd be lost at the bottom of the Mekhong with all his sins come back in the form of river fish, snapping away at his nasty flesh. Or perhaps I just pushed to see what would happen.

It rolled more easily than I'd imagined. I barely leaned against the black boot and the car was on its way down the slope. It seemed to have a mind all its own. I couldn't have stopped it if I'd wanted to. I lost sight of Claude's silhouette when the car reached a sort of shelf and slowed a bit but in seconds it was over the ridge and nose-down headed for the water. The voracious Mekhong took the whole car in one gulp. I hurried to the ledge and looked at the bubbles – big, head-sized globs of air. Every second I expected the evil doctor to burst to the surface, coughing and spluttering and thanking his good Lord for delivering him safely from the edge of death. But he didn't show. I was surprised to see people running past me, down to the river: foreign men and Lao staff and the Vietnamese and the curious girls. They'd seen it happen. And they all ignored me as if I'd had nothing to do with this. As if a car had taken a fancy for a dip all by itself.

Some men jumped into the water. They were probably drunk and showing off because the water was flowing fast and deep at that time of year. In fact the car was no longer where I'd put it. They found it a week later on the way to Basak. There was no ginger-haired man sitting in the front seat. At first that helped me sleep. Imagining my Dr Claude opening his car door, swimming across the river to live a nice life in Thailand. But that guilt didn't last for long. One night, Gulap came to me and in perfect Lao she told me how she could rest much more easily knowing that man was where he deserved to be.

On the first day he arrived in Laos, the man calling himself Hervé Barnard had travelled south to Pakse on a false laissez-passer. He shook his head at how easy the commies made it to falsify documents. How had they ever won the war? It took him only half a day to find the man he was searching for. The Lao was still living at his old address. This information had recently become available following the declassification of official documents in Paris. Most of the material pertaining to the debacle at Dien Bien Phu was now in the public domain. Too bad for anyone mentioned in the files whose life depended on secrecy.

The Lao officer had once been the head of clandestine missions for the Lao Issara resistance movement and subsequently for the Pathet Lao in the south. The years had made him soft. There had probably been a time when he would have died rather than disclose information about his colleagues. But just two hours of torture, not even sophisticated state-of-the-art torture at that, and Barnard had the name he'd wanted: Daeng Keopakam. The Lao had died anyway, but bereft of honour. Barnard spat on his corpse.

Armed with the name, some old French charm and a seductive smile, he'd found the warm trail of Madame Daeng. She'd continued her lunchtime noodle restaurant shift deep into the American occupation. Then, for some pathetic, nostalgic reason, she'd taken over that same restaurant at the ferry crossing. How was that for ambition? What a mind to waste.

He thought back to their last night. He'd awoken and she was there beside him. She'd kissed his cheek and said good morning. She was beautiful, there was no doubt. Those deep dark chocolate eyes could take all the air out of a man in one blink. He'd looked around the room with heavy eyes. Everything seemed normal. His uniform on hangers in the doorless closet. His gun on the desk. His briefcase on the chair. Everything was as it should have been. Apart from an odd feeling at the back of his mind.

He'd heard the code name *Fleur-de-Lis*. It had not come from the French side but from the Lao. It had been given up to interrogators by a captured local spy. But he'd not known the agent's true identity. Only that the *Fleur-de-Lis* had been responsible for most of the mayhem experienced by the French administration in the south. But, like Barnard, they'd all assumed the agent was a French official. A double agent. At the very least, a sophisticated Vietnamese educated in France. Espionage was a career for the upper classes, not the coolies or the *corvée* labourers. Nobody had considered for a second that the bane of all their security troubles could be a native.

And that was why it wasn't until long after the mess to end all messes, after the humiliation, that the man now calling himself Hervé Barnard finally put the pieces together. He was certain who *Fleur-de-Lis* was. He'd been in love with her which made her betrayal even more biting. Yet only he and she knew what had transpired that long sleepy night. And the years passed and he rose through the ranks and became a man with power. But his successes could never satisfy him because of that dreamless night in a bamboo room in Pakse.

And, as a man in his sixties, he was back. He'd stood at the ferry ramp and looked down at the tattered canopy of the noodle stand that had once belonged to Madame Daeng. It was lunchtime but the stools were unoccupied. The pot-bellied patron sat alone eating an orange, wiping his hands on his greasy undershirt. No finesse, thought Barnard. No class. Typical of these disgusting people.

He was back in Vientiane now. He had her name. They'd told him she'd come here twelve months earlier to establish a business in the capital. But the different departments: business registration, migration, housing, medical – none of them was prepared to give out information about a Lao citizen. Not to him. He was the enemy. The officials were cadres from the north-east who'd spent a lifetime fighting his kind. If they spoke French they didn't let him know as much. When he'd returned with a translator they'd interrogated the poor woman about her relationship with this old *farang*. Not even offers of a finder's fee could squeeze a sac of information from these dry old commies. He'd gone to the markets. There were still some French speakers there. Nobody knew of a Madame Keopakam. But Daeng? My word. There were Daengs aplenty, they told him. Fire a bullet in the air and it would likely land on a Daeng. He'd suggested there would be a reward to anyone who could locate his old friend, Daeng Keopakam, from the south and said his name was Hervé and he was staying at the Lane Xang.

And that's where he sat in his hotel room, waiting, choking in the smog of his chain cigarettes, fuming. The only way he could lighten his mood was by imagining Madame Daeng hanging by the ankles from a beam, and him with a brand new tyre iron.

5

The Uphill Rowing Club

On Friday morning, Siri and Daeng awoke to a completely different Mekhong. Far and near, the villages had washed the three years of grime from their longboats and those with leftover paint that hadn't hardened in the cans had spruced up the old ladies of the river. By whatever means, they'd dragged them to the water and, with thirty-six hours to go before the races began, old crewmates with rusty joints were relearning the pleasures of rowing.

Before the change of administration the races had been annual. Betting on the results had become endemic. Wealthy landowners brought in athletes to replace the less serious rowers on their local crew in order to safeguard their bets. One by one the locals lost their seats to outsiders and became viewers. But these were socialist days and an edict had been passed around saying that only those born within the sound of an elephant's trumpet from the village could crew its boat. And on this gloriously sunny but chill morning, the motley crews of out-of-shape villagers puffed steam into the cold air. There was no doubt there were no athletes on display this day. It seemed hardly possible that more incongruous teams would ever be gathered. Different ages, genders, builds, sizes of girth, levels of disability and mental state; all were on display.

The boats were sturdy and long, accommodating anywhere from thirty to fifty rowers in each. Most were hand carved from solid timber and stank from a hundred layers of linseed oil. All of the crews were in need of professional coaching. The starboard to starboard rule of passage had never entered the rule books of the Pak Lai races. They floated sideways. They collided. They laughed. They formed logjams of boats held together with oars and careened downstream. They laughed some more. Siri and Daeng watched the circus with tears of mirth rolling down their cheeks. Their favourite was one bright green boat whose crew seemed to be on the waning side of sixty. Most of the women had a smudge of red where their teeth used to be. They chewed cuds of betel and grinned horribly. One particularly gaunt man appeared to be the village headman and he shouted instructions that were either ignored completely or met with howls of derision. As they seemed to have trouble fighting against the current, Daeng lovingly nicknamed this crew the Uphill Rowing Club.

'Do you suppose they'll get it right by tomorrow?' Daeng laughed.

'I very much doubt a month of practice would improve matters too much,' said Siri.

'I can't–'

Daeng's thought was interrupted by a loud knock at their door. The door wasn't locked so they both shouted, 'Come in!' but the knocker did not do so. Siri was out of breath by the time he reached the handle. He opened the door and was confronted by a short but very attractive woman around Daeng's age. She wore a beautiful Lao *phasin* and a crisp white blouse. Her thick hair was fastened in a chignon with two gold hairpins. Behind her was a Chinese-looking man of the same height. His head was shaven and, for some reason, he wore a long white nightshirt.

'Doctor Siri,' she said, not a question. Her smile was that of a much younger person. If her teeth were false they'd been fashioned by a craftsman.

'Yes?' said Siri, suddenly aware he was dressed in nothing but a threadbare towel.

'I am Madame Peung,' she said in impeccable French. 'People have been calling me Madame Keui of late so that is the person you might have been expecting. But, what's in a name? Please call me whichever you wish.'

Siri was about to hold out his hand but the visitor put her palms together in a *nop*. The authorities had outlawed the bourgeois salute but it still felt right. If he hadn't been holding up his towel with one hand he would have returned it. The bald man merely nodded.

'My brother, Mr Tang, lost the power of speech after

an explosion when he was in the military,' she said. 'Neither can he hear. But he has great sense. He feels our meanings.'

Then, in Vietnamese, she said, 'I hope you're enjoying your retirement. It must be difficult to know what to do with your days now.'

Siri was fluent in both French and Vietnamese but of course both were spiced by his Lao. Yet there was something peculiar about this woman's languages. It was as if . . . as if she were speaking to him with his accent. As if she'd borrowed the words from him.

Madame Daeng joined them at the door.

'We have guests,' she said. 'Why haven't you invited them in?'

Siri made the introductions as they all walked to the veranda. Madame Peung and Tang sat on the deckchairs. Siri sat on the railing, being careful to keep his knees together. Madame Daeng found herself dragging the heavy wooden chair over to join them. Madame Peung proved to be most agreeable for a witch. After talking about their respective journeys, bemoaning the cost of goods at the local markets, and one or two jokes, the three communicators had apparently broken the ice. So much so that Madame Peung decided they were close enough for her to toss a few sticks of dynamite into the embers of bonhomie.

'Before he shot me, I was as Lao as you two,' she said.

'Sorry?' said Daeng.

'You've heard I speak Lao with a Vietnamese accent,'

she said. 'But before the break-in to my house two months ago, my Vietnamese and French had been quite basic. After I was shot I found myself channelling Hong Phouc, a Vietnamese mandarin of the late nineteenth century.'

'How badly were you injured?' Daeng asked.

'Oh, I was killed,' she said.

It's not easy to keep a straight face when the person you're talking to insists they were once dead. She'd delivered the line so deadpan that both Siri and Daeng smiled at her, expecting a punchline. But she continued.

'They still haven't caught him, the murderer. So they don't know why I was targeted. He didn't take anything from the house. Hong Phouc suggests that it was part of the vast cosmic plan. The same man shot me on two separate occasions. The second bullet didn't do any harm at all.'

'Because you were already dead,' smiled Daeng.

Before becoming involved with Siri and his band of merry ghosts, Daeng would probably have made a joke at this juncture and dismissed the woman as a nutcase. But she'd heard of so much weirdness from her husband that almost anything was possible. Almost. Siri, on the other hand, was so engrossed his knees drifted apart.

'Evidently,' said Madame Peung, averting her eyes and letting out a gut laugh that suggested she was every bit as bewildered by it all as Daeng. 'Ridiculous, isn't it? On the night I was shot for the first time, all I remember was looking up from my bed to see a strange man leaning over me. I heard a crash from the gun.

Three days later I awoke in the same bed at exactly the same time. Of course I didn't know then that three days had passed. I thought it was the same night and the shooting was a dream. I took the torch, went to the bathroom and had the longest pee I've ever had in my life. I didn't think it would ever end. I passed the mirror and I was . . . different. I was younger. Oh, not by a lot but enough to notice. And my body was in better shape. I wondered whether that trip to the bathroom was part of the dream. I was confused. I returned to the bed and slept till morning. I was awoken by a scream. My live-in girl was standing in the doorway to my room with her hands over her mouth. I asked her what was wrong. She screamed again and ran off. I didn't see her again.

'I went down to the village to see the headman. But as I walked past the houses all I heard were screams and the slamming of doors. I asked what was wrong but nobody would talk to me. There was one old woman I had befriended many years before. She made charcoal. We used to talk a lot. She was the only one who wasn't afraid of me.

'"Of course they're scared," she said. "The menfolk carried your body down to the pyre yesterday and we watched you go up in smoke. You were killed by an intruder three days ago."

'I was astounded.

'"Of course it's a mistake," I told her. "It must have been somebody else. Someone who looked like me."

'"It was you, sure enough," she said.

'"Then, who am I?" I asked.

'"Who indeed," she said.

'For the next few days I tried to make contact. I went to everybody I knew. People whose children I'd seen as babies, watched them grow up. I'd bought goods from their shops. Some of them had worked for me at the house. Of course I knew all this but I couldn't convince them that I was me. And there was this awful Vietnamese accent. So, slowly, I retreated to my house and started to live like a hermit. Then people began to come. Strangers. They said they'd heard that I'd been reborn and wanted me to help them locate relatives on the other side. The first few visitors I threw out angrily. But after they'd gone I had dreams. It was true. Those lost relatives really did come to me. Hong Phouc introduced them. I really could see them. Talk to them. It frightened me. I didn't know what it all meant so I called for my brother to come and stay with me. He wasn't surprised at all. Our family always knew he had some innate gifts that he could not express. He has been a great comfort to me.

'When more strangers came I listened to them and I helped them find the bodies of their relatives. It was all quite simple. They tried to give me rewards but I didn't want their money or their jewels. Every visitor I swore to secrecy. "Do not tell anyone else what I do here." But still they came. And after two months I got the first visit from Madame Ho, the minister's wife.

And that, dear doctor, is why I am here. And some of your questions at least have been answered.'

'Siri, you're drooling,' said Daeng.

During the remarkable tale, the doctor had lowered himself from the railing and sat cross-legged but discreetly in front of the witch. Madame Daeng retreated inside.

'But how? How do you talk to them?' Siri asked.

'The same way I'm talking to you,' Madame Peung replied, 'except I use my mind. Look down there.'

They looked through the railings towards the river.

'Do you see her?' she asked.

'The woman on the rock?'

'That's the one. Ask her why she's here.'

'I can't. I mean, the only way I know how to ask is with my mouth. I could shout at her.'

'That wouldn't work. She's trying really hard to talk to you.'

'You see? I'm a failure.'

'It will come, brother Siri. I can help you.'

'You don't know how pleased I am to hear that,' said Siri.

They were startled by a flash. Madame Daeng had returned with her favourite Polaroid Instant camera and, before anyone could object, she had snapped the visitors for prosperity. She watched the print come to life in her hand before taking a second photo.

'Just for the family album,' said Daeng.

It was in the second photograph that she noticed the

glint in her husband's eye. It was a twinkle the type of which she hadn't seen for a very long time.

The rest of the morning was spent in what Siri interpreted as a leisurely manner. Once Madame Peung and her brother had left them to return to the old French administration building behind the square, Siri and Daeng went down to one of the tents that had mushroomed along the river bank with Mr Geung and enjoyed some local rice porridge. Ugly stood guard. The minister would be arriving the following day and the witch had told them she had a lot to prepare so she wouldn't be able to join them.

'I don't think you should be so pushy,' said Daeng.

'What do you mean?' Siri asked.

'If she wants to share her secrets with you, she will.'

'I hardly pushed.'

'No? "I would really like to watch your preparations." "Do you need to be in a trance?" "Do they speak to you in voices you can actually hear?" You bombarded the poor woman.'

'Those are the questions I want answers to, Daeng.'

'It was just a little bit demeaning.'

'I don't–'

'Mr Geung. How about another bowl for you?' said Daeng. 'I don't know where you put all that food, really I don't.'

'I'm a va . . . va . . . vacuum cleaner,' said Geung which caused laughter and led on to other subjects. Breakfast was followed by a leisurely stroll downriver followed by Ugly and some eleven disciples. Ever conscious of his wife's arthritis, Siri asked several times whether Daeng would like to rest.

'Siri,' she said. 'This isn't the Olympics. I'm perfectly capable of walking.'

This told the doctor one of two things. One that she was secretly in pain and bluffing. Or, two, that she had remembered to bring her opium and really was feeling nothing. They found an idyllic spot to rest. Siri dozed. Mr Geung skimmed flat stones but was unable to surpass his record of two. And Daeng sat in the shade of a tree and wrote in her notebook. When they returned, it was almost lunchtime and they were all in a relaxed mood. It was too hot for the rowers to practise. A large pirogue was tied up at the dock. It contained just two teak logs but it already sat as low in the water as could be considered safe. Daeng left Siri and Geung and walked over to the pilot of the boat.

'She's probably going to give him a lecture on deforestation,' said Siri.

'It's cruel,' said Geung. 'The tree sssspirits are not happy.'

Siri wondered whether Geung had learned about the malevolent spirits of the forest from him or whether he perhaps saw them himself.

'So, what do you make of the witch, Geung?'

Mr Geung had met her briefly on Siri's balcony.

'She's pretty.'

'Granted. But what do you think of her? She claims

she can talk to spirits just like you and I are talking now. Just one time I would like to grab myself a spirit and have a good old chat over a cup of tea. Maybe even Yeh Ming. Did you know I host a thousand-year-old spirit?'

'Yes.'

'I wonder if she . . . How do you know that?'

'The second bottle of . . . of . . . of Johnny Walker in Xiang Kouang.'

'There, and I used to be so disciplined. So, do you think she can talk to my shaman, Geung? Do you think she can teach me to?'

There was no answer.

'Geung?'

'Comrade Madame Daeng is pr . . . pr . . . prettier.'

'Right.'

That night, Siri dreamed of Frenchmen. They had the appearance of the military. Short hair. Fit. That stature that comes from years of standing to attention. But there were no uniforms to confirm this theory. They were naked but it was certainly not an erotic dream. The Frenchmen were in hell. Despite its reputation as a forgiving religion, Buddhism has a fine selection of hells. There were hot hells and there were cold hells. These poor French blighters were in one of the coldest – Utpala. It was recognizable because their skin had turned the blue of water lilies. There were six of them and they were huddled together for warmth like penguins. As Siri watched, the huddle became a ruck and then a scrum. A rugby match was on in hell. The French played three-a-side. They leaned together and created a tunnel between them. General Charles DeGaulle himself was the scrum half. He leaned over, called out some indecipherable code and threw the ball between the legs. But the ball was not a ball. It was a head. Siri caught a glimpse of it before it disappeared into the scrummage. It was the head of his wife.

Siri awoke with a loud, shuddering sigh. The first thing he saw by the moonlight through the window was Madame Daeng's head on the pillow. He was filled with dread. The eyes were open and shot with blood. Her lips were purple. He poked at her nose and the head rolled to the far side, off the pillow and landed with a clunk on the concrete floor.

Siri awoke with a loud, shuddering sigh. The first thing he saw by the moonlight through the window was Madame Daeng's head on the pillow. She slept peacefully with a blissful smile on her lips. He took hold of the sheet and edged it down. Her head was, thankfully, attached to her neck which in turn held company with the rest of her. He hated those false awakenings. With too much adrenalin coursing through his veins now to sleep he watched his wife's gentle breaths fill her chest before travelling through her body to her magnificent vital organs. She made it look so easy. He never tired of watching her breathe. Every night spent beside her was an honour.

6

Bewitched, Bothered and Bewildered

When Madame Daeng awoke next morning the sun was already smiling full-faced through her window. In Vientiane she awoke naturally before the sun appeared and began her preparations for the restaurant. But here she could sleep soundly, uninterrupted by obligations. She looked to her right. She was alone. The bathroom was one floor down and she assumed her husband's ancient bladder had driven him there. The muscles in her legs contracted and grabbed cruelly at her nerves as she swung them off the mattress. With her feet on the ground she waited for them to announce that they were ready to begin the arduous task of carrying her around for another day. The first half-hour was always the hardest. Momentum took her to the open doorway and on to the balcony. There was a strong flowery scent in the air as if Mother Nature was excited. The air was cool and fresh. It was second honeymoon weather.

She leaned on the balustrade. The regatta practice

had begun. There were signs of improvement. The boats were colliding less frequently. There were fewer men and women overboard. One boat even appeared to have its oars in the air and back in the water in time to the cox's drum. For a while. But the Uphill Rowing Club still splashed around like a drowning cricket. She could hear the sounds of the oars clattering together and the laughter of the old ladies.

She leaned over the rail to see whether she could catch sight of Ugly and his minions on the freshly cut grass below. But there were no dogs. Or perhaps there was one. In the shade of a Rhinoceros-Droppings tree sat Siri on one of their deckchairs. He was staring transfixed at the face of Madame Peung who sat opposite him with her trim old-lady bottom on the other.

My mother and I lived in that small laundry room for the next nine years. All my school years had been spent ironing. I considered myself bright. I'd learned to read and write Lao at the temple but there was nothing to read in my language. So I taught myself to read first French, then Vietnamese and I found a great assortment of books and magazines left behind by travellers. There was no mention of Laos in any of them. It made me feel even more that I was an insignificant person living in an insignificant country. I learned that the world worshipped money. Only the sons and daughters of the royals were sent overseas to study and they came back having laundered out all that dirty Laoness from their personalities. They were more French than Asian.

It saddened me that I had no value. Nothing to contribute. The Vietnamese boys were always trying to date me. I'd been flattered at first. They wore the best clothes, rode new bicycles. A couple even had motorcycles. But they weren't wooing me so we could drink café au lait *and discuss politics. I was Lao. I didn't even make it on to the pecking order. I saw the Lao girls give in to them. They all needed somebody to love them in whatever way was available. But they couldn't have me. They tried but I was handy with a knife even then. Nobody messed with me. I'd inherited my father's fire. My mother told me stories about him. How he marched up to the administrator's office in his handmade straw sandals and announced that there would be no taxes paid that season.*

'What do we get for our taxes?' he'd asked the government interpreter. 'We have no roads. No clean water. No help when the crops fail. You take our men for slave labour to grow your coffee and mine our gems. And then you have the gall to tax us for the privilege.'

My father returned from that first meeting with fifty lashes across his back. That night he sat shirtless at a bonfire and one by one the men walked passed him and spat raw rice liquor into his wounds. They drank through the night heaping curses upon the white gods. By sunlight they were prepared for their first riot. The revolution spread through the hills. The French called in more soldiers. My father recruited more fighters. And for three years they matched the French arms with Lao grit.

He told his men,

'Individually, the French are clerks and bookkeepers. Weedy men resentful at being posted to this sweaty country with its

mosquitoes and biting centipedes and godless brown people. But you put enough clerks and bookkeepers together and arm them and they think they can do whatever they want. One of us is worth ten of them. Twenty.'

But they did put enough clerks and bookkeepers together and they put down the riots and then there were just the women and children. And what could we do against the might of a great European nation?

The official from the department of Housing was short. Not legally a midget but unlikely to reach 140 centimetres in his remaining lifetime. He stood in the open doorway of the hotel room looking up at the tall Frenchman.

'*Oui?*' said the Frenchman.

Comrade Koomki introduced himself in Lao, then broken Vietnamese, then Russian. The Frenchman only knew four words of Russian.

'I don't speak Russian.'

Comrade Koomki shook his head, looked at his shoes, held up one index finger and ran off along the corridor. Ten minutes later there was another knock at Barnard's door. This time there were two visitors. Comrade Koomki had returned with a dirty man in gloves. He was barefooted and wore a large straw hat.

'Who are you?' asked Barnard.

'I am the gardener,' the man replied in very good French. 'My name is Apsara.'

'Why are you here?'

'Because this man asked me to come.'

'And who is he?'

'He would prefer not to say.'

'Why do you speak French?'

'In the old regime I was the night manager here. I'm being retrained from the grass roots up. I shall return.'

'So?'

The gardener and Comrade Koomki spoke together in Lao.

'The comrade's cousin sells spices at the morning market. She heard you asking for Daeng Keopakam. Nobody there knew that name. But the comrade here remembered it. The lady in question has since married and has a new surname. He knows where they live.'

'And when so many comrades in so many government departments refuse to give me this information, why is this nameless comrade prepared to deal with me?'

More Lao.

'The comrade wants to know whether you intend to do any harm.'

'And do you recommend I give him a positive or a negative response to this?'

'The comrade has just lost his position due to them. He is keen to have revenge on your Madame Daeng and her husband. He would be pleased if some ill fortune were to befall them. He would also like a more fiscal reward.'

'Then tell him I can promise both riches and ill fortune in large helpings.'

'Then I believe you two can do business.'

Nurse Dtui had been through a rough day at the chalk face. Her first-year nurses fell into a giggling fit every time Dtui poked her ruler anywhere near the midriff of the plaster dummy of a man with all his organs visible. The spinal injuries teacher was off with malaria so Dtui had to teach back-to-back classes all day. And, not for the first time, the administrators had announced that, due to problems at the treasury, the staff would be receiving its salary in vermicelli rice noodles this month. Even without the rapidly growing daughter strapped to her back, Dtui would have creaked under the weight of responsibility. There was a Lao proverb that called teachers the engineers of the soul and Professor Dtui was starting to wonder whether she had the right nuts and bolts for the job.

She arrived at the police dormitory at nine p.m. The lights were on in every room but hers. Why had she chosen the only conscientious police inspector in Vientiane? She walked past a slim man who was sitting cross-legged on top of the bicycle shed. From a distance he'd looked like some geometrical diagram. As it would have been foolish for a robber to lie in wait in front of the police dormitory, she assumed he was an off-duty policeman and passed him quite calmly.

'You Dtui?' he asked.

'Depends,' she said.

'I've got a letter for Dtui from her Auntie Daeng.'

'You could have slid it under the door,' she said.

'Then I wouldn't have got my other half, would I?'

'Half of what?'

'The five US greenbacks she promised me.'

'Then it's really not your night, is it.'

She fumbled for her door key.

'It might be important,' he said.

'Then I'll find that out when she comes back to Vientiane.'

'Come on. I'm a poor boat pilot. She promised.'

Dtui turned to him and put her fists on her hips.

'You see this uniform?' she asked. 'Am I an airline pilot? No. I'm a nurse. And do you know what that means? If they have money to pay me, I earn twenty of your precious greenbacks a month. If you think I'm going to give you a week's salary for a note, you're dreaming.'

'She promised.'

'No she didn't. Now, go away.'

'I walked up from the port just to give you this. My cargo's still down there. Anyone could walk off with it. I'm doing you a favour.'

'Then you'd better hurry back.'

Dtui inserted the key in the lock and stepped into her room with nothing more to say. She turned on the light and sighed. She missed the old days when people did favours for purely moral credit. Two minutes later, the letter slid under the door and mumbled curses could be heard heading off into the night. She left the letter lying there, plugged in the kettle, untied the knot that held her daughter and lowered a sleeping Malee on to the mattress. She envied her daughter's slumber. She told herself for the millionth time how clever she'd been to produce such a beautiful child and how lucky she was that the father was still around. Distracted, perhaps, but devoted.

Once she'd poured the hot water on to her instant noodles she closed her eyes and imagined grilled chicken and turnip and fresh garden cabbage. But her subconscious did nothing for the rehydrated pasta. She owed socialism a debt of gratitude. She thought how much fatter she'd have been if she actually enjoyed her meals. It wasn't until she was halfway down the bowl of virtual food that she reached for the letter. There were two photographs and a page of handwriting torn from a notebook. Daeng sent her regards. Told her how pleasant Pak Lai was. How much she was looking forward to the boat races. Then she made an unusual request.

The unproductive half of Saturday – unless you happened to be teaching an intensive course to silly nurses – and all of Sunday, were the days the Lao were given to rest their weary joints. To be certain the populace didn't waste this opportunity, the Party had arranged joyful activities during which a comrade might get together with new friends and laugh and sing uplifting songs. Inevitably, the activities involved the use of garden tools or nails or large tubs of wet cement. The Party would provide a packed lunch of sticky rice and foodstuff fermented to the point of micro-organism meltdown. Nobody was forced to enjoy these adventure weekends. Yes, your neighbourhood chicken counter might take note of your name if you were found lounging in your home. Yes, there might be hold-ups with your rice ration at the co-op. Yes, your name might appear on the list of suspected insurgent sympathizers pinned to the village noticeboard. But, yes, a citizen was perfectly free to choose what he and his family did with his weekend. Madame Daeng had asked Dtui and Inspector Phosy to give up an entire Sunday to conduct a little investigation.

Dtui was only too pleased.

The man calling himself Hervé Barnard sat in the closed noodle restaurant on Fahngoum that Madame Keopakam, now Madame Paiboun, aka Daeng, had made her home in Vientiane. The back door hung by its hinges and the bloody tyre iron lay on the table in front of him. He'd already ransacked the upstairs rooms. The bedroom. The messy library with its hundreds of French books. The desk in the small office. There was an album. Black and white photographs of youths at a camp. There was Daeng, the way she'd looked when he'd fallen in love with her. He stared at her. Emotions crashed into him like a multi-vehicle pile-up on an icy motorway.

Before her he'd loved nobody. And since? How could he ever trust a woman after that? In five short months she had taken away all those parts of him that gave a person potential. She had been that moment. The fulcrum. The point when everything became unbalanced. As long as she continued to breathe the same air as him, create currents in the same atmosphere, his ever-shortening life would be intolerable. She needed to be gone so that he could die.

He could already smell the smoke. The album. The books. The desk. Soon the entire restaurant. Not spite, merely a tactic of war. Wherever they were they'd hear about this. They'd hurry back. They'd find the body. She would be distraught and vulnerable and distracted and he would kill her. It was the only way to find peace.

The Minister of Agriculture, ex-General Popkorn, and his wife arrived by helicopter at eleven a.m. The last celebrity to make an appearance in the province had been Ai Dum the country music singer and the crowd then had been marginally smaller. But, of course, back then, there hadn't been cadres going door to door dragging comrades from their hammocks. Back then they hadn't come 'to make a good show for the province'. They'd come because they enjoyed a good dance and a sing-song. The crowd of several hundred this Saturday was subdued because they knew the minister would neither sing nor dance, and just as well, perhaps. As he walked through the aisle they'd created for him they seemed unimpressed. Another old man in a grey safari suit.

But what a wife. Madame Ho was every bit as colourful as the old royal regatta pennants. She dressed in Western style in a white and orange frock daringly short to show her lamb-hock calves, and yellow high heels that defied all the principles of foundation engineering. She was a buffalo teetering on half-centimetre points. She was plastered in make-up that from a far distance might have made her look gorgeous. But as she passed the half-heartedly cheering locals with their little Lao flags, they could all see that the cosmetics did not follow the contours of her features. Hers was a deleted and redrawn face whose pencil lines still showed through.

The ministerial arrival was recorded in photographs and they all knew that the caption – *Local agronomists show their admiration for their minister* – would appear in the next edition of *Siang Pasason*, which nobody ever read. They hurried ex-General Popkorn to the governor's house. Governor Siri was in the dark as to the purpose of the visit and the status of all the players he'd been told to accommodate. The official line was that this was an event to pass on the Party's hopes that the boat races might stimulate camaraderie amongst the proletariat and show the country folk that a little cooperation can achieve a great deal. And that this message would trickle down to cooperative farmers. He had no idea that the minister was in Sanyaburi to evoke a ghost.

After refreshments, the minister went to the river, made a long speech to the assembled boatmen and women, then cut a ribbon suspended between a tree and Miss Sanyaburi, 1978, in traditional dress. And thus the Pak Lai boat race festival was officially opened. The minister waved, shook the governor's hand and told him he needed a private room to speak with his aides. This room had already been organized and tables had been arranged into a rectangle with all the chairs facing inward to an island of imitation flowers and a handwritten card welcoming *Our Dear Friends from Vientiane*. The governor was more than a little miffed to have been excluded from this gathering.

Attending the closed meeting were the minister and his wife, Madame Peung and her brother, Tang, Dr Siri the coroner and his wife, Daeng, and a retarded fellow whom the minister assumed to be some part of the ceremony. The minister sat at a ridiculous teak throne dragged in at great expense to make an impression. To his left sat Siri. The general remembered the old doctor from numerous battlefront campaigns. Like many of his ministerial colleagues he had great respect for the doctor's skills behind the front line, patching up wounded comrades and saving lives. But, also like his colleagues, he found the old man's reluctance to take orders a reflection of his anarchistic leanings. He was to be avoided socially. There had been a circular to that effect. The party line was that Dr Siri Paiboun had been ideologically tainted by too many years in France and the early onset of senility. It didn't however stop them from using his various skills whenever their own were lacking. And, on this day, in this room, Siri was the minister's only ally.

'Stack of lizard poop,' he said, leaning towards Siri.

'I'm sorry?'

'Spirits and digging up the dead. Best left where he fell, as far as I'm concerned, Siri. Rest in peace, isn't that what they say? No need for all this.'

'I was under the impression you'd signed all the travel documents for us to be here,' said Siri.

'Certainly I did. It was the only way I could shut her up.'

On the word 'her', he'd raised his chin in the direction of his colourful wife. Siri looked at the woman. He recalled that the Ministry of Culture had issued a list of culturally unacceptable fashion statements. On it were long hair for men, clipped hair for women, revealing shorts and skirts, uplifting brassieres and, as far as he could remember, make-up. The list had obviously passed Madame Ho going in the wrong direction. She was ablaze with cornfield yellow and fresh-bruise purple and Wattay blue. Siri was certain if anyone struck a match in front of her she'd go up like a rocket. She was loud, too, and spoke Lao with the same linguistic prowess as Yul Brynner speaking Thai.

'I take it this wasn't a love match,' said Siri, not caring in the least how offensive the question might have sounded.

Popkorn glared at him, then smiled.

'Her family had a fleet of cargo ships out of Hai Phong. We needed the concession. They needed someone to marry their daughter.'

Siri admired her hairy ankles and the quote, 'Greater love has no one than this, that one lay down his life for his friends,' sprang into his mind. Undefeated as a general. Massacred as a husband.

The minister leaned forward and addressed the group.

'Can we get this damned thing over with?' he said.

His wife glared at him. Madame Peung stood and smiled at the old soldier.

'Comrade Popkorn,' she said. 'I'm terribly sorry to have imposed this journey upon you. I know you're a busy man. But I needed to be here in person in order to cross-reference the location of your brother's corpse. I know that you believe this is all a lot of nonsense. Three months ago I would have felt exactly the same. Then, suddenly, something remarkable happened. I woke up as a different person. I was, you might say, in another reality. And I suddenly had a gift.'

Siri looked at her. She did not emote. Nor did she prance. She spoke calmly and used simple Lao. She told her story the way a baguette seller might describe the day she'd won a minor prize in the Thai national lottery. There was excitement in her eyes but not boasting. Siri hung on her every word. He might even have been smiling. At least that was how Madame Daeng noticed it. All this and the main feature had not yet begun. Brother Tang sat to one side ripping up crude paper cartoons of money and clothes and gold bullion.

'You're all in doubt,' said Madame Peung. 'I would be too. But the spirits come to me with ease. It's as if I can pluck them out of the air at will. Let me take this one, for example. Madame Ho.'

The minister's wife let out a Pekinese whelp.

'Since our session together when we discussed your sister she has visited me often,' said Madame Peung. 'But I am sorry to tell you her bones will never be reunited with those of your ancestors. She was afraid of the socialist takeover. She boarded a refugee boat headed for Australia. It was not seaworthy and it sank in the deep ocean. I am sorry. Nobody survived.'

The minister's wife gasped then burst into tears.

'Kiang,' she sobbed. 'Kiang. Why didn't you stay? I could have found you a gullible husband in the military. You would have been safe.'

The minister's eyes rolled to the ceiling and back. He rarely travelled with his wife and everyone could see why. Madame Peung left her seat, squeezed through a gap between the tables and knelt in front of the Vietnamese woman. She held her hand.

'Kiang took something of yours to remember you by. Was there something you both treasured?'

'Our cat, TinTin,' said Madame Ho.

'TinTin is there with her,' said Madame Peung. 'They both miss you.'

'That's lov . . . lov . . . lovely,' said Mr Geung.

Madame Daeng's eyes joined the general's on the ceiling.

'I really don't want this to be a circus,' said Madame Peung. 'I'm usually alone with the victim's relatives. But in order to find the minister's brother I need a sympathetic audience. Let's not forget I'm new to all this. I can feel the hostility in the room. It doesn't help. So, excuse me for what I'm about to do.'

She turned and looked directly into Daeng's eyes. It was all the doctor's wife could do not to turn away.

'The red-haired man is with us,' said Madame Peung.

Just that and Daeng closed in on herself like a frond of sensitive grass. She didn't want to hear any more.

'He has been punished over and over for what he did to your sister. He holds no grudge against you. There is no threat from him. From others, yes. But not him.'

Daeng said nothing but the witch had reached an icy hand inside her chest and pulled out her deepest tumour. She could feel the cold space that remained there.

Like a chess master playing several games simultaneously, Madame Peung walked around the rectangle of tables to where Mr Geung sat. She reached out her hand and he looked at it unaware that he was expected to take hold of it.

'Geung,' she said, 'your father is sorry. He will always be ashamed of the way he treated you.'

'My father is . . . is . . . is . . .' said Geung.

'He's gone, Geung,' said Madame Peung. 'I'm sorry.'

'No, he's not,' said Geung.

'Yes.'

'No.'

'I'm sorry.'

Mr Geung surprised everyone by smiling at this news. But he had no more to say. He was a man with an elaborate network of lights and sounds that played inside him like a tightly wrapped pinball table, but few of them could be seen or heard from the outside.

Meanwhile, Madame Peung had arrived at the seat of Dr Siri. She knelt in front of him, smiled and took his hand. He doubted anything she had to say would cause him any great concern. He was wrong.

'Would you like to hear from Boua?' she asked.

'No,' he said, instinctively. His hand now grasping hers tightly.

'I mean . . .' he continued. 'No. But thanks.'

There were any number of reasons why this would not be a particularly appropriate time to chat celestially with his dead wife. Not least of these was the presence of his current wife seated opposite.

'I understand,' said Madame Peung. 'I'm sorry. Perhaps some other time.'

She turned and, still on her knees, crawled before the minister.

'The energy is right now, Comrade,' she said. 'We can find your brother.'

Inspired by the show he'd witnessed, Minister

Popkorn had no hesitation. He pulled the black and white photograph from his top pocket. It showed a dashing Lao soldier, arm in arm with a younger and skinnier Popkorn. They were posed in front of the Hanoi opera house. Attached to the photo with a paper clip was a small plastic photo envelope. She looked at him quizzically.

'My wife thought it might help,' he said, embarrassed. 'He spent–'

'He spent some time as a monk,' Madame Peung interrupted. 'When he was first ordained they cut off his eyebrows. For some reason he kept them. He was a little strange like that. He said that if anything ever happened to him you should plant them and grow a new him.'

The minster was astounded.

'It was . . . a joke,' he said. 'He liked to joke. He was a fun-loving young man.'

Siri, it had to be said, was a little perturbed that the general should hang on to his brother's eyebrows, but he could see a real affection between the two men. He was more impressed with his witch with every revelation. Her melodic laugh. Her matter-of-fact telling of intimacies. The glint in her eye. She was, no doubt, the real thing. Her brother had already sensed that the time was right. He had lit incense sticks on either side of her chair and was tapping gently on a small, handheld drum. The smoke of burning spirit money rose from a large mortar behind him. Madame Peung returned to her seat. With everyone's permission she began the ceremony to locate the body of Major Ly. She started with an explanation.

'Places,' she said. 'All places are governed by the holy mothers of the pantheon. Before we contact them we need to pay homage to the wandering souls. They delight in the ashes of riches and finery. My brother is finding a rhythm that will ease me into a shallow trance, although I have to admit I don't have trouble slipping away. I'm told that normally we need all the trappings and I should wear a red hood and all that, but I think that's for the tourists. I merely wait for my spirit guide like a passenger on a train platform; when he gets here I'll shudder a little as he enters my body and, from there on, he does all the work. If you could just be patient for a few moments. Thank you.'

Siri had been expecting a song and dance act. He'd attended enough exorcisms and séances – had even conducted one of his own, albeit like a drunk attempting to fly a jumbo jet. So he expected that at any minute the kaftaned assistant would drape the red hood over the medium's head and beat the hell out of a tambourine until she fell into her trance. But Madame Peung merely put the brother's photograph on the plastic-covered chair arm beside the minister, took hold of his wrist and found a pulse. She nodded to the beat and Tang the assistant beat in time to it on the drum.

Madame Peung smiled at Siri, sighed and lowered her eyes. The sounds in the room came from the drums and shouts and music speakers back down along the river bank. They all watched the medium. Tang was tapping the drum with two fingers but the sound seemed to vibrate around the room. Then, a hum, a deep melodic hum emerged from the back of his throat. It was unvoiced, monotone, hypnotic and seemed not to need an intake of breath in order to continue its seamless drone. Everyone in the room sank into its warmth. And then the witch shuddered. It was barely noticeable but everyone in the room, on edge, witnessed it. She nodded slowly. Smiled now and then. Laughed silently once. Then, after, some five minutes, she sighed. Her brother ceased his dirge and began to collect together the props. He seemed to know it was all over.

'Hmm,' said Madame Peung, as if mulling over a minor plumbing problem. 'I know now why his body wasn't found.'

'Why?' asked the minister.

'He was trapped on a boat. It was a large boat and he was inside the cabin when the vessel capsized. It flipped over and he was unable to get out. He drowned.'

'Where?' asked the minister.

'Not far from here, as I already intimated. It's about ten kilometres upriver. I am still visualizing the landscape.'

'Why, after all these years, has nobody noticed a boat submerged in the river?' asked Daeng.

'That's a good question, Madame Daeng,' said Madame Peung. 'I think it's because, well, I don't feel water around him. It's more claustrophobic than that.

Perhaps he's in a cave? Or, no. In fact, I believe he and the boat might be encased in mud.'

'That's not unlikely,' said the minister. 'There are long, deep stretches around these parts. In places the river can reach a depth of sixty metres. In some spots you could sink a pirogue and the silt and mud just sucks you down. Over time I wouldn't be at all surprised if a sunken boat vanished completely.'

'Oh, my word. This is a major project,' said Madame Ho. 'Call in the engineers, husband.'

'Now wait!' said the minister. 'I can't requisition a unit of men just like that. What would I tell their commanders?'

'You're the Minister of Agriculture,' she reminded him. 'You don't have to tell them anything. You give the order. They come running. Not terribly complicated.'

Siri let out a silent puff of air. If he'd had a wife like this he would certainly have shot her long ago.

'Before I start calling for reinforcements I hope you don't mind if I go and take a look for myself,' said the minister, although his sarcasm had a pleading element to it. 'Madame Peung, would you care for a short helicopter ride?'

'Oh, that sounds like fun,' she said.

'Right then,' said the minister. 'My helicopter is only fitted with four passenger seats. So that's—'

'I'm so sorry,' said the witch, 'but I'll have to have my brother along. I may be in need of another brief trance as we get closer to the site.'

'Then we're full,' said the minister. 'You, your brother, me and Dr Siri.'

'Why him?' said Madame Ho and Daeng at exactly the same time.

'He's the coroner,' said the minister. 'There might be bodies down there. I've never seen my brother without his skin on, so if we find him I'd need a formal identification. That would avoid having to bring in troops. We can ship his remains home and be done with all this nonsense. You do have his medical records with you, don't you, Siri?'

Siri tapped his shoulder bag.

'I don't actually swim that well,' he said.

'Never mind,' said the minister. 'If there's anything in the water I'll have the pilot and the mechanic bring it up to the bank.'

Siri could see that the minister was sold on the idea that Madame Peung would be able to pinpoint the whereabouts of Major Ly. He'd arrived sceptical but was now a believer. As evening was fast approaching, they scheduled the flight for first thing the following morning. Siri was every bit as excited about the trip as Madame Peung.

It was then that the French made a seriously bad call. The Thais were posturing again, claiming this stretch of land, moving that boundary line. The French knew that we Lao showed little loyalty or gratitude to our colonial leaders. They were certain we were so spineless we would side with anybody, and the Thais – at a great stretch – were our ethnic counterparts. Our histories were interlaced (usually with the Thais sacking and pillaging our cities). But thanks to a little cardsharpery at the diplomatic level, the Thais had claimed the west bank of the Mekhong as their own and a third of our Lao brothers and sisters now found themselves on Thai soil. There were more ethnic Lao in the northeast of Thailand than in Laos itself.

So, in response to this Thai flirtation, the French administrators decided to instil in us a pride in our nation. They organized youth movements across the country. The larger towns held Lao camps where teenagers were gathered to hear about the great Lao kings and famous battles against the cowardly Siamese. They printed anti-Thai propaganda for us to read around the campfire. But something else happened at those camps. The same national pride the French hoped might turn us against the Thais turned round and bit the hand that beat it. The camps formed a foundation for what became a movement to overthrow the colonists. And I was there at the camp in Pakse. Too old to register as a camper, I signed on as a cook.

'I'm not going to let you read any more till it's finished.

'Is this the part where I arrive on the scene?'

'Why on earth would I find that important enough to include in my memoirs?'

'I bet you loved me at first sight.'

'You're so vain.'

When the French and the Vietnamese came to inspect us, we sang Lao songs and learned what native plants could be used as balms against burns, and waved little paper Lao flags we'd made during art and craft sessions. And when they were gone, our teachers told us about the French atrocities.

Like me, the young people there had seen no worth in themselves and the camps gave us a value. And two of our teachers had studied in France but they weren't royals. Through their own hard work and raw ability they'd earned degrees in Paris and even though they could have stayed in Europe and made a lot of money, they came home to help develop their people. One of them, a nurse called Bouasawan, whom I wanted so much to be, taught us about the uprising of the lower classes throughout the world. Her husband, Dr Siri Paiboun (and there was the reason I wanted so much to be Boua), was a dashing, funny, intelligent man who taught us the real reason we should be proud. Not because some ancient king massacred another's army but because we were human beings. We had rights. We deserved respect.

The seeds of the Lao Issara – Free Lao – movement were watered in those camps and many of our youth went on to be leaders in the uprising. The French realized too late that engendering a pride in Lao nationhood was perhaps not such a good idea after all. They disbanded the camps but there was no disbanding the hearts of the Lao now joined in comradeship. The damage was done. We knew who our enemy was, and he wasn't Thai.

7

Village of the Undead

It had been a long time since Inspector Phosy didn't have bad weather to grumble about. Drought had given way to monsoons, to flash floods, to dust storms. Crops had been lost to locusts. Plagues of mosquitoes had been unleashed when they flooded the land for the new dam and with the humidity being what it was, dengue, the bleeding fever plague, was rife.

But here they were on a bright Sunday morning chugging along on his lilac Vespa motor scooter. A cool breeze massaged their faces; Phosy, Dtui and Malee. A family outing that didn't involve digging. Not dirt anyway. They were in no hurry so Phosy sat on 30 k.p.h., which gave him ample time to avoid disappearing into a pit or running into a stray pig or swallowing flies as they sang. Ban Elee, their destination for the day, was forty-eight kilometres from Vientiane off Route Thirteen, an unspectacular straight road passing lookalike villages every ten minutes or so. Once Phosy had read Daeng's letter, there was no question that he would make this trip. Madame Daeng wasn't one to waste anybody's time.

They arrived stiff from the ride and stretched and clicked joints and walked around the bike to get the circulation back in their legs. There was nothing to confirm that they'd arrived at their destination apart from the odometer on the Vespa and the word of a farmer they'd spoken to earlier. There was no signpost and nothing remarkable about Ban Elee to distinguish it from every other village.

'You lost?' called a woman who sat on a flimsy balcony threading jasmine on to a garland string.

'Can't be lost if you have no idea where you're going,' Dtui replied and smiled at her.

This was to be their tactic for the day. Unplanned tourism.

'From Vientiane, are you?' asked the woman.

'How'd you know?'

'It's only city people would waste good petrol going on a joyride in this day and age.'

'We saved up for it,' said Dtui. 'We wanted our daughter to see the countryside while there's still some here to see. Introduce her to some good country people.'

'And where's that accent from?'

'Udomxai. I'm a northerner. I miss the countryside too.'

The woman chuckled. Her large breasts jiggled as she did so.

'You know? My husband just brought us down some custard apples. Sweetest little buggers you ever tasted.

Come up and sample a few, why don't you?'

Ten minutes later there was a good-sized gathering on that small balcony and Malee was being bounced from lap to lap, showing no preference for stranger or relative. A dozen villagers had naturally gravitated to the lei-threader's hut and they already knew that Dtui was a nurse, Phosy was a policeman, and Malee would be either a doctor or a psychologist. The latter was something of a gamble as Laos didn't have a psychologist but Dtui predicted there'd be a huge demand by the time her daughter graduated. This was the village life that Dtui so missed. These people were four hundred kilometres from her own village but they were still her people. There was an old saying: people of a different village are herbs of a different garden. But she knew that wasn't true. She believed that somewhere in a sixty-people grass hut village in Kenya there was a lei-threader and a bicycle repair man and a seller of zinc watering cans, and if some cosmic lightning strike were to magically transport her there, she'd know exactly how to act and she'd be accepted. Villages were about people.

Phosy was advising some elder about the construction of a dyke. Dtui took advantage of his distraction by leading them in to the investigation.

'That's a splendid house up there on the buff,' she said. 'I wouldn't mind living in a place like that. Is it yours, Headman Gop?'

The old man laughed.

'I wouldn't want to live there,' he said. 'Neither would you.'

'Why not?' Dtui asked.

'It's haunted,' said one teenage girl, as skinny as a raindrop down a window.

There were a few nervous laughs. Some looked at her as if she'd spoken out of turn. But Dtui knew they'd be unable to resist the country habit of telling a good yarn.

'Don't make fun of me now, girl,' said Dtui.

'Do you not believe in ghosts then, Nurse Dtui?' asked the headman, his good eye attempting to pick her out amid the crowd.

'I've never seen any nor heard a story that could convince me,' said Dtui.

'Then hear this one,' he said. 'That house you covet up there on the hill, it belonged to a royalist general and his wife. Like most of 'em, the general was more intent on making money than on soldiering. They say he got a small fortune tucked away. All he had to do was stay alive and they'd have enjoyed a very comfortable retirement. But he went and stepped on a mine instead and left the woman a rich widow. He was from here, a son of the earth, but she saw herself being a cut above all us. Plastered her face in make-up just to let us know she could afford it. She lived in that house up there with one live-in girl – hired us to do all the manual work: cut down her papayas, clean her toilet. So we weren't what you'd call close. Then, three months ago, give or take a week, she got herself killed.'

'No? How?' Dtui asked.

'She'd been away on one of her business trips,' said the lei-threader, taking over the story. 'She was gone longer than usual. Wouldn't have known she was back if it weren't for that noisy old truck she arrived in. She had a girl working for her at the house. Lived in a single room at the back. She'd be the one come down to do the shopping. But that evening, the girl didn't come down to get the old lady any food. Just picked up some petrol at the hand pump. So we assumed her majesty had brought something back from the town. We all went to bed, as normal. When the fighting was on we didn't take much notice of shots in the night. But there were these two shots and we all woke up. It sounded close, you see. We have our own, what you'd call, security force. We take it in turns to patrol with a rifle. We thought it was the guard shooting at something. But one of our lads who was in the military said it sounded more like a handgun.'

'I knew it was a handgun,' said the headman.

'So, we all ask around and see that everyone in the village was accounted for,' the lei-threader continued. 'And Ott, who was on duty that night, comes running from the back fields and says he thinks the shot was from the hill. From Madame Peung's house. So up we all go, none of us in a hurry to run into a gunman. And the live-in girl comes running out of the bushes in a red fit. "She's dead," she shouts. "The widow's dead and they took my pig." We had no idea why she was going on about pigs but sure enough, there's the widow's body lying in a pool of blood on her bed. Hole through her head.'

'We didn't catch the gunman,' said the headman. 'We assumed it was a burglar. There are a lot of old soldiers begging and living rough. Madame Peung's house would have been an inviting target, away from the village as it is. We heard the truck drive off so he must have stolen that. We took the widow's body down to the temple and sent a message on to kilometre fifty-six. That's the nearest police box to here. What we'd normally do is contact the family of the deceased and get them to organize the cremation.'

'But we didn't know anything about her,' said the lei-threader. 'There weren't any papers or identifications in the house. Not so much as a photograph album. So we had to do it all ourselves. We had her laid out for three days in case anyone wanted to pay their respects . . .'

'There wasn't exactly a rush,' said the skinny girl.

'Then the boys carried her down to the pyre and up she went,' said the headman. 'It was all over. Or so we thought.'

'It was the next morning we hear another scream,' said the lei-threader. 'The live-in girl had stayed on in the maid's room up there and she comes running down the hill again. "She's not dead," she screams. "Madame Peung isn't dead." We assumed she'd been hitting the turnip wine early and went about our business. But then, what do we see but this figure walking down the hill. And the closer it gets, the more certainly it looks like the widow.'

'We all pissed off inside our houses and barred the doors,' said the skinny girl.

'I didn't,' said the headman.

'I was so scared my tongue curled back on itself and came out my rear end,' said the lei-threader. 'She walked right up here on the balcony. I could see her through that crack there as clear as I'm seeing you.'

'You're sure it was her?' Phosy asked.

'Not a doubt in my mind,' she told him.

'She came to me, of course,' said the headman. 'Which was only proper. But I was indisposed.'

'You were hiding in your outhouse,' said the lei-threader. 'I could see you from the back window.'

'Just taking care of my ablutions, is all.'

'So, what did she do?' Dtui asked.

'She came to me,' said a wrinkled old woman who had been camouflaged thus far by the grain of the wood. 'She got her oven charcoal from me. I didn't mind her, not like this lot. She'd give me a bonus at Lao new year. Nothing wrong with her. And she says, "Bung," she says. "What's going on here? Why's everybody screaming and hiding from me?" Well, I told her, didn't I? I told her, "Of course they're scared," I said. "The men folk carried your body down to the pyre yesterday and we watched you go up in smoke. You were killed by an intruder three days ago. You're dead, madam." And, you know? She turned as white as ... well, she was really white. Can't say I've been that close to a ghost before but she was so shocked she was dead I even felt sorry for her. She went from door to door calling out people's names. Insisting there'd been some mistake. That she wasn't dead at all. She tried for a few days. She was polite about it. Friendly even. But nobody dared come out to greet her.'

'I would have done,' said the headman.

'She seemed really confused,' said the lei-threader. 'Like she wasn't prepared to admit she was dead. And I must say there was a lot about her that didn't seem dead at all. She could ride a bicycle, for one. I mean, how many spirits do you know that can ride a bicycle? And she could write. She'd pin a note on the central pillar at the market with her grocery list on it. One of the cabbage women would take it halfway to the house and leave it under a tree on a chair. The money would be there waiting.'

'So, is there no chance it could have been a mistake?' Dtui asked.

'Well, that's what we were starting to think,' said the headman. 'That perhaps the woman who was shot wasn't Madame Peung at all.'

'It was,' said the skinny girl. 'We all saw her.'

'And something like that,' said the lei-threader, 'and word gets around. People from the neighbouring villages came by to get a look at the used-to-be woman: Madame

Keui. That's what we all started calling her. And I suppose it was about a week after she was reborn that this drugged, crazy man staggers into the village holding a pistol. Dirty runt, he was. He stank to high heaven and must have been completely off his head. "Where is she?" he shouts. "Where is the woman who can't be killed? I didn't miss, you know? Never miss." He was a serious gunman, that one. He had another pistol in the back of his belt. He meant business. We reckoned he had to be Hmong with that accent. Lot of Hmong round here.'

'You see?' said the skinny girl. 'Word had reached the bandit who'd shot her in the first place. He'd been haunted ever since he first killed her and he was back to finish the job. Is that creepy or what?'

'He runs up the hill to the house and we're all milling about wondering what we should do,' said the lei-threader. 'We probably didn't do as much as we could have to overpower him. We'd seen enough maniacs with guns over the years. But we found the security rifle and some of the younger ones grabbed machetes and we all marched up there. We were about twenty metres from the house when the front door bursts open and there he is with the widow. He has hold of her by the hair and he's dragging her out to the veranda. She doesn't scream, though. Very calm, I'd say. "Does this look like a spirit to you lot?" shouts the lunatic. "Do I not have hold of real hair? Is this not a real bruise on her eye? Do you not smell the stench of sweat and fear on her? Why would anyone think I was afraid of this?"

'We all stood back and watched, not knowing which of them to feel sorry for. "And if she was a spirit, could I do this?" he shouts and laughs like some imbecile and points the pistol barrel to the side of her head. He lets go of her hair and she just kneels there, calm as you like. We knew he was going to do it. We all stepped back at the sound. Bang! Most of us turned away.'

'I didn't,' said the headman.

'When we turned back we all expected to see her head all over the front step,' said the old woman. 'But nothing had happened. She just turned to him and smiled. He tried to scream but nothing came out. Then he was gone. I've never seen anyone run that fast in all my days.'

'Are you sure he didn't just miss?' Dtui asked.

'I saw the bullet hole where it went in her head,' said the skinny girl. 'Blood trickling down.'

'We all did,' said the headman.

'How did the widow react when she was shot this second time?' Phosy asked. Baby Malee had done a complete lap of laps and was happy to suck her thumb against her father's chest.

'She just rubbed her temples like she had a migraine or something,' said the skinny girl. 'She went to have a lie down. When we saw her next day there were no wounds. It was a miracle.'

'It didn't actually bring us closer to her,' said the

lei-threader, 'but getting killed twice left her with this . . . this gift. She stands there in the middle of the village and starts telling us about dead relatives who want to get in touch with us.'

'Claims she saw my wife who still hadn't forgiven me for a little purported rendezvous I had with a lady-boy down in the capital when I was a lad,' said the headman. 'Complete rubbish, of course. But she yells it out to everyone.'

'But she knew stuff only our dead kin could know,' said the skinny girl.

'We couldn't shut her up,' said the headman. 'She went on about a lot of personal things and said if we wanted to talk to our relatives we could go up to the house. I didn't talk to my wife that much when she was alive so I wasn't about to go up there and talk to her spirit. I don't know anyone who'd be brave enough to go up there talking to ghosts. Not that I was afraid, of course. Just not interested.'

'I went up there,' said the skinny girl.

They looked at her with shocked expressions.

'You never did?' said the headman.

'Yeah, I did. I wanted to know about my dad.'

'And could she tell you anything?' asked Phosy.

'A lot. She really could talk to ghosts. I guess that's what she was doing for the strangers too.'

'Strangers?'

'We started to get visitors,' said the headman. 'They'd get off the bus or walk in or arrive on motorcycles, like you. They'd stay for an hour or so then leave. But they wouldn't tell us what they'd been doing.'

'Was there anybody with her up in the house?' Dtui asked, remembering the note on the back of Madame Daeng's photos about the mute brother.

'I don't recall seeing anyone,' said the headman. 'But then again, the live-in girl was long gone before the second killing and none of us went up there. There could have been someone. Could have been a whole coven of witches for all we know.'

'I never saw nobody when I went up there,' said the skinny girl.

'Were there any major differences between Madame Peung and your Madame Keui?' Dtui asked.

'The voice was the same, but there was the accent,' said the old lady. 'You can't hide a Vietnamese accent. The district shaman said it was very likely she picked it up in limbo. Lot of Vietnamese stuck in limbo, he says.'

'Did your shaman have any other comments?' asked Dtui.

'He did mention that we might have been the victims of mass hysteria,' said the lei-threader. 'That we'd all inhaled some natural gas escaping from the earth or listened to some demon music and ... imagined the first murder.'

'What do you think?'

'It was her,' said the old lady. 'No question. The live-in girl had spent all that time in the house with her. She was in no doubt. It was the same woman.'

'And where's the live-in girl now?' asked Phosy.

'Long gone,' said the skinny girl. 'Probably still running if I know her.'

On the journey back to Vientiane Dtui and Phosy had gone over the story looking for logical, non-supernatural explanations for what had happened. In his pocket, Phosy had the bullet the headman had gouged out of the front post. That was real enough. Their suggestions were even more far-fetched than the events themselves. But, short of the entire village stringing them along in an elaborate joke, there was no explanation. It jarred every joint, nipped at every nerve in his policeman's body, but Phosy was forced to agree with the remote likelihood that Madame Keui was indeed a born-again medium. It was not an admission he'd be sharing with anyone at police headquarters. And, besides, there were still a number of smaller questions pending that begged an explanation. He often found that pulling on a loose end unravelled the whole story. But, for the meanwhile, the note Dtui and Phosy would be sending upriver with the next boat would be to the effect that, although their investigation had discovered layer upon layer of mystery, they had uncovered no obvious deceit. As far as they could tell, and as bizarre as it sounded, Madame Peung, aka Madame Keui, was everything she claimed to be. As it turned out, it was a note that would never be sent.

The Vespa pulled up in front of the police dormitory where a small throng of uniformed policemen stood.

Upon seeing Phosy they hurried over to him. They were supposed to salute a senior officer, even if he was wearing Bermuda shorts and a nylon jacket. They'd had training courses on police etiquette. But this was often forgotten, especially during moments of urgency.

'Brother,' said Sergeant Sihot. He was solid as a tank and permanently dishevelled. 'There's been a crime committed. Two, if you count them separately.'

'Sihot, can you not call me brother in front of the men?'

'What?'

'The training?'

'Oh, right. But, someone's torched Madame Daeng's noodle shop.'

'What?' shouted Phosy and Dtui at the same time. They were too shocked to dismount.

'It and the buildings either side of it are gutted.'

'What makes you think it was torched?' Phosy asked.

'Strong stink of petrol in the upstairs rooms,' said Sihot. 'And, look, Brother Phosy, I . . . I don't suppose you know where Dr Siri and Madame Daeng are right now, do you?'

'They're off in Pak Lai,' said Dtui.

'Oh, well. That's a relief.'

He turned to smile at his men. They all seemed suddenly delighted that Daeng's shop had been burned to the ground.

'How could that be a relief?' Phosy asked.

'Because there's a body in there.'

8

1910

It wouldn't officially go on record as Nurse Dtui's first solo autopsy. Judge Haeng had reluctantly given the go-ahead but there would be no permission slip with his signature on it. If anything went wrong he would know nothing about it. That was good enough for Phosy.

After an idle month, the morgue smelled . . . well, like a morgue. Opening the doors and windows did nothing to remove the musty stench. Turning on the light in the late evening succeeded only in filling the place with flying beetles the size of pecan nuts and a cloud of mosquitoes. Only the corpse would escape this onslaught as it had no blood to suck. It had arrived in a large tote bag and been poured on to the cutting room table with the sound of mah-jong tiles. The bones were black. The few that had still been connected at the site were now separated. It was more a puzzle than an autopsy.

'What do you need to know?' Dtui asked. She wore a fresh, green operating theatre robe that reached her feet. Four hundred of them were stacked in the corner, donations from the Soviet Union. There were a matching number of masks and twice as many little rubber boots but she hadn't bothered with them.

'Who he or she is,' said Phosy.

Dtui leaned over the pile of bones and poked around with a pencil.

'Oh, well. We're in luck,' she said. 'Look at this.'

Phosy leaned in to look.

'What is it?'

'It's his name card. It miraculously survived the fire.'

'All right. Then just tell me whatever you can.'

'That's more like it.'

While she was shuffling the parts around she came across the pelvis.

'I'm quite good at the easy parts,' she said. 'And this is one pelvis that was never designed to give birth. And this little fellow over here is probably an eye ridge. All of which tells me our friend here, is . . . or was, male.'

One femur was intact. She measured it. She hmmed.

'I was about to suggest it was a child,' she said. 'He's short. But there's a lot of wear and tear on these joints. And look, the sternum end of the clavicle is fused. So our man here was over thirty. There's a lot of pitting on the rib so he might even have been over forty. So it's a short, middle-aged man.'

'Good job, Dr Dtui,' said Phosy. 'Anything else?'

She liked that title. With a broad smile on her face she swatted a menagerie of flying beasts away from the standard lamp and swung its arm over the bone pile. She picked out fragments of the skull and started to put them together. It was particularly difficult. But after ten minutes of shuffling she looked at her husband.

'I don't think he was killed by the fire,' she said.

'You don't?'

'Well, to be certain we'd have to look at his lungs. As his lungs are deep-fried and indistinguishable from his kneecaps, we'll never know. But I'm prepared to stake my reputation on it. And don't say I don't have one.'

'OK, let's hear it.'

'If he died in the fire I can't think of any reason why anyone would wait until the charred building was cool enough to clamber up to the second floor with no wooden staircase and beat the living daylights out of a corpse.'

'He's been hit?'

'Blunt object. Half a dozen times. Maybe more.'

One problem with communication between Vientiane and Sanyaburi was the absence of a telephone line. Phosy had tried to link through military channels only to discover there were no army units stationed there. It would have been easier to call Thailand on the solitary Lao overseas telephone line and ask someone to run a message across the border. His last hope had been a channel directly to the helicopter which had transported the Minister of Agriculture to Pak Lai but the crew had closed down the equipment for the night. Few boats plied that section of the river after dark as there were still bandits about. So it wouldn't be until the next morning that a message could be sent to Dr Siri and Madame Daeng telling them that their home and all their possessions were gone.

After the autopsy, Phosy had combed through the skeleton of the shop and found nothing of importance. He'd watched them spoon the remains of the victim into the large bag. At the back of his mind was Dr Siri's story about the midget from Housing and the late-night raid. The man had probably lost his job as a result of Siri's complaint. If the body were his it would look very bad for the doctor, especially as there was no way of estimating the time of death. One more thing the inspector had noticed before heading for home was a car parked some fifty metres away on the river bank. Obviously somebody of influence had got wind of the fire and come to observe. The sleek government ZiL limousine sat in the shadows like the devil's own hearse. Nobody got out to discuss matters and Phosy wasn't about to tap on the window and say hello. It was best left alone. It was late and nothing else could be done. Perhaps, by morning, some loved ones would have reported the disappearance of a completely different short, middle-aged man.

How far could they have gone? he wondered. Not for the first time. Hervé Barnard sat in the driver's seat of the black ZiL. Its windows were so darkly tinted he could barely see the statuette on the bonnet. But the point was that nobody could see in. It was a politburo car he'd stolen directly from the parking lot behind the parliament building. The ZiLs the Russians sent to their Third World comrades were a far cry from those that travelled in their own lanes in downtown Moscow. These shoddy rip-off versions leaked petrol and were incredibly easy to break into and hot-wire. The Lao, not realizing this, had felt it safe to leave a fleet of them unguarded behind a bamboo gate.

Barnard had been given little choice. He'd needed to be at the scene of the fire to identify the old whore from her recent photograph. He'd needed to be here to follow her and to kill her. But there were few Westerners in Vientiane and his presence amongst the gawking crowd would have stood out. Hence the car. He'd watched the flames. They were a spectacular sight. Fire had a hunger for old buildings. Most of the properties along the river were closed but a group of onlookers had appeared from nowhere and stood and watched. They'd oohed when a window popped and ahhed with every falling rafter. He'd expected a human chain with buckets. The river was just across from the fire. But, no. They stood. And they watched until the last flaming moth flew off to the heavens and there was only smoke. And not until then did the insignificant policemen arrive. And then the more important ones. And then the boss, resplendent in Bermuda shorts and sandshoes, came to conduct an unimpressive investigation in the dark with failing torches. But where, oh where, were the owners?

Barnard had arrived at eight for his appointment with the little man at the address he'd been given. There were no lights on in the shop or upstairs. No sound. No passers-by. There was a note pinned to the metal grate. He couldn't read it but he assumed it to say the owner was out. Barnard didn't know where she'd gone or for how long but he had only three more days before he was out of medication. He'd had to expedite matters. The fire would bring her back in a hurry. If not this evening, then the next day. She'd travel home to mourn for her little shop and he'd have her.

He couldn't stay at the Lane Xang now, of course. He'd drawn attention to himself by handing out his room number at the market. He doubted this God-awful place would have an efficient police force but, even if it did, he'd done enough to cover his tracks. They'd find the body in the burned-out building. The comrade's little wife or his little mother would report him missing and, assuming they could count, the police would put two and two together. The dead man had an ongoing feud with the couple. Barnard didn't know why and didn't care. The little comrade had burned down the shop in revenge and was trapped by his own fire. Or, with a bit of luck, they'd suspect the shop owners of murdering him. Even more reason for them to return to clear their names. In a civilized country they would perform a post-mortem investigation and make the gruesome discovery of his death. But a country ruled by a university dropout half-breed was hardly likely to know what a pathologist was. He felt the odds had finally swung in his favour.

The flight following the course of the Mekhong was a hairy one. The young pilot lacked the confidence you'd like to sense in someone controlling, what Civilai often called, a heavy metal coffin with an egg whisk on the top. The boy pilot had been set the challenge of navigating the river as low and as slowly as possible. Somebody had been attempting to talk to him on the radio but he'd ripped off his headphones as the tension dug in. No longer connected by microphone, the mechanic was yelling at the top of his voice, pointing this way and that. The Mi-2 helicopter was cleverly designed so as not to be able to look downward without balancing on its nose in mid-air. The mute brother clung to the back of the seat, his knuckles as white as the bones they contained. But Madame Peung rode the air currents like a girl at the funfair. She whooped and laughed and would, no doubt, describe her flight as exhilarating.

Siri was too preoccupied to be nervous. Not for the first time in the past three years, as Yeh Ming, the one-thousand-and-two-year-old shaman, slowly moved into Siri's life, the doctor was pondering yet another dream mystery. They'd been there again, the naked Frenchmen.

Not a pretty sight. They were huddled together for warmth, staring directly into the lens of the dream camera, yelling their *têtes* off, shouting directly at Siri. It was as if they knew he was there watching but they couldn't understand why he wasn't taking notice of them. Why he wasn't acting on what they were telling him. But for Siri it was exactly like watching a television with the sound off. He could hear nothing. He saw the Frenchmen break out of their penguin huddle in order to use their hands, because what true Frenchman could make himself understood without hand gestures? This was even more confusing. Six mimes all backward-walking and imaginary-wall-feeling and banana-unpeeling. Siri had no idea where to look. But the bitter cold proved too much for them. Their joints froze. They turned frosty white. They crumbled to the ground like crushed ice and were blown away. Siri felt somehow responsible. He found himself looking at a snow storm. Waiting. He was contemplating what he'd have to do to change the channel when he was suddenly aware of the shape of a figure walking through the blizzard in his direction. It was a man's outline trudging slowly through the snow. As he walked closer, Siri could see a long white gown edged in gold. A white suit beneath. But who . . . ?

The man stood directly in front of the lens, his face filling the screen. Siri recognized him, an acquaintance who had become significant in Siri's personal Otherworld. During his cynical years, Siri had always mocked the fact that mediums throughout Asia had a hierarchy of spirits. Shamans might dress like a king or a royal consort and messages to the beyond would begin through the ear of the departed aristocracy. He'd always considered that to be somewhat classist. But, of late, he'd come to realize there was some logic in it. The kings and princes always surrounded themselves with the most powerful shamans. Thus they had a direct line to the beyond. It was only natural that the royal courts would have a thriving afterlife community. In death as in life, the royals would rule the roost.

The recently departed king's face hogged the screen. He spoke. Siri heard nothing. But this was not the usual contact where the spirits came into the doctor's world through his head and spoke using his voice. This was more a portal that he was being invited to step into. He had no idea how. He wanted to get closer but this was a dream. There was no actual television. No sofa. No living room. The king raised his voice. There was something. It was faint, like listening to the neighbour through a drinking glass pushed up against the wall. He couldn't make out words but there were sounds. This was a breakthrough. But the king soon became frustrated as he realized his words were not passing over. He stepped back and considered the situation. He then held up one finger. Then nine, one, and then he formed a zero with his index finger and thumb. 1910. It was a year. Siri committed it to memory. Before the king turned back into the blizzard, there may have been a roll of the eyes, a dip of the head. The gestures a schoolmaster might make in the presence of a remedial pupil.

When he woke that morning, Siri had prodded his wife's shoulder but she was already awake. He'd asked her, 'Daeng, what happened in 1910?'

She'd smiled and turned to him.

'Most women are awoken first thing on a Sunday morning with erotic requests and all I get is a history test.'

'Consider the erotic request the first prize for the first person in this bed who can tell me what happened in 1910.'

'Siri, I don't know. I wasn't born yet.'

'Damn. I need an historian.'

'You've had a dream.'

He sat up on one elbow.

'Just once,' he said. 'Just once I'd like to decipher the dream clues before I'm forced to resort to my huge intellect. Because it won't be very long before my intellect goes the way of my ebony-black hair and rock-hard pectorals. Life would be so much easier if I could just wake up with the answers.'

So, Siri had told Daeng all about the frozen Frenchmen and the king. They wracked their brains as to how this might be connected to their latest mission. And, leaving Daeng to discover what had happened in 1910, Siri had departed for his helicopter flight. But then it was, with the helicopter swinging back and forth like a fat sailor on a hammock in a high sea, that Siri recalled one other memory from his dream. One that had remained suppressed during his discussion with Daeng. There hadn't been six Frenchmen but seven. One sat to one side just as naked as the rest and he'd borne a remarkable but incongruous resemblance to Comrade Koomki from Housing.

Siri was snapped from his reverie by the sight of Madame Peung slapping the young pilot on the back and pointing. The pilot panicked and threw the craft into a rapid spiral descent they all doubted he'd pull out of in time. Miraculously, at the last second, he had the beast under control and hovered a few metres above the bank. The sound of sighs could be heard over the growl of the engine. But Siri was trying desperately to recall what it was that had transpired just before the shoulder slap. There had been a gesture, a moment between Madame Peung and her brother. It was something that looked trivial but Siri's instinct told him that it was significant. But, there and then he wasn't able to untangle it from his dream recollections. It would come to him, he was sure.

Despite its gentle hover at two metres, the Mi-2 dropped so heavily to the ground it bounced, not once but three times. Had Siri's teeth been false they would now be embedded in the inside of his skull. The minister swore like a twisted bantam but Madame Peung squealed with delight. They alighted, all but the chastised pilot, on to a patch of grass on a bank that dived steeply down to the water. There were hills on both banks and a sharp turn that threw the mighty Mekhong into a wall of rock.

'It'll be deep here,' said the minister, once the engine noise had been extinguished. 'The river has nowhere to go but down.'

'This ... this is where it happened,' said Madame Peung. She walked down the slope to the water's edge and closed her eyes. A breeze off the water sent ripples through her loose-fitting satin trouser suit. 'Major Ly is here. He's so pleased to feel your presence, Minister.'

The minister stood beside her and looked out at the swirling water.

'Prove it,' he said.

His tone was sceptical but Siri knew he'd been convinced long before this.

'I know,' said Madame Peung, but not to the minister. 'So give me something.'

She raised her head and listened to the Mekhong. Siri fancied he could hear voices too but it was likely just the swirl of the water through the rocks.

'Minister,' said Madame Peung. 'Are you sure you want to test him here, like this?'

'Yes.'

'In front of strangers?'

'I have nothing to ... Why? What did he say?'

'You and your brother had a tent when you were young. It was pitched in the back yard. One game you played was called Arabia.'

'How . . . ?'

'You would take it in turns to be the erotic female dancer. You would tuck your–'

'Enough. All right.'

He looked around. Four of the five litres of blood in his body had found their way to his cheeks. Only Siri had been close enough to hear. The doctor filed it away.

'That's ridiculous,' said the minister. 'But, well I suppose we might as well get on with this. Hey, you.'

He called to the mechanic. The young man jogged down to the group.

'You told me you could swim,' said the minister.

'Like a fish, Comrade.'

'Right. Let's hope you swim better than your pilot flies. Get yourself in the water down there and see what you can find.'

The boy stripped off his shirt and boots and confidently dived into the choppy flow. To everyone's surprise, Tang, the witch's brother, strode down the bank, peeled off his long robe and jumped into the water also. Siri and the minister looked at Madame Peung incredulously.

'He looks unathletic,' she smiled, 'but he's a remarkable swimmer.'

The doctor and the minister exchanged another look but the brother did indeed appear to be very happy in the water. He it was who reached the middle first and his was the first duck-dive sending him deep into the river. Madame Peung walked over to sit on a large boulder that hung over the swirl. It was an idyllic spot surrounded by thick jungle and probably inaccessible by land. Siri thought it would be a great location to photograph a Bière Lao advertisement or a pornographic movie. He clambered over the smaller rocks and sat next to the medium.

'Ah, Siri,' she said. 'You are full to bursting with questions.'

'I could burp them out one at a time,' he told her.

'Keep a cool heart, Doctor. There's no hurry. Why were you so reluctant to hear from your first wife?'

'It seemed ... I don't know ... disrespectful to Madame Daeng.'

'Aren't you curious at all?'

'I'm ...' Siri reached for his missing earlobe. It was a habit he'd developed whenever verging on the supernatural. 'I'm so curious I could scream. You probably know about my shaman-in-residence, Yeh Ming?'

'Of course.'

'Well, whether I like it or not he's in me somewhere. But, for reasons I don't really understand, he's putting down barriers between me and the departed. I know they're there. I see them. But I can't talk to them.'

'What can I do for you, Siri?'

'Teach me.'

'To make contact?'

'Yes.'

She smiled.

'Can you teach somebody not to be colour-blind?' she

asked. 'To not grow hair out of their ears?'

'I'm not sure what that means.'

'Dr Siri. You are a man of science. Your education gave you proof that there was only one world. This physical one we see all around us. Yet, without warning, you were tossed into this other dimension. You see it just as I do. You experience it. And, even though you can't deny it's there, your incorrectly educated self is always at odds with it. It's there but it cannot possibly be there.'

'So, how do I . . . ?'

'It might be too late, Siri, my darling. Cynicism is a big part of who you are. It's the shutter you pull down to keep out the storms you can't weather. As long as that shutter is down, your ghost friends will be on the other side of it.'

She stood and started back over the rocks. As she passed Siri she stumbled and he caught her. She looked into his eyes.

'You know, I'm probably not the most qualified guru to be working with you on this problem. What makes me flesh and blood and them not, I have no idea. But I cannot deny they're there nor can I deny my role in their unsettled state. The moment you're able to do the same, that's when you'll communicate with them. It's standing-room only out there, doctor. Your waiting room is full. I see them.'

The two divers had returned to the river's edge. She released his hand and continued along the bank. There had been something déjà vu about her words. He'd had this conversation before in this same place. But not in the waking world. The divers' return was an annoyance. He hurried along behind her to where the minister leaned over the mechanic.

'Anything?' shouted the old general.

'A lot of mud down there,' said the mechanic. 'No sign of a wreck.'

But Tang was out of the water and ripping branches from the nearest tree. He returned with two, handed the pilot one and dived back in.

'I think he wants you to follow him,' said Siri.

The mechanic shrugged and swam out after the brother. Once more they duck-dived at the deepest point. The onlookers stood still and silent watching the surface of the Mekhong. Siri, with his troubled lungs and his modest beginner swimming ability, could only marvel at how the two could be so comfortable under thousands of kilograms of water. In fact they were down so long he was starting to get anxious. Not so anxious that he might rip off his shirt and dive in to rescue them, but enough that he asked the minister how well he could swim.

But then the divers' heads appeared above the choppy water and each had a broad smile on his face.

'Have a nice time?' asked Madame Daeng, sniffing the air around Siri like a dog taking in the hindquarters of an interloper.

'I'm lucky to be alive,' he told her. 'Our pilot trained on Dumbo the elephant.'

'This Dumbo wears lavender perfume?'

Siri didn't hear. He looked out over the balcony. The river was so crowded with craft you could step from one to the next and reach the far bank. Daeng wore sunglasses and had a half-empty beaker beside her on the rattan table. There too sat her notebook and a pen.

'Ice tea?' he asked.

'Mekhong whisky and water,' she told him.

'At eleven a.m.?'

'I'm on vacation.'

'Are your legs playing up?'

'Will you stop talking about my damned legs,' she growled. 'My legs are fine. I'm more than just a pair of legs, you know? Ask about my elbow, why don't you? My fish-gutting skills. My ability at mental arithmetic. Just leave my bloody legs alone.'

'I . . . how many glasses have you had?'

She ignored the question. Siri brought over the second deckchair and set it up beside hers. He sat. Silent. Decided this was as good a time as any to keep his mouth shut. They watched the chaos on the river for a good ten minutes.

'I'm sorry,' she said.

'No problem.'

'So. What happened upriver?'

'Are there any other words I shouldn't use? Buttocks, for example.'

She smiled.

'Just shut up and tell me about the trip,' she said.

'How can I shut up and–?'

'Siri!'

'We had a lovely time, impending death notwithstanding.'

'Did you find the brother?'

'We're not sure. There is something just below the mud.'

'A boat?'

'It's likely. They poked it with sticks and estimated it was about five metres long. The mechanic said it might be a rock but the deaf and dumb fellow seemed pretty excited.'

'So, she's legitimate then, your witch.'

'It's too early to confirm but too eerie to ignore.'

'But you have a gut feeling.'

'She is rather impressive.'

Daeng took up her glass and drank from it.

'Right,' she said.

'Any luck with 1910?'

'I found the one and only Pak Lai schoolteacher.'

'Oh, well done.'

'He graduated from fifth grade. Didn't make it as far as high school history.'

'Oh.'

'And, are you sure it was a date?'

'What else might it be?'

'A telephone number?'

'I just couldn't imagine a royal spirit giving me his telephone number. Did you . . . ?'

'There's no phone here. Or, rather, there are four phones but no line. This area isn't a priority ... for anything. Do you think we might use the helicopter radio to call Phosy?'

'They've gone already. Popkorn and his frightful wife went directly back to Vientiane after dropping us off.'

'Madame Peung didn't go with them?'

'No, the minister said he'd send a team of military engineers. Madame Peung will greet them and lead them to the site. Could be tomorrow or the day after. Meanwhile, she's invited us to dinner at the governor's house tonight.'

'You naturally accepted.'

'Would have been rude not to. And it's an opportunity to talk. We had precious little time this morning and it was hellish noisy on the flight. She's a difficult woman to tie down. If I'm lucky I'll be able to get her alone for a little while and do a bit of probing.'

Madame Daeng knocked back her drink and stood.

'Steady on, *ma fille*,' said Siri.

'I can look after myself,' she snapped. 'Always could.'

9

The Cadaver of Short Stature

Nobody had laid claim to the cadaver of short stature. It was Monday and Inspector Phosy had left a number of messages with the Housing Department asking them to let him know whether Comrade Koomki turned up for work that morning. There had been no reply. And so he sat at his desk. He'd progressed to a rank where a quick response to a call for help was no longer his concern. This was largely a desk job. Promotion generally led one away from the work one enjoyed and into a state of inertia.

Still unable to get word to Siri and Daeng in Sanyaburi, Phosy had nothing to do other than thumb through the incident files on his desk. It had been a weekend of misadventure rather than crime. A grandmother in Amone had made a cake. She had mistakenly mixed the eggs and lard with gunpowder instead of flour. The oven blew up but as she had rushed to the bathroom to take care of business she was unharmed. Then there was the gardener at the Lane Xang hotel who had slipped on wet leaves and broken his head in the empty swimming pool. And the mysterious disappearance of one of the three hundred stone busts of the president recently arrived from Romania. More likely a miscounting of stock than a theft.

Nothing there called for his professional expertise. So he allowed himself some time to mull over the odd situation they'd encountered in Ban Elee. Phosy was a simple policeman – a hero of the revolution perhaps but uncomplicated in terms of seeing and believing. He could gather facts, analyse them and draw conclusions. Perhaps the only man he'd met who could better him at detection was Dr Siri himself.

The fact that such a logical man as Siri claimed to see ghosts had always been a mystery to the inspector. Phosy had no personal contact with the spirits. He didn't pay homage to his ancestors or apologize to the land spirits for cutting down a tree. On his trip out to Ban Elee, he had encountered ten villagers who claimed to have witnessed a reincarnation. He knew uneducated people were given to animist beliefs and leaned on the side of gullibility. But what did they have to gain by inventing this bizarre story? What would be the point of setting up such an elaborate scam? No, unlike Siri and Dtui who were prepared to accept such events as paranormal, Phosy was an investigator. He would investigate until there was nothing left unexplained and only then would he be prepared to join the ranks of the unhinged.

'The facts,' he said out loud, then internalized the rest when he saw the clerks were looking at him. The wife of a royalist general most certainly had a security file and he'd gone in early this morning to dig it out. It sat beside the incident reports on his desk. He'd been through it already. It wasn't particularly meaty. As a widow she'd continued to export timber to Thailand through old contacts in the Thai military. This with the blessing of the Party. The wealthy had not been summarily shipped off to re-education and stripped of their belongings. The Pathet Lao had a country to run and they needed this back-up capitalist base to be able to afford to do so. Not all the successful business people fled across the Mekhong. Many were courted and encouraged.

Madame Peung was one such socialist socialite. A few years ago she'd been introduced to similarly well-heeled capitalists in Vietnam and import–export deals had been signed. Following her last business trip to Hanoi she was shot and killed. This is where the personal information file ended. There was a police report paper-clipped to the cover. The killing had been investigated by a cadre called Ekapat, serving as district police officer at kilometre fifty-six. Phosy had Ekapat's file at hand also. He had been transferred from military unit eighty-seven in Houaphan. He had spent most of his army service in the catering corps and attended the rapid conversion course to make him a policeman just four months earlier. To his credit, he did travel a great distance on his bicycle to reach Ban Elee. These were his findings:

'The murder took place at about one a.m. The attractive maid said she heard two shots some two minutes apart but I didn't see any bullets at the scene. They were probably still in the victim's head. I didn't look. She didn't see the intruder so there was no description I could post. Nu, the maid, who is single, said she went to the victim's room and the door was open. It's normally locked, she said. The victim lay in a pool of blood on the mattress. Later questioning of the villagers confirmed they too had not seen the assassin. It was not ascert . . . asser . . . as . . . Nobody knows what was taken 'cause they didn't know what was in the house to start with. The maid wasn't allowed in some rooms so she didn't know either. But I imagine it was a robbery. I may have to interview the maid again. The end.'

Real policeman Phosy paused at this point to ask a few questions. He wondered why there had been such a gap between the first and second shots. Why the victim's door was open. Did she open it because she knew the killer or did he break it down? If the latter, why didn't the maid hear the sound of wood splintering? The same applied to how the killer got into the house. Did he break a window? Were there signs of a break-in around the front or back doors? Phosy wished now he'd gone up to look at the house when he had the chance.

He'd been too quick to accept Dtui's opinion that

this was an example of the supernatural. He sharpened his pencil and made a list of more earthly possibilities on the back of the incident sheets.

The widow was not killed, only injured in the first attack. The bullet did not damage any vital passages in her brain, in fact it gave her heightened sensitivity.
There was a mix-up of bodies at the temple and the person the villagers took to the pyre was not in fact the widow.
The burning of the corpse was symbolic rather than actual.
The person who was killed was not the widow but a friend who looked like her.
The widow was killed and replaced by an imposter who claimed to have psychic powers for the purpose of ... (He drew a blank on that one.)
The whole thing was conspired by the villagers for the purpose of ... (He had no idea how to get out of that one either.)

This was a rather humble list but it made Phosy feel better that there were straws to clutch at. And there was one more straw. The brother. Why hadn't they seen him in the village? Was he holed up in the house that whole time, afraid to go out? He wondered whether any of the bereaved families who visited the witch had seen anything or anybody in the house. He'd need to contact them. Yes, a start. He went straight to the communications room and sent a wire to his counterpart in Ho Chi Minh. The wire would be diverted via the Vietnamese Secret Service Unit in Vientiane where it would be translated. A background check would be run on Phosy and eventually the request would be sent off to the Department of Justice in Vietnam. All this just to find out what Madame Peung had been doing on her last visit to Ho Chi Minh. Did she upset anyone enough to want her executed? It was one of Phosy's favourite ploys to start with the paranoid and work backwards. Conspiracy theories weren't always far-fetched. Not in this day and age.

The underground movement against the French was expanding. The Lao Issara organized acts of sabotage. We collected intelligence on troop movement through networks of observers in the villages. We lured the clumsy French militia into the jungles where they were ill-equipped to compete with nature. A platoon could often be defeated by dysentery alone and we would retreat not from the enemy but from the stench. We left the politics to the elders. Our job was to remind the French that they weren't welcome. To let them know that Laos was no longer a cushy posting. We were angry and we wanted to fight. Once or twice our cell would meet up with the medical unit of Bouasawan and Siri. It was heartbreaking. He loved his wife so much he couldn't see me at all. He was the first man I'd loved and he had no idea.

The guerrilla skirmishes went badly. We suffered losses. Then came a war in Europe. The French were distracted. And suddenly there was another monster in the mix. South-east Asia was invaded from the north by the Japanese. In no time at all, that little Asian country had taken over half a continent. If nothing else, the Japanese dominance around that time showed us that Asians could be more powerful than Europeans. They gave us hope. But they frightened me even more than the French. We were told to cooperate with them but they didn't look at us . . . at me, like an ally should. We were still not equals and our fighting girls were seen as fair game by the randy Japanese. I once had to kill one to remind them we had rights and we deserved respect. By then, killing had become second nature to me, but this was the first time I'd had to use my knife on what was technically a partner. I knew he would have gladly done the same to me once he'd had his way, so it was no great moral jerk. But he'd worn those three stars on his shoulder and it was suggested I disappear for a while. I became quite adept at disappearing. In fact, although I was in contact with my commanders the whole time, I only reappeared once during that period.

In October 1945 we all joined together in Savanaketh town and heard the joyous announcement that France, somewhat tired after fighting off Germany, had graciously granted us a flimsy independence. We were a sort of free nation. I kissed Nurse Bouasawan on the cheek that afternoon and shook Dr Siri's hand. I could feel his palm in mine for many months after. It was the last time we would meet for over thirty years. I loved again after that but never as deeply or sincerely as I had with my doctor. We all celebrated long and hard and started to plan the new nation. But it turned out to be a brief freedom. With the war in Europe won, the French returned to renew old friendships. And this was when the horror years started. The

Japanese were defeated. The French returned in great numbers and the clearing up of troublesome elements began. The Frenchmen still had blood in their teeth from the European campaign and they swept through Laos like angry dogs reclaiming their bones. We were scattered off to the jungle where we had to rethink, replan, reorganize. It was there that the whore in me was born.

Barnard had pushed his luck far enough. He was starting to question his strategy. It was Monday morning and he knew they'd be missing the car soon. He couldn't sit there indefinitely. He assumed that if the old couple was in Vientiane they would have come by to inspect the damage. So they must be away and he needed to find out where. He was used to having people around him who could gather information. Spies who could move about unnoticed. Technology that would allow him to listen to private conversations and interpreters who could fill in the gaps. But here he was alone and conspicuous and he had little to fall back on but experience and the fact that he had nothing to lose.

The short man had told him that the husband was a doctor at Mahosot Hospital. Siri, his name was. That would be the next move. He removed the lighter fluid from his bag and sprinkled it around the interior of the limousine. He wound down the window, opened the door, and stepped out into a blinding sunshine. He looked up and down the deserted road, struck a match and tossed it into the car which was puddled with petrol from the slashed feed pipe. No point really but old habits died hard. He was a block away when he heard the petrol tank explode.

The hospital had been built by the French and all the signs were still posted in the French language. But as he didn't know in which section this Dr Siri worked, he had no choice but to ask. He produced his most charming smile and stopped an elderly nurse.

'I am looking for Dr Siri,' he said, in French.

She shook her hands as if to wave off this foreign attack and hurried away. But then, her steps slowed. She seemed to have gleaned something from the question. She turned.

'Dr Siri?' she said.

He nodded.

'*La morgue*,' she said.

It took Barnard only five minutes to find the small building, its impressive French name plate with *La Morgue* written in comic green and red letters over the door. He reached into his bag and took hold of the tyre iron. It should take him far less time to beat the information he needed out of the staff there.

The preliminary heats of the boat races started early. Two boats would start together to the sound of a pistol shot. They travelled five hundred metres to a point where the judges sat on a tin barge anchored midstream. For the finals the teams were dressed in gaudy almost-matching uniforms and an array of straw hats. As the Peace Hotel blocked the view from the administration buildings, the governor and all his guests invited themselves to Siri's balcony. The only good news was that they arrived with several crates of beer. The close proximity to Thailand meant the governor had a healthy supply of exotic foods and drinks on hand. The size of his gut suggested the Singha Beer importation was not a once-in-a-blue-moon occurrence. The man had no shame. He stood at the railing with his bottle in his hand saluting the peasants below like some red-nosed Mussolini. A month earlier he'd announced to these same peasants that the boat race festival would be dry this year. Due to the rice harvest disaster, no rice had been diverted for the production of whisky. Anyone caught moonshining would be arrested. Yet, to the trained eye, it was clear the boat crews and their cheerleaders were 'on' something.

The guests had brought along a few dozen stackable chairs but Siri and Madame Peung had grabbed two of the comfortable deckchairs and were deep in conversation, ignoring the races below. His wife, Madame Daeng, hovering a few metres away, squeezed the paper cup that contained her beer until a little tsunami of foam splashed over the rim. The previous evening, with her husband locked in conversation with the witch at the dinner table, she'd been forced to listen to the other Siri amusing his hand-picked guests with bawdy stories. The thought of it brought about another involuntary squeeze of the cup. Another spill.

'Steady, old girl,' came the overly familiar voice of the governor from behind her. 'That stuff doesn't come cheap, you know?'

'Sometimes I don't know my own strength,' she told him without looking around.

'So, are you going to tell me, or not?' he asked.

She turned towards his ruddy face.

'What do you need to know, Comrade Governor?'

'What this top secret mission of yours is all about. I'd ask your husband but I can never tear him away from his girlfriend.'

'There is no mission,' she said angrily. 'We're all just here to enjoy the races.'

'Bull. There's more to it than that. A week away from race day and I'm requested . . . no, I'm bloody ordered to give up my two best rooms to important people from Vientiane. I even have to give up another room to a moron. None of you seem to be reaching into your pockets as far as I see. Where am I supposed to get the budget to cover the lost tourist revenue, eh?'

She eyed the distance to the railing and wondered whether he weighed as much as he appeared to.

'And after all this generosity,' he went on, 'I'm not even let in on the secret. Clandestine flights upriver. Special transportation requests. Hushed Vietnamese conversations late at night. And now I'm told to expect a unit of army engineers that I'm supposed to feed and billet somewhere. Again, I ask, where's the bloody money coming from?'

She turned square on and pulled back her shoulders.

'You have resources, you slimy man.'

'What did you . . . ?'

'Illegal smuggling, for one. A thriving import business no doubt paid for from illegal logging. Perhaps the odd gem. I've seen all those crates in the chicken shed. I wouldn't be surprised if you've been trafficking girls over the border to brothels on the other side. That would be your style. But, we'll get you. When my report goes in you'll–'

'Listen, you . . .'

'Yes, I know what you'd like to say but, how sad, you can't say it because you don't know just how VIP we are, do you? You'll just have to suck up to me for another day or two. And that includes making sure I have enough to drink.' She was about to turn away but had an afterthought. 'And this is a "love me, love my dog and my Down Syndrome friend" deal. If I hear of you kicking either of them, I promise you there will be a full-scale enquiry into where all this booze came from. You do understand what I'm saying, don't you?'

She smiled at him. His mouth was ajar enough to see the brown roots of his teeth. He most certainly was not used to being spoken to in such a manner. She could see the rage in him. He wanted to kill her. That was a particularly common male way of solving a problem. But she knew she held the bloody plums in her hand.

'Were they women's voices?' she asked.

'What?' He wiped the drool from his lips.

'The hushed Vietnamese voices. Were they female?'

'I don't . . . Yes. One was, I suppose.'

'Good boy,' she said, and turned her back on him. 'You can leave me alone now.'

She marched across the balcony on heavy legs to where her husband was sitting. She could see him transfixed by the face of the beautiful witch, adoring her words. It was disgusting.

'Excuse me, dear Madame Peung,' she said in Vietnamese. 'I am in need of a husband.'

She hooked a finger into the neck of Siri's collarless shirt and yanked. He laughed, apologized to Madame Peung and took Daeng's hand as they walked across the crowded balcony. Their room was filled with even more strangers so they kept going out the door and down the staircase.

'What's so urgent?' Siri laughed.

She didn't speak until they reached the landing one flight down.

'Siri,' she said, stepping up to his face. 'Do you trust me?'

'Absolutely not. You'd kill me as soon as—'

'Siri. Stop it. I'm not joking. Do you trust my judgement?'

'Of course.'

'Will you listen to me without saying, "But, Daeng!"?'

He laughed again.

'I swear,' he said.

'That woman.'

'Madame Peung?'

'She's up to something.'

Siri was nodding.

'Don't do that,' said Daeng.

'What did I do?'

'That sympathetic counsellor nod. You do it when you're talking to idiots.'

'I do not, and you're not, so why . . . ? All right. What makes you think she's up to something?'

'You said you trust me.'

'And I do.'

'Then, if I say she's up to no good – as a loving husband you would simply tell me you believe me and be in my corner.'

Siri reached for her hand but she pulled it away. He smiled.

'Daeng,' he said. 'I'm seventy-four. I have all the woman I need in you. It's sweet. In fact it's very flattering, but surely we're both a bit over the hill for jealousy. There's noth–'

'You ass!' she said, and started down the stairs, passing Ugly on his way up.

'But Daeng? Daeng?' he called. She didn't stop. He considered going after her but he wasn't certain what rules they were playing under here in the wilds. Even though there hadn't been any punches thrown, this probably counted as a fight. It was their first. He sat on the step. As the staircase was open, Ugly didn't consider it part of the building. He sat beside his master.

'I take full responsibility,' Siri said to the dog. 'In fact, if there were a flower stand and a retailer of chocolates, I would spend the last of my wages on them. It always worked with my first wife. Jealousy is a fleeting emotion. Of course, all she's seen here is me with a very attractive other woman whom I suppose you could say I pursued. Engaged her in lengthy conversations. And that, my dear Ugly, is why Daeng was angry. But anger is just one more incarnation of love. She loves me and that makes me happy. I shall repair the damage. But not yet. I'm too close to answers to give up on my witch.'

Ugly, as may have been expected, licked his undercarriage noisily.

10

Hanoiance

'Do you speak French?' asked the man.

The baby was awoken by his gruff voice and started to cry. Nurse Dtui went to comfort her. After the autopsy it had been two a.m. before mother, father and daughter finally got to sleep that morning. But, as always, they were up with the chickens and working on the police vegetable lot with the other families. This was the first chance Dtui had found to put her daughter down to catch up on her sleep. The morgue was usually such a quiet place. She had bones to label and a report to write. Her classes didn't begin until the afternoon and she'd been giving thought to the state of the skull on the aluminium table. The ferocity of the attack. The number of unnecessary blows when one or two probably did enough damage. But the attacker had continued as if to vent some pent-up anger. She wouldn't want to meet such a person.

With her hands around the tiny fingers of Malee she looked up at the tall Westerner who stood in the doorway. He was probably seventy but she'd never been able to estimate the age of foreigners with any accuracy. He smiled warmly and she wondered whether the neat teeth were his own. He'd probably been a handsome young man. Not even the star of an old smallpox scar over his right eyebrow detracted from his natural good looks. But she had no idea what he was saying.

In Lao, she said, 'Who are you looking for?'

She tried the same question in Russian but the look on his face suggested they were to be marooned on their separate islands in a vast linguistic sea.

But then, in English, he said, 'I don't suppose there's any chance you speak English?'

Dtui's English came from a dictionary and several textbooks. She had few chances to use it. The phonetic alphabet had taught her how the words were supposed to sound but few speakers of English consulted the phonetic alphabet. Consequently she had a problem with accents. It took her some time to digest the Westerner's words. He was reaching for something in his satchel.

'I speak a little,' she said, relieved to have removed the cork that held in her English.

'Then you must be Vietnamese,' said the man.

'Vietnam? No. I am Lao.'

'Well, wonders will never cease.'

'I'm sorry, I . . .'

'Never mind.' Again the smile. 'I was hoping to find my good friend, Dr Siri,' he said.

'You know Dr Siri?'

'We were best friends, before. In France.'

'Really?'

Malee had continued her gentle wail. It was unusual for her not to fall back into the depths of sleep. Dtui was concerned as a mother but failed to recognize the animal instinct with which a baby is born but sheds over time. The awareness of danger.

'Is he here?' the man asked, looking around the room.

'No. He is in Pak Lai.'

'Is that far?'

'Is it . . . ? No. On the Mekhong about seven hours.'

'Oh, too bad. Then perhaps I can talk to his wife?'

'Madame Daeng, also . . .'

'In Pak Lai?'

'Yes.'

'Then that's all I need you for.' The smile was gone. 'Far too easy,' he said, and walked to the table where Comrade Koomki lay in charred lumps.

'I . . .' Dtui had started to pick up the anxiety in her daughter's tears.

'You are a doctor?' he asked.

'Nurse.'

She took a step backwards to the dolly where her instruments were laid out.

'A nurse?' he repeated. 'And such a pretty nurse.'

Dtui had a scalpel in her hand behind her back. She tried to make the three steps to Malee's hammock look natural but her bladder suddenly ached and her legs began to wobble. Acting natural could only be acting at this point. The foreigner picked up a short length of bone with his left hand and again reached into his satchel with his right. To Dtui's disgust, the man put the bone between his teeth and began to chew.

'No better combination,' he said. 'Calcium and charcoal. The arsonist's snack of choice. But, of course, as a nurse you know this already.'

His right hand emerged from the satchel holding a metal bar. He looked at Malee suddenly silent in her hammock. Dtui stepped between her and the man and held the scalpel in front of her. Barnard laughed.

'Ooh! Such a small knife compared to my big iron,' he said. 'Nurse of the morgue. Nurse who deals with the dead. Do you know what cancer is, my pretty nurse? Certainly you do. Cancer is a contract that states categorically how long you have remaining to complete all of your business. It allows you a small portal of time to avenge all the wrongs you have suffered. To find peace from the demons that live beneath your skin.'

He took a step towards Dtui. She held her ground and brandished her scalpel. He seemed not to care. He had a lot to say. Dr Siri had often told her that it's only in the movies that crazed killers explain everything before that final blow. That actual killers just got it over with and fled. She had no idea what the Frenchman was saying but she was certain he had murder in mind.

'And when you realize your future is measurable in hours rather than dreams,' he continued. 'That is when you seek out the moment in time when everything changed. When everything became shit. You go back to that moment and do what you can to delete it so you can sleep through those infinite hours of death without nightmares.'

With no warning, he smashed the tyre iron on to the aluminium dolly, sending the bones flying across the room. Those that were left he crushed with three manic blows. Dtui swept her daughter into her arms and stepped back to the wall. She knew the tiny blade would offer no defence at all against this maniac with his metal bar. Her only hope was to attack. Thus far, the man's face had shown no emotion, no anger, no excitement. His was a temperate, dull expression like the mask of the dead.

He turned to her as if suddenly remembering she was in the room.

Dtui lunged with the knife.

He held up his left hand like a policeman stopping traffic.

She lunged again and the blade cut a ribbon of red across his palm.

He looked disappointed. His hand gushed blood but he seemed not to care.

Dtui felt this was all without hope. He was a living cadaver and there was nothing she could do to frighten him. Still he talked.

'It is a shame,' he said, his bloody dripping hand still held aloft. 'Two generations of lotus eaters gone in one small massacre. It will never make the newspapers in Europe.'

He took that decisive step forward just as the louvres above Dtui's head shattered, sending a hailstorm of glass across the room. The Frenchman showed no defensive instincts. It was as if he were staring into snow. Glass pierced the skin of his face as he looked up towards the source of this interruption.

'You're surrounded,' came a deep male voice speaking English from beyond the window.

This was followed by the sound of a gunshot.

'We know you're in there. Come out with your hands in the air.'

Barnard sighed. He looked at the mother and daughter as if contemplating whether he might have time to beat them to death. He twirled the metal bar around like a conductor exercising his baton and he pouted. Then, he turned and walked calmly to the door with his weapon held above his head.

Dtui's knees buckled and she slid down the wall to the concrete floor. Malee, who had held back her tears this whole time, suddenly released a flood. Dtui willed her own breath to return. Her heart to beat. The ink blots to clear from before her eyes. She waited for the sounds of yells and gunshots from outside. Of a chase. Of a killing. But there was nothing. In fact there were no sounds beyond the cries of her daughter. She calmed the girl with a lullaby and, some five minutes later, eased herself back to her feet. She placed Malee in her hammock and walked on unsure legs to the exit. She peeked nervously around the door frame. There was nothing untoward. Mahosot was its normal sleepy self. There was no sign of the crazed Frenchman.

A nurse emerged from the midday shadows of the canteen, her crisp white uniform reflecting the sun like a solar panel.

'How are you, Dtui?' she called, calmly, as if the world had not, five minutes earlier, been about to end.

'Did you see a . . . a *farang*, just now?' Dtui asked.

'The Soviet doctor was just . . .' the nurse began.

'No. A tall, old man. Blue shirt. Carrying a leather satchel.'

'Nope.'

'Anything unusual? Police? People running?'

'Dtui, are you all right?' asked the nurse.

'I don't know,' Dtui confessed.

Something had happened that she couldn't explain. A broken window. A voice she'd never heard before. A gunshot. Two lives saved. A miracle.

At first it might have seemed odd that a landlocked country should have a navy. It was something like tropical Singapore listing a snow plough amongst its official vehicles – which it did. But when one considered the fact that Laos had a five-thousand kilometre border to police, a thousand of which was river, it began to make more sense. The Lao People's Navy comprised twenty US-made river patrol boats, sixteen amphibious landing craft and two fairly large cruisers that couldn't be used in the dry season.

When one of the cruisers arrived in Pak Lai mid-Monday afternoon, the crowd cheered, believing it was part of the celebrations. The vessel ignored the current race and ploughed between the two longboats, causing both to capsize in its wake. The crowd went wild with enthusiasm. They seemed to cheer every damned thing. There wasn't a bottle to be seen anywhere but those Sanyaburans were most certainly on something.

The cruiser reached the wooden dock and, unlike the ferry, did not berth politely. It seemed to use the flimsy structure as a brake to arrest its charge upriver. The pier creaked and leaned at a precarious forty-five degree angle but did not give up its moorings. Sailors fore and aft tied off on the wooden posts. Ten unenthusiastic army engineers in a mismatch of uniforms ambled across the deck and strolled along the jetty. The boat was piled high with heavy equipment, even a bulldozer rocked precariously at the stern. The engineers had arrived.

At almost the same time, met with the same frenzied cheers, the ferry appeared upstream. It had left Luang Prabang with Comrade Civilai as its only passenger but was now full to the brim. At every turn in the river, every small village, it had taken on revellers intent on enjoying the Pak Lai boat races. None of them had laissez-passers but who was checking? At heart, the Lao were party animals and the zoo had been quiet of late.

The ferry leaned against the dock from the north side, setting it upright. The passengers were off the boat in seconds and mingling with the huge crowd. Civilai, who was absolutely, most certainly, and definitely on something, staggered to the wrong side of the ferry and was about to step into the Mekhong. The pilot rescued him in time and deposited the old politburo man and his travel bag on the shifting jetty. Siri was there to meet him.

'Have a rough cruise did you, skipper?' Siri smiled.

Civilai's eyes were no longer coordinated. The cord seemed to have snapped. One was overseeing the river while the other honed in on Siri.

'Those ... these Sayabung people,' he slurred, 'are all nuts. You wouldn't believe how ... how ... who much a person could smoke, and snort and ingest in a four horse period. Or, hours, of course – even.'

'Oh, I believe it, old brother,' said Siri. 'In fact your eyes have no pupils.'

Civilai began to scan the jetty beneath his feet and check his pockets.

'I had them,' he said. 'I know I left Lang Praboon with them. And did I say ... passionate?'

'Who?'

'The Sangbarani women.'

'Say no more, old man. I know your wife.'

'I need ...'

'Some sleep.'

'How ...?'

'I'm psychic.'

'You're not. You're a–'

'I know. Let's go.'

Siri propped up his friend as they walked the short walk to the guest house.

'Who are you taking me, you villain?' Civilai asked.

'To my bed.'

'Good. Will Mademoiselle Daeng be joining us?'

'I doubt it. She's not talking to me.'

'At last a natural marriage. All this lalalala love at your age. *Totalement* obscene. Did you take on a concubine, you old snakehead? That's the test.'

Civilai had apparently lost the use of his legs as Siri was now dragging him along the gravel path. Despite his large stomach he weighed surprisingly little.

'What would I do with a concubine at my age?' Siri asked.

'Nothing. That's the point. You just dress her up sexy and walk her around around town and everyone thinks you're Valentino. At your dis . . . discreet love nest you sit and play backgammonon and on and you eat scones.'

They were passing the engineers. Young men. Undisciplined. Rude.

'Looks like the old queens are going to get lucky this afternoon,' shouted one of them to a parry of laughter.

Siri stopped and Civilai almost slipped through his grasp. It wasn't the comment that caused Siri to pause

– although he would normally take a few moments to make mincemeat of the young soldier – it was the language he'd spoken. Siri looked around at the boys in the unit. Sharp, angular cheekbones. Chinese eyes. The engineers were all Vietnamese.

To come across a unit of Vietnamese soldiers at that time would not have been unexpected. There were an estimated forty thousand of them on Lao soil 'easing the transition'. When still active and able to stand, Civilai had once stood up in front of the committee and suggested that the Vietnamese invasion of Laos had already happened but nobody was prepared to admit it, particularly the numerous party members of mixed, Vietnamese–Lao ethnicity. The Vietnamese labour force dragged in by the French oppressors had been encouraged to spread its seed, one might say, at the grass roots level. There were currently 'advisors' in each of the ministries and the recent memorandum of understanding had given Vietnam a licence to trade and pillage.

But Sanyaburi was a province as far from the Vietnamese border as it was possible to get. There were no security issues that might trouble Hanoi. The Vietnamese military experts had supposedly been training Lao troops for ten years. Lao engineers were every bit as competent as their trainers. Why would a Lao minister order in a Vietnamese unit in what was basically a personal matter?

Siri walked on, dragging Civilai as he went.

'Aren't you going to smaggle his face into a billion billion little pieces?' Civilai slurred.

'No, brother. I have to think this out.'

Civilai slept like a man full of conflicting stimulants, oblivious to the fact that his bedroom was crowded with party-goers. Not even hearing the cheers from the river below. Siri dumped him on the penthouse suite bed and went off in search of his bride. He found her on a swinging wooden seat in the garden behind the governor's house. She didn't seem to be enjoying her beer. Her husband was five metres from her when he dropped to the ground and walked up to her on his knees. Ugly, the dog, followed the cue and dragged his bottom across the short grass one metre behind. When Siri was close enough he gave Daeng a *nop* fit for a queen.

'My love,' he said, his head bowed in shame. 'You were right.'

She laughed.

'You were right too,' she said.

'I was?'

'I was. I am . . . jealous,' she told him.

'You are?'

'It's irrational and unwarranted and a product of my own imagination, and I should be old enough to know better. But . . . yes. I hated seeing you with that beautiful woman. I wanted to drown her in the river.'

'Then . . . why didn't you?' he smiled.

'She weighs more than I can comfortably drag. I'm not as young as I was. And . . . perhaps that's my problem. Perhaps it isn't her who is the used-to-be woman, but me. Because of this annoying biography you've had me put together, I've been remembering me. I mean, what I consider to be the real me. Doing a lot of probing into my soul. Asking, was that me or is this me? Was I immoral? Did I actually achieve anything? What have I become as a result of it all? And there she is, this successful businesswoman who has conquered the material world, and now is in control of the afterlife . . . and you. What was I compared to that?'

This time, Daeng's hand was more than pleased to be in his.

'The answer isn't nearly as complicated as the question,' Siri told her. 'You were great. You always have been great. And you always will be great. There is no woman who can compare to you because you are unique. And that makes me great too because I ended up with you.'

He watched the tears race one another down her face. He rarely saw her cry. He never cried himself so he put the dampness on his cheeks down to an early dew.

'And what am I right about?' she asked.

'What?'

'When you grovelled over to me a few minutes ago you said I was right.'

'Ah, yes. There's something going on.'

'I told you.'

'I never doubted you. Did you witness the arrival of the engineers just now?'

'No.'

'They're Vietnamese.'

'No? All of them?'

'I swear.'

'What the hell are they doing here?'

'It might have been the minister's doing. Trying to keep this secret, so he brings in foreigners. Word's less likely to get around.'

'That's a lot of trouble to go to just to keep a secret, Siri. What if there's a completely different motive? Something totally unrelated to the brother and the sunken boat.'

'Like what?'

'I don't know. Perhaps it's the only way they could get Vietnamese troops into Sanyaburi.'

'There's hardly enough of them for an invasion.'

'But if they're engineers they might be here to do some surveying? A bit of spying on the Thai border?'

'Then that would mean the whole performance with Madame Peung was just to win the minister over and get him to make the call to bring in soldiers.'

'Siri, how certain are you that she's legitimate?'

Siri got off his knees and sat on the swing beside his wife. He looked off towards the river, mentally thumbing through his conversations with the witch.

'She talks about things as if . . . as if she's seen what

I've seen. She's shown me how she makes contact, or rather how she opens herself to be contacted. She's been teaching me how to relax and accept whatever comes my way. There's just so much evidence. All that display in the governor's meeting room on Saturday. It was too natural. Too spontaneous. I mean, how could she know all those things? She hadn't been told who would be there in the room.'

'All right. So she's really a medium. Then we'd have to assume someone harnessed her skills to meet outside objectives. Blackmail? Threats?'

'The brother. What if he's not her brother? What if he's a minder? By her side all the time to make her say what someone wants her to say.'

'All right. We might be getting somewhere.'

'And we might be going there for no reason.'

'What do you mean?'

'Just that this could all be exactly what it seems. The Vietnamese unit was the only one available. We'll all go and dig up the boat and we'll find the remains of the minister's brother. No mystery at all.'

'And do you honestly think that's all there is to it?'

'No. But I do think this whole thing can be explained if we can discover what happened in 1910.'

'Where are we going to find an historian in Pak Lai?'

'You know? I think there might be one sleeping in our bed this very minute.'

11

Wake Me Up Before You Gogo

'I told him. I told him where they were,' she said.

Dtui and Phosy lay side by side and wide awake on their thin mattress on the floor. Malee was sound asleep. She was apparently not nearly as traumatized by the morning's events as her mother.

'Stop it,' said Phosy. 'You couldn't know.'

'I'm sure he'll go there.'

'You can't be certain. You know how hard it is for a foreigner to travel around the country unaccompanied by some Lao official. Even if he tried there are checkpoints all the way. Without a travel document he won't get past any of them.'

'He'll find a way. I looked into his eyes, Phosy. He's crazy but he's calculating. I think he was talking about his cancer and how little time it had given him. I'm sure Dr Siri did something to him in the past and this insane man wants revenge.'

'Look, first thing tomorrow I'll go to the German embassy. They handle French visas now the French embassy is shut. I'll see if they have copies of visa applications. They should have a photo attached. I'll bring what they have and show you. We'll find him.'

'That's no help at all to Siri and Daeng. I know what this man is capable of, Phosy. I was this close to the metal bar that beat the hell out of the fire victim. He burned down Daeng's shop. He was going to kill your wife and daughter for no other reason than that I knew Siri. If it weren't for the glass breaking . . .'

'Stop thinking about it. You're safe. Malee's safe.'

'But who could it have been? The voice?'

'I imagine someone overheard the conversation and decided to help.'

'Phosy. How many people do you know who speak English? I mean, those that haven't already swum across the river. This man was fluent. And he had a gun. He saved our lives.'

'And if we ever find him I'll pin a medal on him. But, in the mean time, how about trying to get some sleep?'

'I won't sleep until I know they're safe.'

Phosy raised himself on to one elbow and smiled at his wife. By the light of the moon he could see the dark shadows around her eyes.

'We'll get them out of there and back to Vientiane long before the Frenchman finds them,' he said. 'I put Sergeant Sihot on a boat this afternoon. It'll stop overnight in Xanakham but tomorrow morning he'll be in Pak Lai. They can all take the first ferry back here. In fact, I wouldn't be surprised if they weren't back already.'

'How could they be?'

'I contacted Comrade Civilai before he left Luang Prabang and told him about the fire. They have working telephones up there. He should have arrived in Pak Lai around midday. Once Siri and Daeng hear what happened I wouldn't be surprised if they jumped straight on the ferry and headed home.'

The only indication that Comrade Civilai wasn't dead was the occasional fart loud enough to cause the boat-race guests to turn in his direction. Madame Daeng shook her head.

'He's not going to be much use to us until at least tomorrow morning,' she said.

'I'm not so sure,' said Siri. 'I reckon we could bottle that flatulence and sell it as cooking gas.'

'There. That's why I married you. Class.'

'I thought you married me because I have an enormous intellect.'

'I've known much bigger intellects,' she smiled. 'Intellects that can maintain their intelligence all through the night. Intellects that—'

'All right. You've made your point most eloquently. Meanwhile, the Vietnamese invasion of Sanyaburi; how do you propose we find out what they're really up to?'

'I think we can arrange it so that the engineers tell you themselves.'

'They're hardly likely to just blurt it out.'

'Not to you directly, but to each other.'

'Ah! Once more she thrusts me into the enemy camp as a spy. No fear for my life.'

'They didn't hear you speak Vietnamese, did they?'

'I wanted to. I bit my tongue.'

'Then you should hang around them.'

'What is my motivation? What Sherlockian disguise should I don?'

'You could play drunk.'

'Ah, a challenge.'

'What challenge? You do it all the time.'

'Do it, yes. But act it? That's a different kettle of gin completely.'

It was late evening. Siri and Ugly approached the small tent compound with two purloined bottles of Mekhong whisky.

'If you insist on coming along,' Siri whispered, 'the least you can do is stagger.'

When Siri started to trip over his own feet, Ugly did the same. Siri decided there was something particularly eerie about that dog.

'One more step and you're dead,' came a voice. Siri looked to one side and saw a sentry sitting cross-legged beneath a Leaning-Egg tree, an AK-47 on his lap. He'd spoken in Vietnamese and, as Siri wasn't supposed to know the language, he waved and staggered on. Not even the sight of the weapon being raised and trained in his direction caused him to halt. In fact it brought on a song which Siri belted out in grand voice for all to hear. The men sitting around the campfire jumped to their feet. Some reached for their weapons. Siri threw his hands into the air, a bottle in each.

'I bring alms from the secret capitalists,' Siri shouted in Lao, 'to share with my Vietnamese brothers.'

'What's he prattling on about?' someone asked.

'No idea. He's as drunk as a wonky fishing rod,' said another.

Good, thought Siri. They don't speak Lao.

He performed a little jig in the light of the bonfire.

'Shoot him,' someone said as the majority returned to their places around the fire.

'Take the bottles from him and then shoot him,' someone else suggested.

Then he noticed Ugly.

'Look at that damned dog. He's even more drunk than the old fella.'

From Siri's lead, Ugly was reeling this way and that and enjoying the laughs he got from his audience. The only officer in the group stepped up to the old drunk and relieved him of his bottles.

'You speak Vietnamese, Granddad?' he shouted.

Siri replied with the first verse of 'They stand to conquer. They squat to pee.' A rude song the Lao enjoyed singing about their Vietnamese counterparts. The young engineers had obviously never heard it. The bottles, uncapped, were working their ways in conflicting circles around the fire gazers. Each man took a generous swig to impress his mates.

'OK, you can piss off now,' said the officer to Siri. 'Job done. Go back to your intestine-eating, monkey Lao.'

Siri laughed heartily and repeated the sentence with awful pronunciation. The engineers cheered.

'Monkey Lao,' they toasted.

'Monkey Lao,' Siri laughed. He reached into his shoulder bag and produced a smaller bottle of whisky. He took great pains to unscrew the top. Once decapitated, he held the bottle aloft.

'Monkey Lao!' he shouted.

'Monkey Lao,' they all repeated.

He was the star turn in this evening's cabaret. The Vietnamese were laughing and pointing at him and his inebriated dog. Siri began to glug down the drink like a man with a great thirst. They all watched in amazement.

'He can drink,' said one of the soldiers.

'Twenty *dong* says he falls on his face before he gets to the bottom of the bottle,' said the officer.

'I'll take that bet,' said one young man.

He clapped a beat for Siri to swallow to and the others joined in. The pace slowed as the doctor's Adam's apple began to rise and descend more laboriously but still he swallowed. And, with his eyes closed, he drained the last of the cold tea and overturned the empty bottle above his head. He smiled, bowed to acknowledge the applause of the soldiers, and fell nose first into the recently mown grass. Ugly took a few tentative steps towards him before lying down and playing dead.

*

The grass had actually been quite comfortable. Siri had fought off sleep until the last engineer had retired to his tent. He was about to return to the guest house when he looked to his left to see Ugly twitching through a deep dream and smiling as if it were a naughty one. Siri paused for a moment too long and he too was plunging through layers of places he'd never seen in real life, only to land in a den of iniquity. He was in a gogo bar in Thailand. The signs were in Thai. The girls on the stage in front of him were in bikinis and stiletto heels. It was certainly a step up from naked Frenchmen. All around him were Western men in loud Hawaiian shirts. But the greatest shock of all was the soundtrack. He could hear everything.

'See all this?' came a voice, shouted above the ear-splitting music.

Siri turned to see an old man staring out over the dance floor. He was dressed well in a dazzling flowery tie and a starched white shirt, but there was little of him inside it. He seemed frail and used up. In his hand was something that looked like Coca-Cola but it was in a beer mug and had a straw poking out of it.

'All this is mine,' said the man. His voice was that of somebody who couldn't hear himself talk. Like a man listening to loud music on headphones.

Siri was delighted. Just as Madame Peung had taught him, by not fighting it he was able to attain other elements. The sound was unpleasant – some awful pop thing – but it was an achievement. He hardly dared talk to the old man in the hibiscus tie for fear that it would all go away. But he knew he had to.

'Who are you?' Siri thought he'd said, but nothing came out of his mouth. He yelled his question. 'WHO ARE YOU?' but again he produced not a sound.

'Relax, Siri,' he told himself. 'Don't fight. Enjoy the show. Smell the tobacco. Order something.'

He looked around for a beer mat and a pen.

'That one over there,' said the old man, pointing at one of the dancers. 'She arrived yesterday. She's a beauty. I get to interview them all, if you know what I mean. She'll be raking it in once she gets the countryside out of her skin.'

Siri breathed. Relaxed. Paid attention. He looked around for clues. Why was he here? Madame Peung had told him to take charge of moments like these. Not to sit and watch the show but to direct it. So he left his seat. The scenery had trouble keeping up with him as he walked to the stage. Here and there he'd see a gap into the next dream. Fat men lined the bar like brooding chickens in a coop. Young girls, fresh from the farm, massaged the fat thighs and squeezed the fat cheeks. He looked at their faces. Did he recognize anyone? Would somebody pass him a note? What was the message here? He turned back to look at his seat and the old man in the white shirt sitting beside it. He was sipping his Coke through a straw. The strobe lights lit him in blues and reds and blinding whites and in one of those flashes, just for a second, there was something familiar about him. Where had he . . . ?

Siri smiled. He went to a vacant stool in front of the stage and watched the dancers. He had his answer. There was nothing to do now but enjoy the show. Or so he thought.

He felt a tap on his shoulder – another new dream experience; touch. He turned to see Comrade Koomki of Housing with a beer in his hand. Only his head looked different somehow, as if it had been reassembled without care: a puzzle whose unmatching pieces had been forced to fit together. He had a marvellous suntan. Siri, for want of a better response, gave him a polite *nop*. It was courtesy. It seemed likely, having seen the comrade in two spirit dreams now, that the poor man was dead. Koomki did not return the *nop*. In fact he took a mouthful of his beer and spat it at the doctor. If it had ever been wet it was no longer so when it reached Siri.

'I'm here because of you,' said Koomki.

Siri didn't immediately see the problem. He was in a bar full of beautiful women and he had a cold beer. It was hardly purgatory. But, as yet, Siri couldn't tell him so. With every second that passed, Koomki's tan grew darker. It was currently burnt sienna heading towards oak. Siri willed himself to speak.

'How did you die?'

But nothing came out.

'They say I have to tell you this,' said the diminutive

comrade. 'They say it might chalk up a few points in my favour. You see? I might have inadvertently been responsible for something that will happen to Madame Daeng. I'm not particularly sorry but I put one of the living angels of hell on to her. He'll be–'

They were interrupted by an elderly woman in a miniskirt who asked whether either of them would be interested in the 'special show' that was about to start upstairs. Siri declined and she started to lick his nose. It wasn't an unpleasant experience. Comrade Koomki was indigo and the bar had started to smell of hay. Ugly's tongue was as soggy as an overripe durian. When Siri opened his eyes the dog stopped licking.

'I got sound,' Siri told him.

Siri arrived at his room at six to find the door open, the floor littered with empty bottles and cigarette butts, and Civilai sleeping peacefully in the bed beside a rather good-looking man with a moustache. Both were, fortunately, fully dressed. There was no Madame Daeng to be seen but Siri wasn't overly concerned. She had set out the night before with two more bottles of Mekhong whisky to lure the cruiser captain and his mate into a confessional. She had a way with sailors. Siri took his toilet bag down to the communal bathroom to shower and freshen himself for what would likely be a full day. When he returned to the room, Civilai was sitting up in the bed rigid as an old hinge, eyes bulging, with a ghastly pallor on his face.

'Good morning,' said Siri. 'Are you going to introduce me to your boyfriend?'

'Siri,' said Civilai, 'Madame Daeng's shop has been burned down. Everything in it has been destroyed.'

Siri stared at his friend, wondering whether he'd just returned from a frightening dream. He sat on the edge of the bed and tightened the cap of his toothpaste before returning it to the pink plastic container Daeng had bought for him.

'I should have told you when I arrived,' said Civilai. 'God, how many days ago was that? I should have grabbed you both and taken you back to Vientiane on the ferry. I forgot all about it. I don't know what they gave me on that boat but . . . Siri?'

'Yes?'

'Are you in shock?'

'I don't believe so.'

'You don't seem that upset.'

'If it's true . . .'

'It's true. Phosy phoned me before I left Luang Prabang.'

'Well, then it's just a building. It wouldn't be the first building I've lost. Do you know if the chickens got out all right? That's the first thing Geung will ask.'

'Siri, are you mad? All your papers. Your books.'

'Just things. They came to me by chance. They left me by chance. Madame Daeng is safe. As long as nobody was hurt.'

'Siri . . . there was a body in there.'

Siri bowed his head and nodded.

'Comrade Koomki.'

'Good Lord. How did you know . . . ?'

'I had a visit last night. In a dream,' said Siri. 'I imagine he set fire to the place. Can't say I blame him. He probably lost his job because of me. I'd most likely set fire to your house if you ruined my life.'

'That's good to know. But listen. Dtui did an autopsy on the—'

'She did? That's excellent. Good for her.'

'But she seems to believe the little comrade was beaten to death before the fire was lit.'

'Ah. Then it's true.' Siri nodded.

'What's true?'

'The Frenchman.'

'What Frenchman?'

'The one who came looking for my wife.'

'That Frenchman?' said Civilai. 'Last thing I knew, that Frenchman was an old flame.'

'Yes. It appears it might be a little bit more complicated than that. There's a chance he might be here to . . . hurt her. If Dtui was right, and I'm certain she was, it wouldn't surprise me if the Frenchman was responsible for both the fire and the death.'

'You've been holding something back, haven't you?'

'I did a touch of research. My good lady wife has a file at the French embassy as thick as an Angkor lintel. Or, rather, the mysterious *Fleur-de-Lis* has a file. In all that time nobody linked Daeng to the famous spy. It was astounding how much chaos one woman can cause. I was barely twenty pages into the file and she'd already reduced De Gaulle to tears.'

'Wait! How could you do research at the French . . . ?'

'The mind is such a terrible thing to steep in alcohol.'

'That's where you put them, you sly old bastard. That's where you hid all your housemates. Slap in the middle of the city.'

Civilai started to laugh but his throbbing head caused him to stand down.

'My goodness, how I love you,' he said.

At this point the hungover bed mate slipped from the mattress, nodded and fled for the door.

'I hope I haven't come between you two,' Siri laughed.

'So, the files,' said Civilai.

'I had nothing to go on, really. I looked for the name Hervé Barnard. Nothing. I'm sure there'll some day be a way to cross-reference piles of paper without licking your forefinger so many times you become dehydrated. I spent most of the night in the archive room. It was quite by chance that I found the letters. I didn't want to waste time reading other people's private correspondence, but there was one box file full of letters all from the same person. They dated back to 1956. His name was Olivier Guittard. The earliest was sent from Saigon and it asked casually whether the French post in Pakse had garnered any more recent intelligence on the person they referred to as the *Fleur-de-Lis*. I didn't go through the whole lot but those I scanned read like a growing obsession. This Guittard character seemed to have been seeking out French officials and military personnel who were, or had been, stationed in the south of Laos. Even back then Guittard had started to collect reports and anecdotes. He'd taken it upon himself to reinvestigate every case that was attributed to *Fleur-de-Lis*.

'He stayed with the French foreign service and was transferred hither and thither. But still he kept up this correspondence with the French embassy. The stamps are collectors' items. Istanbul. Mauritius. West Africa. The writer spent most of his life on the road. Each letter was headed with a code number which I assume referred to his security clearance. If he was just a stalking nutcase, I doubt they would have kept his mail. Somewhere down the track he had an epiphany. Either that or he was prepared to state something he'd suspected all along. He wrote, "I have finally caught up with two ex-military men I had been seeking for some time. I am now convinced that *Fleur-de-Lis* was not an expatriate French or Vietnamese but a local. A Lao. An attractive female. She went by many names but operated out of a noodle shop in Pakse. It was at the ferry that she found her marks and wheedled her way into the inner circle of French administration."

'There were no internal memos attached to these letters so I doubt anyone took notice of them. They bore the initials of the clerk that received them and stuck them in the box file. The embassy in Vientiane had more important matters to deal with than the investigation of an ex-underground agent. All told, over the period 1954 to 1978, I counted fifty-nine letters. I looked up the writer in the files and found a record dating back to 1953. It was a notification of courier status that Olivier Guittard should be afforded all convenience to speed his travel between Saigon and Europe. He wasn't even based here. But there was strict security around the couriers. They had to be clearly identified. I found his personnel file. The paper had greyed over time. The ink sucked back into it. It was hard to make out the words, but under "Physical description" I could just about read the sentence, "Distinguishing marks – smallpox scar over right eye". It's just as well you didn't put us on the ferry back to Vientiane.'

'Why?'

'Because I imagine that was exactly what he wanted. Why else would he burn down Daeng's shop if not to have us hurry back to salvage our lives from the ruins?'

'You'd fly straight into his web.'

'Quite so.'

'Gad, I'm stupid.'

'Only moderately. My guess is that being here is the safest place for Daeng.'

'I . . . I think I have to throw up,' said Civilai.

'Downstairs,' said Siri. 'Second door on . . .' But the old boy was gone and probably wouldn't make it.

Siri picked his way through the atolls of empty beer bottles and the corpses of a million fire ants lured by the nirvana of lamplight the night before only to be denied enlightenment. He went to the balcony and breathed in the fresh sunrise. It was the day of the finals. The previous day's losers were already working on their oarsmanship so they might grab a wild card entry to the final round. Even at this early hour they were laughing and exchanging insults.

Some twenty elephants on the far bank were knee-deep in the river, providing hosing services to one another. They'd been there since Siri first arrived, their mahout drowsing beneath a Laundry-Fruit tree with no particular hurry to move on.

And, upstream, he caught sight of the tail end of the naval cruiser before it made that long, sweeping turn east. And something inside him gave way like floors in a dynamited building. Daeng. Daeng would befriend the crew of that boat. Daeng would drink with them and get their information. With Civilai and a hundred revellers in Siri's room, she would curl up on the deck of the boat and sleep off the booze. That was what they'd planned. But the boat had left and there was no sign of Daeng. He thought of Guittard and the twenty-year fixation. And he considered how a little money could secure the services of a pilot and pay off police checkpoints. And a sudden panic flooded over him. All the faith and admiration he had for his wife's survival skills were suddenly hanging by a thread. She wouldn't have been prepared. She's out of practice. She's not the woman she used to be. All these thoughts and the fear of spending the rest of his life without her coursed like a flash flood through his veins as he ran out of the room. He pushed past Civilai in the doorway and made for the stairs. Already his ailing lungs squeezed in on themselves. His breath came in short wheezy puffs. On the second floor landing he ran into Mr Geung coming out of his room. He too was in a panic. He hadn't even stopped to dress. His neat pot belly hung over his Minnie Mouse undershorts. He looked petrified.

'Geung,' said Siri, taking his friend by the shoulders. 'What is it?'

'Co . . . co . . . co . . . co . . .'

'Slow down.'

'Comrade Mad . . . Mad . . . Madame Daeng.'

'Yes, what about her?'

Civilai had caught up with them.

'She . . . she . . .' Geung was trying his hardest. Siri massaged his shoulders.

'That's all right, Geung. Take your time. What about Madame Daeng?'

'She . . . she slept with me.'

My spoken French and listening skills were a lot better than I let on. I could read well enough. I was working at the ferry noodle stand breakfast and lunchtime. It meant I got to see a lot of the French administrators and military as they waited in the short queue to cross on the car ferry. I'd go from jeep to truck selling little plastic bags of noodles or iced drinks. I'd sell little. Most of the foreigners thought our food was unhealthy and tasteless. But that wasn't why I walked the queue. The point was to get noticed. My faltering French was better than most and the French housewives were always looking for staff. My selling point was that I was slow, borderline retarded – an act I worked on. They knew they could get me cheap. 'Poor mental girl would just be so grateful for the opportunity.'

My looks were my Achilles heel. The frumpy foreign women didn't hire anyone too good looking to tempt their husbands. So I made myself look as dowdy as possible. I dressed to appear fat. Wouldn't wash my hair for weeks at a time. Blacked out a couple of teeth. But that wasn't necessarily enough to stop the randy Frenchmen from having a go at me. The older military types were the worst. I had one or two tricks up my sleeve for them. My favourite was a letter I carried with me all the time. It was typed in French and signed – so it claimed – by a doctor. It said that this woman, Saifon (I had many names back then), was suffering from a highly contagious and incurable cocktail of vaginal herpes and syphilis. If any of my suitors doubted the veracity of this document, I had discovered a wild pomegranate that, when smeared on the skin, dried to a repugnant, pus-like finish. It was quite harmless but the looks on the faces often made me wish I carried a camera.

Only twice did I have to resort to the razorblade trick. In my lunchbox I carried a blood orange, two plums, and a sweet local turnip. When working as a domestic servant in the French houses I was searched every day by the Vietnamese security guards. It was often no more than an excuse for the sleazy little men to have a feel. My fruit and vegetable lunch pack never caused alarm. They never looked closely enough at the sweet turnip to notice the fine slit into which I had inserted the razorblade. I always kept my bag close when I knew my master was on heat.

The early afternoon following too many glasses of Bordeaux at lunch is often the time their penises become larger than their brains – although neither would achieve record dimensions at the best of times. The moment arrives when he comes at you like a wild boar. He would prefer you begging and screaming, 'Non, monsieur, je suis vierge.' *But if you share his enthusiasm it stops being rape in his mind and becomes passion. The French love that transition. His ego then readjusts his modus operandi. Your satisfaction becomes part of the show, a chance to let you see what a real man can do for a girl. And that, invariably, gives you a moment. As he removes his boots you reach for your lunch pack. He dives, panting, on top of you. His stinky sweat like a putrid bog. You reach for his testicles. He feels a warm flood of dampness . . . down there.*

'Oh, monsieur,*' you say.*

'Oui?' *he grunts.*

'Did you know that in a passionate state, pain inflicted in the area of the groin does not reach the brain for a full minute?' (Of course my speech isn't quite as eloquent as that but men rarely give thought to syntax at such a moment.)

'What are you . . . ?'

You hold up the blade in front of his eyes until he can focus. In your other hand the orange-bloody plums can only be two things. There is a moment of horror frozen on his face. He rolls to one side and looks down to where the crushed orange looks like the after-effects of a machete attack. He staggers bow-legged to the bathroom giving you time to adjust your clothing and leave the room, your dignity intact.

Of course, you are then looking for another job but it's worth it.

They sat under one of the recycled parachute tents by the river; Siri, Daeng, Mr Geung, Comrade Civilai and Ugly, drinking truly horrible coffee.

'All right,' said Civilai. 'Forget the fact that your boat has gone without you. Let's look at the positives.'

'All right,' said Siri. 'I'm looking. No, it's dark. What are they?'

'For one, we have time to strategize.'

On the walk from the guest house – a walk during which Daeng apologized numerous times to Geung for curling up in his bed that morning – they had briefed her on the horrors that had occurred in Vientiane. Like Siri, she'd taken the news quite calmly. In fact she seemed more interested in the drama unfolding upstream than in her lost livelihood.

'What is it with you two?' Civilai asked.

'So, this is the way it looks,' said Daeng, ignoring the question. 'The cruiser has indeed headed upstream, presumably with Madame Peung who has a Vietnamese accent and her deaf and dumb brother who may or may not whisper in Vietnamese late at night, and a unit of Vietnamese soldiers, but without their unbiased medical observer. I take it everyone has spotted the Vietnamese connection here.'

'Did you get anything from the cruiser's Lao captain?' Civilai asked.

'All I could tell was that he'd been briefed privately by the minister. He was under the impression they were there to retrieve the remains of Lao soldiers trapped in the hull of a boat. The minister's brother was one of them. They'd bring out all the remains and have the coroner sort out who was who. He was told not to interact with the Vietnamese engineers which wasn't that hard considering he couldn't speak Vietnamese and they can't speak Lao. He was angry about being the taxi service.'

'Then that would suggest the minister believes that's why they're here,' said Civilai. 'What news from the engineers?'

'They think it's a boat rescue too,' said Siri. 'They were instructed to free a small vessel from the mud at the bottom of the river and winch it to the bank. They have sub-aqua equipment. They aren't particularly happy about it. They were complaining about all that effort and manpower just for a few Lao bones.'

'So, there you have it,' said Civilai. 'What's the mystery here? It all fits. Brother. Bones. Ancestors. Happiness. Wife stops nagging. Minister gets some sleep.'

'What do you make of it, Geung?' Siri asked.

Mr Geung's insights were invariably right on the money. Except he hadn't spoken since his confession to the doctor that he'd slept with his wife. It was obviously worrying him. He had yet to stop blushing. There was, of course, nothing to be embarrassed about. Madame Daeng returns home after a late-night tipple with the navy to find two men asleep in her bed. Neither is her husband. She goes downstairs. Geung's room is unlocked. She crawls beneath the mosquito netting, curls up in an empty space on the vast mattress and sleeps like a babe. Had she been less tipsy she would have considered Mr Geung's fragile emotions and the fact that he had a fiancée back in Vientiane. Mr Geung, being Mr Geung, would have no choice but to tell Tukda of his indiscretion and the relationship would be on shaky ground.

'You have to pun ... punish Madame Daeng,' said Geung as if the party in question were not sitting there in front of him.

'I promise. I shall,' said Siri.

'She was bad.'

'I know she was. I shall take the leather thong to her this very night.' (She kicked him under the table.) 'But in the meantime we're working here. We are presented with a mystery which appears not to be mysterious. Given all we've been through, that in itself is mysterious. If everything is going as expected, why do we all feel so uncomfortable? Something is wrong, Geung. Tell us what it is.'

Geung looked away from the doctor and stared out across the river. The new day's races were about to start but he wasn't focused on the boats. He was quiet for so long they thought he was still sulking, until he said, 'The ele-phants.'

'What about them?' Civilai asked.

'Why are the elephants here?'

They all looked at the small herd, all bloated with water and the mahout rocking in the breeze in his hammock.

'Of course,' said Civilai. 'That's it.'

12

A Mekhong Wave

'But he knew,' said Phosy.

'Keep your voice down,' whispered Dtui. 'I've finally got her to sleep.'

'If he knew' – his voice was lower but no less angry – 'why in hell's name didn't he tell me?'

'Well, firstly because you were off in Vieng Xai at one of your midweek junkets.'

'It was a training course. And that's irrelevant. He could have left a note. He could have told you.'

'Secondly, there wasn't actually anything to tell. The Frenchman wasn't a menace at that stage. Siri was making enquiries because an old friend of Madame Daeng was trying to get in touch.'

'You think Siri would go to all the trouble of talking to the German second secretary and the head of the Roads Project if he wasn't suspicious? They were tight-lipped about it until I told them what their lost tourist had achieved in a few short days. That's when they put me on to the caretaker at the French embassy. He admitted Siri had been there to look at the archives. He said he didn't know what the doctor had found and he wouldn't let me go in to take a look. Said I needed a higher level of clearance. And he was jumpy. He was hiding something. I know he was.'

Dtui turned her smile towards her sleeping child. She and Madame Daeng had few secrets. She knew exactly what the caretaker was hiding.

'So what do we have on our evil Frenchman?' she asked.

'Just his fake name and the fact that he forged his travel documents and his work placement. The French embassy in Bangkok faxed a photograph. I've sent copies of it everywhere. Nobody answering to that name has left the country by air or by ferry so I'm working on the theory that he's still around. He's gone to ground. We've searched every boat out of the city. Road blocks on every track heading west. If he's on his way to Pak Lai he must be on foot. And if that's the case, Siri and Daeng will be back anytime soon.'

'So you keep saying. Civilai will bring them back. Sergeant Sihot will bring them back. Where are they then?'

'I don't know, Dtui. I don't know.'

It hadn't been so hard. A fistful of American dollars and a modest fishing boat became a moonlit ferry. You could get shot from either bank of the Mekhong but even soldiers had to sleep. You picked your moment.

The fisherman was nervous about rowing across on such a clear night with sentries dotted along the bank. The nerves were misplaced. He should have been focused on his passenger. That's where the real danger lay. Twenty metres from Thailand and the tyre iron had sent the wiry brown man to the bottom of the great river.

He knew they'd be watching for him on the way to Pak Lai. The west was closed to him. But the south was hospitable. Thailand needed its tourist dollars and it honed its Thai smiles and its few words of English to suck out every last coin. Foreigners were shown respect, even the ones who deserved none. Barnard had no entry permit, but nobody asked. Transport was efficient and trouble free. He took the local bus to Chiang Khan and on to Bo Phak. And in under six hours he was in Boh Bia staring at a line of forest which the locals told him was the border with Laos. You could pick your spot. More dollars bought an unnecessary porter and a guide and three asses. It seemed no time at all before they had negotiated the heavily wooded trail through Sanyaburi and arrived at the Mekhong at a spot upriver from some madness of a festival. Cancer will take you the moment you yield to it, but he had that one motivating factor that could drive the terminally ill – that kept them going against all the odds. For some it was love. Family. For some it was a simple thing like adding to the count of bird songs and sunrises. For Barnard it was the dream of leaning over the dead body of

Madame Daeng with the blood still warm on his tyre iron.

'It could easily take us a few months, you realize?' said Madame Daeng.

They sat dead centre in the longboat of the Uphill Rowing Club. It had taken the crew only five minutes to lose their first heat of the day which sent their average to zero points. Despite the generous atmosphere of a Lao boat race, losing every event and causing damage to others meant that you were disqualified from even the losers' wooden spoon race in which both boats won a prize. The URC was just about to return home with nothing to show for its efforts until Madame Daeng made them a proposition.

'If we asked them to pull in their oars and let us row we'd be there in half the time,' said Civilai. 'They do realize that only sailing boats have a need to tack, don't they?'

'Where else were we going to find a boat to take us upriver?' Daeng asked. 'And look at them. They're all so happy.'

'They're on something,' said Civilai, who spoke from experience.

When Daeng and her team had first approached the URC and suggested a journey upstream, she'd expected to haggle a price. But the crew was so pumped with adrenalin from the races, it was up for anything. They'd booted out half a dozen rowers who seemed not to care in the least and made space for the guests. Against the current they barely caused a breeze but Ugly's tongue unfurled above the cool water as he scanned the bank ahead for hostiles. Daeng leaned back against Siri's chest. Mr Geung rehearsed the words he'd use to placate his fiancée. The crew was passing around several plastic bottles from which they swigged with great enthusiasm.

'I could use some of that,' shouted Civilai.

A housewife handed him one of the containers and winked. He took a swig and spat it out. Coconut water.

'This is all you're drinking?' he said with amazement.

'Of course,' said the old village headman.

'But you all seem so . . . stoned. How can that be?'

'We work hard,' said the old man. 'We don't have a lot of chance to play, but when it comes, we play hard too. We don't need stimulants.'

'Remarkable,' said Civilai.

'Adrenalin,' said Siri. 'If only you could mix it with soda and ice.' He watched the elderly lady in front of him who paddled with gusto even though her oar was too short to reach the water.

'Has anyone considered what we might do when we get there?' Civilai asked.

'We might ask someone whether back in 1978 they remember seeing a naval vessel full of engineers,' said Siri, prompting laughter from his shipmates.

'Then perhaps there'll be enough time for someone to explain why the elephant thing was so relevant,' said Daeng.

'The elephant,' Civilai began. 'A noble creature used for hundreds of years as a pack animal. Its courtship has been compared by many to the politburo. Much show and trumpeting but you don't see any results for two years. Moody beasts whose strength is all in the neck with a surprisingly weak back. They were gradually replaced by asses and ponies and trucks. During the war – hard times – some were eaten. Nutritious but a bit like chewing on one's favourite shoe. The population dwindled but you'll find more here in Sanyaburi than any other province. That is largely because it's one of only two border provinces you don't have to swim to from Thailand. A lot of our most profitable smuggling of goods takes place right here and much of the jungle is only accessible by elephant. Lesser pack animals are easily spooked and unwilling to cut new swathes through dense undergrowth.

'Once the Thailand trade was squeezed out by the Party and diverted to the Vietnamese border, business over on the west flank changed direction. Export switched to import. Black market goods flooded in across this porous border with the tacit knowledge of the local administrators. The things we lacked – which are many – they had. But it's very much a one way trade. Empty elephants to Thailand. Full elephants to Laos. So, the question is, why have fifteen elephants been showering and frolicking at the riverside for three days when there's smuggling to be done? It can only be because they've been booked. They're waiting for a delivery. Something to take to Thailand.'

'It could be something completely unrelated,' said Daeng. 'The sleazy governor might be exporting something.'

'Very true, Madame Daeng,' Civilai agreed. 'But the governor has to maintain his position. Has to show his loyalty to the Party. He's not going to blatantly load up fifteen elephants in the middle of the boat races with all us outsiders around. No, I'd say this is a private booking and I bet you it has something to do with your witch. For some reason, she's prepared to risk everyone seeing and I bet it's because she has a very narrow aperture of opportunity. This has to be done now. There's something they want to ship to Thailand in a hurry.'

'What?' asked Daeng.

'I think that's a question we might get answers for if ever we catch up with the cruiser,' said Siri. 'And, brother . . .'

'Yes?'

'You did so well with the elephant question, here's your bonus history question for two hundred points.'

'I'm ready.'

'What of significance happened in this country in 1910?'

'1910? Let me see, France and Siam were busy slicing us up and winning parts of us like poker chips. Sanyaburi found itself back in French hands.'

'I wonder if that's got anything to do with it?' said Siri.

'The resident general experimented with making the whole country a free trade area. No notable battles, births or deaths as far as I know.'

'Boring. That's all?' said Daeng.

'It's quite a significant amount,' Civilai pointed out. 'And I've given you more than you'd learn at a Convenient History 101 course you might study at Dong Dok College. The world began in 1975 as far as they're concerned. What did you want exactly?'

'I was hoping for a key,' said Siri. '1910 was the clue.'

'I still think it's a phone number,' said Daeng. '1910.'

'Not an active one,' Civilai told her. 'Numbers 1000 to 2000 were decommissioned after the takeover. That was the French network.'

'There it is,' said Siri. 'The French connection again.'

'So we'd not be able to discover which department or household used that number before it was decommissioned?' asked Daeng.

'Not on a leaky boat in the middle of the Mekhong,' said Civilai. 'When we get back to Vientiane we can go through the files at the central post office.'

'No. It's a date,' said Siri. 'I'm sure of it.'

The rowers at the front of the boat were yelling excitedly. They'd seen something in the water. Some tried to stand to see over the heads in front but the movement unsettled the fine balance.

'What is it?' Civilai asked.

'No idea,' said Siri.

The URC boat was steered without a rudder through

some group osmosis which explained why it spent so much time zagging. But somehow it found its way to the left bank and defied the current that was so eager to send it home. Ugly barked. Everyone stared to the right. Nobody spoke. There was no breeze, no cloud, seemingly no weather at all.

'My heavens,' said Siri.

'It . . . it's waving,' said Mr Geung.

Despite the fact that nobody was rowing, the boat held its place in the river and angled towards the open water where a hand protruded, its fingers splayed. It seemed to be telling them to stop.

A cacophony of sound drummed through Siri's head: screams and gunshots and loud Chinese music. He pressed his palms against his ears, closed his eyes, and straight away he knew whose hand this was.

'Grab it,' he shouted.

They all looked at him as if he were mad. Nobody in their right mind would invite the Siren of the water to drag them down into the depths. Nobody would take hold of that dead hand and allow the evil spirits to escape into a live body. Reluctantly they rowed towards the hand. Siri dared touch it. He reached over the side of the longboat, lunged but missed. But Daeng behind him was more successful. She caught hold of the wrist with two hands. To everyone's shock the hand arrested the flow of the heavy teak vessel like an anchor. The longboat wheeled around and Siri scurried back to help his wife. He took hold of the slender hand.

'Row to the bank,' he cried.

And row they did, as hard as they were able. But the hand in the river was stronger. Siri and Daeng held on with all their might but the boat was going nowhere.

'Put your backs into it,' Civilai shouted.

Every man, woman, amputee and child leaned into their oars if only to get away from that horrifying hand. After several minutes, the rowers were panting but the hand held firm.

'It . . . it must be a very heavy hand,' said Mr Geung.

'Again,' Civilai shouted.

The oars dug in with unprecedented coordination. The boat lunged. The hand conceded. It took some ten minutes to reach the bank. If the team had put this much effort into the races they would certainly have fared better. At the bank, the water they bailed out of the craft was half sweat.

Siri and Daeng were out of the boat and up to their waists in the river. Still they held the delicate hand between them.

'This is who I think it is, isn't it?' said Daeng.

'Yes,' Siri replied.

Two of the few crew members under fifty jumped from the boat and, careful not to touch the body, they ducked below the surface. When they re-emerged, one of them said, 'It's no wonder we had trouble. She's roped to some bloody great hunk of machinery.'

The two men dragged it to the bank and Siri and Daeng found Madame Peung's body much easier to slide up on to the grass. Her ankle was tied by a short rope to an air compressor. Daeng told them she'd seen it the night before, stowed to the stern of the frigate. Siri could see no wounds. There were no bloodstains on her clothes. If her raised arm was a conscious effort, he had to assume she'd died from drowning. Yet in most cases, the victim's face would be contorted in agony. Madame Peung seemed almost to be smiling. Even in death she was beautiful.

'Awfully bad luck,' said Civilai, who leaned from the longboat. 'Fancy her getting her foot tangled up in the rope just as the compressor was about to fall overboard.'

'You'd think she'd have seen it coming,' said Daeng, and winced at her own insensitivity.

Siri felt a good deal sorrier for the death of Madame Peung than he had been for the loss of his books. She'd been kind to him. He liked her. But, quite clearly, the villains had no further use for her. If the water at that spot had been just twenty centimetres deeper, they'd have passed her by. But had she made some supernatural afterlife effort to raise her arm? To be seen? To have her body put down with respect so her spirit might move on? He wouldn't have put it past her.

With the compressor as their reward – thirty kilograms of scrap metal – the two men agreed to sit with the corpse until the longboat passed on the return journey. They kept their distance from her. Siri had considered it disrespectful to go into battle with a body on board. Daeng and Geung took the two empty paddle spots and joined the uncoordinated splash upriver. Siri had several excuses for not picking up an oar, not least of these his injuries sustained in a run-in with the Khmer Rouge. Any other man would have enjoyed the three months of bed rest the doctors had recommended. Siri had been repainting the bathroom Wattay blue after only a week. A bathroom that was now in ruins. A good enough reason not to waste time painting bathrooms. Civilai cited the loss of his right earlobe as the reason why he didn't rush for the vacant paddles.

The conversation amongst the rowers had taken a more serious tone. The discovery of the body had shifted them into a superstitious frame of mind. There was speculation that the great naga had taken another soul because the race organizers had banned the final party. This was where everyone took to the river in anything that could float to thank the great serpent for not flooding them the previous year. There would always be a lot of drinking and at least one near-fatality.

'Civilai?' said Siri.

'Yes, brother?'

'We're heading after a boat with a machine gun attached to it and ten armed soldiers on board.'

'It won't come to that, Siri.'

'If we happen to round a bend and there they are, they might come at us.'

'And?'

'And I think we should at least explain to our shipmates what we're doing here.'

'They didn't ask when we set off.'

'They hadn't seen a dead body tied to an air compressor when we set off. We might need their help.'

And so, with the oars raised and their chests heaving, the crew listened to Civilai's abridged version of why they were pursuing a Lao naval vessel.

'Where would they be heading?' asked one shirtless fat man with stomachs piled on his lap like hillside paddy fields.

'It's a point exactly twenty-two kilometres upriver,' said Siri.

This was followed by a mass exchange of nods and a soundtrack of 'Oh, yes.'

'Sharp bend in the river? Rock cliff?' asked the fat man.

'Well, yes,' said Siri.

Smiles. Chuckles. Knowing looks.

'Frenchy's Elbow. Might as well just leave your Vietnamese to it,' said the old lady with the short oar. 'They'll be taken care of, all right.'

'I don't understand,' said Daeng.

'It's started,' said the headman. 'One body already and they haven't even arrived there.'

'Is there something at this place?' Siri asked, although he knew there was.

'Not something you could poke in the eye with a stick,' said one woman. 'But something just the same.'

'Are there bodies there?' Siri asked.

'Oh, yes,' said the headman. 'Plenty. But your minister

won't be finding his brother at Frenchy's Elbow.'

'Why not?'

'Because the boat at the bottom of the river there went down about the same time your minister was born.'

A shudder ran up Siri's neck. Nobody was rowing. The river was running fast from the floods in China. Yet they were floating at some speed ... against the current.

'Frenchmen?' Siri asked.

'Ah, there's one with the gift,' said the old lady.

'Well, here's one without,' said Civilai. 'What are we talking about here?'

'Everyone in these parts knows the story,' said the fat man. 'It was the year of our Lord Buddha 2543 ...'

'Of course, it would be,' said Civilai. 'Better known as 1910.'

'You can't get reliable intelligence these days,' said Siri.

'The French bastards convinced the King of Luang Prabang that he should lend them his crown jewels for some world fair over in Europe somewhere,' said the fat man. 'In fact it seems pretty damned obvious that they were stealing them. But, what can you do when you've got a dozen muskets pointed at your head? They loaded it on a French gunboat called *La Grandière*, guarded by six French soldiers, and they set off down-river to Vientiane. But that treasure was cursed. They say a whirlpool surged up out of that deep water and swallowed the boat down in a spot they now call Frenchy's Elbow. Drowned, all of 'em. In the early days you could see the hull from the bank. Locals passing it on the river would swing by to take a look. They might dive down to see if there was anything to salvage. But every one of them that tried suffered personal or family ills straight after. Deaths or sickness or crop failure. They say one boy got all the way down there into the cabin. It was dark and he was feeling around and his hand fell on the face of a man. He fought the urge to flee and took the man's hand. He helped himself to a ring. Perhaps that was what triggered the curse. 'Cause when he first dived down there he was just a lad, but when he surfaced with the ring in his hand, he was a grey-haired old man. That was the last time anyone went down there.'

'And he had a unicorn horn sticking out of his back,' whispered Daeng to her husband. She too had noticed their upriver floatation.

'You not buying any of this?' Siri asked her.

'The Curse of Frenchy's Elbow? Come on, Siri. Everyone living near water goes nutty eventually. Loch Ness monsters and Sirens and Great Nagas. It's a symptom of water vapour inhalation.'

Civilai crawled back to join them.

'Have you noticed we're floating against the current?' he said.

Siri ignored him.

'What about my dreams?' said Siri. 'The naked

Frenchmen. You don't think there could be a boat laden with the crown jewels of Laos down there?'

'Whether there is or there isn't,' said Daeng, 'some silly curse isn't going to stop that unit of engineers from digging it out. But I'll tell you one thing. If there is treasure down there it all makes a lot more sense than a search for a minister's dead brother. A lot of effort has gone into organizing this and we can't leave it up to your spirit friends to stop them shipping our treasure off to Thailand.'

'Irrespective of the fact our old kings pilfered it from some other old kings in the first place?' said Civilai.

'It belongs – through the statute of limitations on the possession of regal booty – to Laos,' she told him.

'You just made that up,' said Civilai. 'It's extortion paid by vassal states to a tyrant. At the worst they're stolen goods.'

'And they're our stolen goods and I'm not handing them over to the Vietnamese without a fight. Siri?'

'Yes, my love?'

'What are you grinning about?'

'It's not a grin. It's a smile of admiration. There's nothing "used to be" about you. The fire never burned out. You're as much in love with Laos as you were back then.'

'And you, old man?' she said. 'Are you tired of fighting for this nation of lotus eaters?'

'Never.'

'Then let's not invest all our faith in this stupid curse. Let's put together a plan B.'

'I think a plan B might involve a lot of sleeping under trees,' said Civilai. 'Digging a boat out of sixty-eight years of silt is no easy matter.'

Like the north-easterly monsoons and feather-duster salesmen, Inspector Phosy was relentless. If something was blocking his path he would chip a way into it until a breakthrough could be made. There were two large rocks currently sitting in front of him and he hadn't made much of an impression on either of them. The Housing Department had confirmed that Comrade Koomki was missing. The inspector had collected a good deal of evidence that Dr Siri was a mortal enemy of the Housing Allocations head but nothing at all to tie the deceased to the Frenchman. One more setback was that Sergeant Sihot was stuck in a clinic in Xanakham with chronic diarrhoea. He didn't make it to Pak Lai.

Phosy had also heard back from Vietnam. The reply came via their Intelligence Unit. They had a sprawling complex behind their embassy but seemed to operate independently. Nobody knew what intelligence was being gathered there or why they'd been allowed to set it up in the first place. Phosy recalled that Civilai had lobbied without success to have it shut down.

One result of the recent agreement of friendship and cooperation signed with Hanoi was that the Vietnamese were reluctantly obliged to be friendly and cooperative. This extended to a relationship between law enforcers in both countries. The fax he held in his hand was a perfect example of 'minimum cooperation':

> Madame Saigna Peung, a Lao citizen, was in possession of a multiple laissez-passer to the Socialist Republic of Vietnam. In the past twelve months she has made eight visits. Her papers were cleared each time at Hanoi International Airport. Before this last trip the average time of her stay was three days. Her last recorded visit was in July 1978 and she was in the country for eighteen days.
>
> Madame Saigna Peung had dealings with the Socialist Republic of Vietnam trade office and was involved in importing goods to Vietnam. There is no record of appointments after the third day of this most recent trip. No more information is available.
>
> Signed, Dac Kien. Hanoi Police and International Cooperation and Friendship Representative.

'No more information is being released, more like it,' thought Phosy as he walked up the hill to Madame Peung's luxury house with a view. And what was she doing there for such a long time on this last trip? He doubted she wouldn't have been followed at least some of that time. It was the socialist way. Surely she hadn't just disappeared. Phosy had said his hellos in the village, told them he'd be interviewing them individually later, but declined company to visit the house. His first action was to sit in the wooden recliner on the veranda looking down at the village and across the fields to the mountains of Ban Elee. Marx had said, 'The rich will do anything for the poor but get off their backs.' Phosy felt the rich on his back as he sat there in front of the big house. What happened to the even distribution of wealth they'd crooned about at the seminars?

But this was not his concern today. He stood and asked the building what had happened on those two weird nights of August. There was no evidence of a break-in at the front door. In fact, you'd probably have needed an armoured car to get through it as the iron latch on the inside had apparently been welded together by a team of swarthy blacksmiths. The rear door had the same impressive apparatus. The windows were all barred. The widow was clearly afraid of losing her money. But there was no evidence anywhere of a forced break-in. He thought about the live-in girl. Whether she might have opened the door for her boyfriend and made up the whole story about being asleep when it happened. On his way to Ban Elee, Phosy had stopped off at the district administration office. He knew a young girl with no travel papers wouldn't be very far from her residence. In fact she was still registered in her grandmother's house and hadn't applied for transit papers. The house was only four kilometres away. He would visit her next.

But, for now, he sat in the main bedroom where a killing had purportedly taken place there on the double bed. The mattress was uncovered now and a bloodstain had taken a huge bite out of it around the area of the pillow. This meant that the victim was either asleep or calmly lying back in her bed when she was shot. So it was unlikely she'd opened the door to her killer, and more likely that the door was unlocked or the killer was in there with her.

The distance from the door to the bed was only four metres, yet there was no bullet embedded in the wooden wall behind the bed. Again it was conceivable the bullet bounced around inside the skull and did indeed go to the pyre with the victim but so much blood suggested an exit wound. There should have been a bullet.

Finally, back on the porch. Here it was that the drugged robber had supposedly dragged the widow to the front steps and, in front of the entire village, shot her for the second time. 'The bullet went into the wooden post,' they'd said. The village headman had retrieved a .45 bullet and given it to the policeman as a souvenir. Phosy found the hole. It was a teak post so the bullet hadn't sunk deeply into it. It would have been retrievable with a penknife. But there was something far more telling than the bullet: the hole itself. He turned back towards the house but something odd on the wooden step caught his attention. It was a second hole, easily missed, neat, the same size as the one in the post. And, after a few minutes of gouging with his penknife, it was here that Phosy found a second bullet. It was a .45.

A picture was forming in Phosy's mind. A scenario so bizarre no fiction writer would insult his readers by offering it up as a plausible plot. To make it credible, there had to be more, much more, going on here in Ban Elee than a meeting with the supernatural. Madame Daeng's instincts had been fired by accounts of events that appeared to be impossible. Now, Phosy was charged with the task of proving that the impossible wasn't so hard after all. Down in the village, his questions were simple. Did Madame Peung shop at the market? No, not since her husband died. She'd become something of a recluse. She sent her live-in girl. Did anybody else have cause to go to the house? No. Apart from the fact that she suddenly had a Vietnamese accent, did you notice any changes between Madame Peung and Madame Keui? Perhaps she'd put on a little weight. Oh, and she'd started using more make-up. She'd always liked to slap on the colour but she'd never used that much before.

Phosy was on his way to meet the live-in girl but he was quite sure he knew what had transpired there in Ban Elee. The only thing he lacked was a motive.

13

Frenchy's Elbow

It was nine thirty a.m. when Barnard arrived at the small outpost they laughingly called a town, Pak Lai. There were thousands of people. In a civilized country that would have worked to his advantage. He could blend in, vanish in the crowd. But this was the opposite. As soon as he'd stepped from the forest, they'd seen him. They were pointing. Calling him over. He was a good thirty centimetres taller than any of them. He ignored them as best he could.

'Hey, Soviet,' they cried. The latest salute to invaders.

He made out not to hear. They smiled and pushed sweets into his hand and coconuts with straws sticking out of them. He brushed them off. So much for his discreet arrival. He made for the old French administration building at the far side of the green and walked confidently through the main door as if he belonged there. The place was deserted. He walked upstairs and into an office full of well-worn French desks and Russian typewriters. Framed photographs of nondescript Asians hung in a line across the back wall. He took a wooden chair and placed it at a window from which he might best view the festivities. He took the binoculars from his satchel. They'd belonged to the guide who now lay battered in a shallow grave beside the porter. The spoils of war.

His heart was palpitating. His breath, irregular. He could feel every scuffled step his body took at the end of its journey. But there was time. He scanned the childish revellers. He'd see her soon enough. Before he set light to the restaurant, he'd found a photograph of the shrivelled hag standing with a scarred old man and a moron. There was enough of her recognizable behind that cruel disguise. The young beauty. The innocent with child. The first love. It was all in there. And no matter how desperately she shrouded herself in wrinkles and flab, he knew that his heart would pick her out of the crowd.

'What do we do if she comes back again?' Civilai asked.

'Who?' said Siri.

'Madame Peung.'

The longboat was making good speed against the flow of the river. On some stretches it felt as if they were merely riding the eddies. The boat was doing most of the work. Siri breathed in the sweet scent of the American Metal-Filing trees along the bank. He stared at his beautiful wife two seats ahead rowing with the grace of a swan ballerina. He doubted swan ballerinas could row but he liked his simile. She was singing the rowing song she'd learned just ten minutes earlier and making up verses when called upon.

'Why should she come back?' Siri asked.

'She did it once before.'

'Water's a tough one, Civilai. Not even Houdini could beat the water torture.'

'I think you'll find that was only in the movie, Siri.'

'Either way, spirits don't . . .'

'What?'

'That's why the Frenchmen have been stuck in hell. They are down there. They're trapped under water. Their souls have no way to go wherever French souls go to. There are six French bodies down there at Frenchy's Elbow. That confirms it.'

'Good, but if she does?'

'Madame Peung?'

'If she comes back?'

'What's your point?'

'*King Kong.*'

'That's a point?'

'We saw it. Remember?'

As Siri and Civilai were movie junkies it was only natural that many of their conversations turned to the cinema.

'How could I forget? What's her name? Fay something.'

'But they captured this giant gorilla, took it to New York and made a fortune from public performances.'

'And Madame Peung is our Kong?'

'Shot through the head, twice, drowned in the Mekhong. She's star material. We could take her to Bangkok and guillotine her on national television. Next night there she is, good as new.'

Madame Daeng's shoulders were rocking with laughter. Civilai was about to continue with the image when, without a word of instruction, all the rowers put up their oars. The fat man looked around and nodded at Siri.

'About a kilometre,' he said. 'Less overland. Better we pull in here. You can walk over the crest. There's a spot up there you can look down at Frenchy's Elbow without being seen.'

All the crew members wanted to go and have a look, of course. But the headman selected two, as well as himself, to accompany the Vientiane people. These guides led them through the thick undergrowth as if they'd spent much of their time escorting tourists to the Elbow. Civilai said he expected to find a souvenir shop set up on the ridge. But what they did get was a spectacular eyrie looking directly down at the bend in the river. The Lao cruiser had moored on exactly the same sandbank that the minister's helicopter had first landed on. The equipment was laid out methodically along the shore. Some of the men were setting up an elaborate winch-and-pulley system using two huge old teak trees as anchors. The bulldozer was lined up between them. All in all, it looked like a very competent operation.

Like synchronized swimmers, three divers emerged from the water with heavy oxygen tanks strapped to their backs. All three held up their thumbs to the officer on the bank. He, in turn, put up his own thumb and gestured for the men to leave the river. The other engineers helped them remove their tanks and they all retreated to behind the tree line. There followed half a dozen muted explosions that belched silt and rocks from the river. Even at such a high elevation, Siri and the team were showered with pebbles and mud. The explosions echoed around the rock faces, the sound getting louder as it travelled, taking on the form of an angry voice, not just to Siri, but to all of them.

One diver went back into the water, swam to the deepest point and dived to the depths. Then, an amazing thing happened. Fish – tens, then hundreds, then thousands – floated to the surface. Stunned by the blasts. Drowned by the air, and carried away on the current. It was remarkable how many fish had made Frenchy's Elbow their home. One of the guides got to his feet and hurried back through the jungle to his boat.

'Looks like they have a net on board,' said Daeng.

Her plan B had been to avoid putting the Uphill Rowing Club in harm's way. They all doubted the Vietnamese would accompany the treasure to the border. After it had been transferred to the elephants the convoy would be at its most vulnerable. They would return to Pak Lai and drum up a village militia to intercept it.

Meanwhile, the show continued. The explosions had been the highlight. For the next hour it was a slow, laborious process of diving and winching. And there at the officer's side the whole time, yelling instructions, pointing this way and that, was Madame Peung's brother.

'He seems to have found his voice,' said Siri.

'Yet another miracle,' said Civilai.

'It's him,' said Daeng. 'This is his party. He's the boss.'

And right away Siri remembered the moment on the helicopter that had almost escaped him. The nudge. The brother had nudged Madame Peung. It wasn't her who recognized the spot on the river. It was him. He was the one who knew the terrain. Madame Peung had just been along for the ride. And no longer of use, there was no doubt in Siri's mind that Tang had lured the woman to the back of the cruiser and dispatched her unseen into the river.

'He'd planned this all along,' said Daeng. 'It's been made to look like a series of unrelated, spontaneous events. The resurrection. The approach by the minister's wife. The location of the body. But it's all been laid out. This is the penultimate scene.'

'And here we are with balcony seats to the grand finale,' said Civilai.

'If that's so, you'll have to agree it's brilliant,' said Siri. 'Although I don't see how it could be possible.'

'It's booooring,' said Geung.

'Patience,' said Civilai. 'They're Vietnamese. Eventually

we'll have something to cry over or laugh at.'

And, as he spoke, something did happen. Cables heading in three directions rose from the water, leading to two winches attached to the trees on the east side and to the tail end of the bulldozer which acted as a counterpoint, pulling southwards from further down the bank. All three were coordinated with whistles. The long ratchet handles clicked a few centimetres at a time and the bulldozer tugged to the whistle. Nothing else appeared to be happening but there was a confident air amongst the soldiers. It was half an hour before the first glimpse of the hull appeared above the surface. It was upside down.

'My word, they've done it,' said Civilai.

After another twenty minutes of patient winching, half the boat was on the steep bank and a gap had opened up above the gunwales. The years had been kind to the heavy metal craft. Being submerged in mud had preserved it admirably.

'I bet some French naval museum would pay a lot of money for that,' said Civilai.

'They're going d . . . down,' said Geung.

With miners' lamps attached to their helmets, two of the engineers crawled on to the space between the bank and the deck of the upside-down craft.

'Where would you store cargo in something like that?' Daeng asked.

'The hold is buried in the deck at the forward end,' said Civilai. 'There should be a couple of metal doors leading down to it. That isn't where those boys are going. They're heading into the cabin.'

'That's where they were,' said Siri.

The others looked at him.

'That's where the Frenchmen were,' he said. 'They're free now.'

They watched as the engineers passed large cotton sacks to the men inside. One by one the bags re-emerged, not full, but with sufficient bulk to suggest each contained the remains of a crew member. Obviously the Vietnamese were not as squeamish at touching the remains of the dead as the Lao. There were six bodies, all told.

All this time the bulldozer and the other equipment were being reloaded on to the cruiser until only the cables that stayed the boat remained. The bodies were carried to the Lao boat and laid side by side at the stern. The skipper cast off and the boat headed back downstream.

'Did anybody notice anything peculiar about that?' Civilai asked.

'I don't get it,' said Siri.

'They came to recover bodies,' said Daeng. 'They salvaged the boat. They went inside. They brought out the dead. They took them back. Everything was exactly according to plan. They've done what the minister asked them to do. I wouldn't be surprised if they came looking for you, Siri, to make an identification.'

'And once more we are dumbfounded by a mystery that is not at all mysterious,' said Civilai.

'Not exactly,' said Siri. 'All it means is that the engineers were only told to recover the boat and bring out the bodies. That they weren't a party to the secret of what could be found in the hold. It's a legitimate rescue mission.'

'So why didn't anyone notice that Madame Peung was missing?' asked Civilai.

'Ah, brother,' said Daeng. 'Nobody notices old women. And nobody misses them when they're gone.'

Civilai looked at her querulously.

'But it looks like somebody else is missing in action,' said Siri.

He pointed to a lone figure on the rocks below the karst. It was Tang, the non-brother, non-assistant of Madame Peung. He was adjusting scuba equipment.

'Who is he?' asked Civilai. 'They were taking orders from him. He'd have to be in some position of authority for a uniformed officer to kowtow to him. And they've left him equipment.'

'What is that over there behind him?' Daeng asked.

'It looks like a parachute,' said Civilai.

'No,' said Siri. 'It's a dinghy. They come with a foot pump. We used to use them on late-night river forays during the wars. That's how he'll be getting his booty back downriver. This really is a one-man show.'

Tang put on his breathing mask and dropped into the water. He carried a small underwater acetylene torch and a pack. He swam alongside the cruiser to a point that was still submerged and down he went. He was under water for a long time. They supposed that the fastening on the hold was rusted and difficult to open. He re-emerged without his blow torch but with a wooden casket about the size of a radio. It was floating on a life vest.

'Every eventuality,' said Phosy. 'What a planner.'

The casket was heavy after all those years in the water. He lugged it out of the river and on to the sandbank. He seemed to pause then, probably deciding whether to open it, but there were obviously more down below.

'He doesn't seem to be afraid of being seen, does he?' said Daeng.

'Everyone for a hundred kilometres around is at the races,' said Siri. 'He picked his day, too. He really has thought of everything. He'll unload the treasure, disconnect the cables and watch the boat slide back to the depths. I bet he has his elephant route all planned out.'

'Do you think we should go down there and overpower him while he's not expecting it?' Civilai asked. 'He is alone, after all.'

'You're never alone with an AK-47,' said Daeng. 'He's got a couple, as far as I can see. One on the bank. Another by the dinghy. Maybe a pistol too. But I think we can probably get down there and surprise him while he's diving. I call this Plan C.'

'We'll let him tire himself out with the caskets,' said Siri. 'Then we'll think of something. None of us is as young as we think we are.'

There were seven caskets in all. Tang crawled up on

to the sandbank and collapsed on to his side as he collected his breath. He didn't even have the strength to remove his oxygen tanks. He had a short stout knife in his belt which he used to prise open the first casket which sat beside him. The lock and the hinges were rusty so it didn't present any problems. From their point of view, the team could not see into the box and they were too far away to notice the expression on the face of the Vietnamese.

But Siri did see something else. A shadow was emerging from the woods on the far bank. It blended into the foliage and when it stopped moving he lost sight of it completely. He knew there was nothing human about the shadow. He was used to such sights but had never sensed such a feeling of foreboding.

Tang turned to another cask and wrenched off its lid with more urgency. Something appeared to be wrong. He turned to a third casket.

The shape in the woods shifted slightly and caught Siri's gaze once more. Then he spotted a second to its left. Larger, this one, and without question the form of a person.

The diver was on the fifth casket. He was clearly not enjoying the task. The last two lids he ripped off with his bare hands. He threw down the knife and reached into the last box and produced a black Buddha image

– the type one might find in any village temple in the land. He fumbled around for the knife and began to hack away at the statuette.

'Wh . . . what's he doing?' Geung asked.

Ugly growled as he scanned the woods down below. He was sensing what Siri could see, hundreds upon hundreds of human shapes emerging from the forest. Once they left the camouflage of the jungle they seemed to have no colour at all. Like viewers at a tennis match, they sat on the grass bank and watched the diver overturn every last casket and empty hundreds of images on to the ground. He hacked at them with his knife. Smashed one against another.

'They aren't going to like that,' said Siri.

Daeng looked up to see her husband staring in the wrong direction.

'See something?' she asked.

'It's like a Cecil B. DeMille ghost epic,' said Siri.

Daeng had long since stopped asking, 'Who the hell is . . . ?'

'Cast of thousands,' said Siri. 'It's a bit frightening. I'm not sure how any of these fit into my "Waiting room to the beyond" theory. They're connected to the Buddha images somehow.'

'What are you seeing there?' Civilai asked.

'All sssitting down,' said Mr Geung.

They looked at him. He shrugged.

'Ah, he sees 'em too,' said the headman. 'There's them that can.'

The diver was beside himself with anger. He paced back and forth with the canisters still attached to his back. This obviously wasn't the type of treasure he'd been expecting. He hurried back to the river, reattached his mask, and threw himself into the water.

'He thinks he missed something,' said Daeng. 'But he didn't. Now's our chance. We can get down there and grab the guns.'

They all stood and worked their way down a steep rocky path that led to the Elbow.

'Probably expecting something more royal,' said Civilai. 'Crowns with rubies and mitres and pouches of diamonds. We talk about our national treasure and naturally everyone thinks of jewels. But each to his own. To the royals, these images were priceless because they'd been worshipped for hundreds of years. They'd clocked up a lot of merit. The king probably had them locked in a vault somewhere and kept the emeralds and pearls in his sock drawer.'

Small rocks were dislodged by their descent.

'All that planning,' said Daeng. 'How frustrating would that be? The unnecessary deaths. The investment. You'd have to feel sorry for him. I wonder who he is; how he achieved all this.'

'I was about to say that it probably couldn't get any worse,' said Siri who had stopped to watch the gallery of observers. They were standing now and moving towards the boat. Moving like trees swept up in a lava flow.

'What is it, Siri?' Daeng asked.

'I wish I could sell tickets,' he said.

'Come on,' she told him. 'No time for ghosties.'

The grey spirits of antiquity usually had little to do with the malevolent spirits of the forest – nasty bastards who had made Siri's life a misery on several occasions. But somebody had cut a deal somewhere in the jungle and the spirits that resided in the images began to merge into the two huge teak trees that anchored the cables. Within seconds, every last one of them had been absorbed into the wood.

'That's a good trick,' said Siri.

'Don't keep it to yourself, old man,' said Civilai.

'Just keep your eyes on the two old teaks that the cables are tied around,' said Siri.

But only he could see what was happening. Only he had stopped to view the show. He was left behind at the rear as the others hurried down the dirt path. He leaned against a large boulder that overhung the river and noticed the lack of sounds. There were no birds. No insects. Even the rumble of water as the river rounded the bend had become silent. There was an imbalance between nature and the supernatural. The first sound to invade this silence was a creak. Perhaps it was more a groan as the old trees strained against the weight of the boat. It was as if they could no longer hold it. Then, one after the other, the cables began to slice through the trees like cheese wires through Camembert. Siri looked down to see whether the others had noticed but he was alone. One second the boat was anchored, the next it was loose. At first it lurched to one side. Then it slid rapidly into the water, dragging its cables behind it. In a single breath it had vanished beneath the water and a bubble the size of a small whale belched to the surface. The gunboat was back at its resting place. Siri's eyes returned to the two old trees. He expected them to topple to the ground like candles sliced through by a Douglas Fairbanks Jr sword. But they stood firm.

He heard the voices of his colleagues below.

'They couldn't have been tied very tight,' said the headman.

'Funny they should both come undone at the same time,' said Civilai.

'I think they must have snapped,' said Daeng.

Siri looked on in amazement. Had they not seen the cables slice through the teak? Was he the only one who knew what had actually happened? In fact . . . had it happened?

When he reached the bank at the Elbow, all was quiet. His colleagues were standing on the bank looking out across the water. There was nothing to see. Nobody really expected the diver to reappear, but for ten minutes they watched with their AK-47s trained on the Mekhong as it passed on its way to Vientiane. But, in some way, the diver did return to the bank. And he did look forlornly at the piles of iron Buddha images before stepping into the forest to face whatever retribution the spirits might have for him. Without the air-compressor to replenish the supply, there had been barely a minute's worth of oxygen in Tang's tank. He'd died an agonizing death trapped in the cargo hold of the gunboat. But only Dr Siri knew any of this. If, in fact, he really did.

'We should go now,' said Siri.

'He might still be alive down there,' said the headman.

'No, he's gone,' said Siri.

They all turned around and looked at the doctor.

'What about the images?' Daeng asked.

Siri looked at the boatman and smiled.

'If I were a lost Buddha,' he said. 'And I found myself far from home for many years, I would look very kindly on anyone who volunteered to take me back to Luang Prabang. The palace is a museum now but one of the old royal temples would gladly take them in.'

'I doubt one person could handle so much merit,' said the headman. 'Bit of an overload.'

'You're right,' said Civilai. 'But fifty people could share it.'

'Aye, that they could,' agreed the old man. 'That they could.'

Siri headed for the trees and studied the point where the cable wound around them. He saw no evidence of magic. Madame Daeng made for the Buddha idols. When she returned she had a small package wrapped in cloth.

'What's that then?' Siri asked.

'Surely we couldn't go through all this excitement without claiming one little souvenir,' she smiled.

'Daeng, you've seen what the curse can do.'

'All I saw were two cables snap. Bad quality.'

'I strongly recommend you don't take that souvenir out of this valley.'

'Recommendation noted. Let's go.'

'Be it on your own head.'

'I suppose the saddest part of all this is that the minister didn't get to find his brother,' said Daeng as they walked along the bank on their way back to the longboat.

Siri laughed.

'Something funny?' she asked.

'You know I wonder whether anyone actually read the Cuban medical report of Major Ly's jaw surgery.'

'It provided some insight into his whereabouts?'

'Pretty much pinpointed the location. I read through it last night. The last page of the file is a letter to the Cuban surgeon from a private hospital in Bangkok. They very politely requested a copy of the surgeon's report and the X-ray, which I doubt he sent.'

'Bangkok? What's Bangkok got to do with all this?'

'Oh, I have a feeling the minister's brother might have had enough of all the warring over here and popped across the border. I imagine he'd collected himself a little nest egg from war booty which he used to establish himself in Thailand.'

'As what?'

'Ooh, at a guess I'd say he bought himself a gogo bar and drank and fornicated himself to death. I doubt he ever got his jaw working properly.'

'That's not a guess, is it?'

'I might have dreamed some of it.'

'Siri.'

'Yes, dear?'

'I will not have you dreaming of gogo bars.'

'Sorry.'

When we fought hand to hand in the jungle I became aware that I was killing the children of parents. Young men who were stuck for a job so joined the army expecting a few years of pineapple eating in the tropics. It concerned me that killing was becoming second nature to me. Indifferent. Indiscriminate. Anyone in a French uniform. That wasn't the way to do it. You needed to operate at a different level to make a difference. I made the decision to leave the jungle and my rebel friends and dig in undercover in the heart of the French administration in the south: back in Pakse where my mother and I had sweated in the steam of boiled bedsheets for twenty years. Like many who feared the reprisals of the French, my mother had returned to what was left of our village. In fact, a lot of the old faces of Pakse had disappeared. I suppose my old face had disappeared with them. Nobody recognized me. I'd become hard, my features angular. My hair was short and my body was lean and muscular. If I'd made myself up with some cosmetics and dressed like the French mademoiselles, I could have had my pick of the French administrators. I could have been the mistress of any one of them. But that wouldn't have worked. It was a small town. Belonging publicly to one man would have closed the door on others. And I would have drawn ire from the Lao. I needed to merge. Be invisible again.

There were men. There were handsome ones and there were ugly ones. Cruel and kind ones. But, to a man, they had something in common. They were always superior. I was never more than an aperitif. I wasn't in their class. I was an ignorant brown-skinned girl they sought to rescue. And so, they were clumsy. They released secrets through the sluice gates of cheap wine. They boasted over the telephone. They left documents lying around. In the beginning I was clumsy too. I hadn't yet learned how to love mine enemy in order to garrotte him in his sleep. I needed to become an actress to mask the disgust that rose in my throat whenever I witnessed the excesses of our gods. Everything could have collapsed in that first week back in the town. It was as if all the trains of fate collided in one day in Pakse and there was only one survivor.

I was told of an agency that recruited French-speaking menial staff for the gods. I was interviewed by an officious Vietnamese woman whose French was awful. I had to match her mistakes and dumb myself down in order to sound competent. It was established from the beginning that she would be receiving 50 per cent of my income as an agency fee. I agreed gladly and noted her address. She sent me to the home of a Vietnamese couple. The wife met me at the front door of their fine wooden home on the bank of the Mekhong. She announced her name and status as if reciting lines in a school play. She couldn't have been much older than sixteen. She called me 'big sister' and showed me to the servants' quarters. There was a fat Lao cook, female but balding, a Vietnamese male driver with an abundance of female hormones, and me.

I still wasn't sure what I was supposed to learn by being in the home of a high-ranking Vietnamese official. I had no guidance. We were hardly the French underground. This was all my idea and it was an idea that felt heavier with every passing day. I was to clean the house, keep the garden and serve food when there were guests. One of the first questions the bitch at the agency had asked was whether I could read. It was a question I got to hear often. I'd told her 'no'. Thus I was allowed access to the master's office. There were so many documents scattered here and there and my French was basic back then. I didn't know where to start. I knew somewhere in the piles of papers there would be information I could pass on but I was so raw that all I could do was start at the top and work my way slowly down.

I was halfway through that very first pile on my very first day when my heart was wrenched out of its socket. A deep male voice from behind me said, 'What do you think you're doing?'

I retreated from the documents with my head bowed. Didn't dare look at the man who had caught me out. I cowered in a corner. Took courage from the knife between the folds of my phasin *skirt.*

'I asked you what in hell's name you think you're doing?'

'Cleaning, sir,' I said, glaring at his boots – boots that should by rights have been taken off at the front step.

'That did not look like cleaning,' he said. 'That looked like reading.'

I had an act already by then. I spoke slowly as if I were backward, blew into my lips as if every word was an effort.

'I . . . I wish, sir,' I said. 'I wish I could read. The characters look so beautiful on the paper. I wish I could turn them into words.'

I shook with fear as might have been expected. He shocked me by kneeling in front of me but I kept my eyes trained on the parquet flooring.

'You're the new girl,' he said.

'Yes, sir.'

'What's your name?'

I had so many.

'Sik,' I said.

His hand reached for my chin and yanked it up so he could see my face. Still I forced my eyes downward.

'Girls as pretty as you don't need an education,' he said. His Lao was competent but he was undeniably Vietnamese. There was something familiar about his accent.

'You can make your way in the world with these.'

He grabbed my tit with his free hand and squeezed hard. I let my hand gently slide beneath the fold of my skirt. That was when I first doubted my ability to be what was expected of me. My life was already sacrificed for the fight of our people, but how could I ever allow myself to succumb to this?

His hand gripped my chin tighter and his face came closer to mine. I could smell the garlic and wine of his lunch and the grease that encased his hair. For the first time, I looked at him. And I knew him. A flash-flood of awful memories whisked me away from that room. Rolled me over and over in the swirl.

Back there somewhere in the room he pushed his lips on to mine and forced his tongue against my teeth. And I let him kiss me. I let him because my mind was elsewhere and it was the means to an end. I knew he wouldn't hear another cockerel crow nor abuse another girl. Suddenly, I had the will.

I awoke next morning to the screams of the thin-haired cook. I ran to the yard with the flowery driver one pace behind me. We stood at the chicken coop crying and screaming intermittently. The driver's horror seemed sincere as, I hoped, did mine. The French militia came and the administrator and the local Lao headman. And they carried away the body of the poor deputy requisitions director who had been so horribly mutilated – down there, as they say. They suspected the young wife who remained sitting impassive on the top step of the front porch the whole time. But for the French to arrest someone for a crime of passion, they had to sense some . . . passion. The little Madame showed none. Felt none. As neither the cook, the driver nor the chambermaid had a motive, everything was once again laid in the lap of the bastard insurgents who lurked in the night shadows.

That night I burned sixteen candles at the temple; one for each year of Gulap's short life to let her know the last of her tormentors was off the streets. I lit one more as a general thank you to whichever god had put me in the house of the Vietnamese. I never did learn how he'd wangled his way into a government position but, I suppose, if a man like that can sell toilets, he can sell himself.

14

Daeng's Big Finish

The sun was setting behind the buildings when the rubber dinghy floated into Pak Lai. With the Uphill Rowing Club continuing its journey to Luang Prabang transporting the Buddha images, Siri and his team had inflated the dinghy and made good time downriver. The current had apparently noticed its mistake and was flowing fast towards the south. They'd collected the body of Madame Peung and the two boatmen had taken over the rowing. Near the town, they'd passed the elephants heading upriver for their rendezvous with Tang and told the mahout he was out of luck. There would be no delivery to Thailand. Pak Lai was rocking with the euphoria of finals day. Music came from every direction and villagers were slowly stirring the air in front of them with fanned fingers as they danced in time to the beat from the invisible instruments. When the dinghy docked opposite the Lao navy cruiser, Governor Siri, drunk as a lord, was on the wonky jetty.

'Have a nice day out, did you, Comrade Coroner?' he slurred.

'Yes, thanks,' said Dr Siri, grabbing the governor's arm to help himself out of the boat.

The governor yanked his elbow away indignantly.

'You do realize there's a unit of soldiers here waiting for your professional self to identify a body.'

'Yes.'

'And?'

'They can leave. It's not the man we were looking for.'

He helped Daeng and Geung out of the unstable craft leaving Civilai to sort it out for himself. The governor didn't like being dismissed.

'How can you be so sure? You haven't even looked at the bodies.'

Siri walked away. Daeng was on the river bank picking out a large stone that seemed to have taken her fancy. She turned back and smiled at the governor.

'It's nothing you need to concern yourself with,' she said. 'You're just the governor. But here's a coup for you. Down there in the dinghy is the body of the woman, Madame Peung, who was invited here by the minister. About ten kilometres upstream is the air compressor she was tied to before she was thrown into the river. She was killed by somebody on that boat. So you have a murder inquiry to conduct. Good luck.'

'I . . . I . . .'

'Yes?'

'We don't have any police stationed here.'

'Well, you're going to have to find some,' said Civilai, clambering out of the boat. 'The minister's going to want answers.'

'It's the last night of the races,' said Governor Siri.

'Then you'd better get some coffee inside you and get cracking.'

'Oh, by the way,' said Daeng. 'The doctor and I will be changing our room. The one we're in is crowded and smells of beer. We'll take the room Madame Peung was in. She won't be using it.'

'What about the brother?' asked the governor.

'Oh, right. Forgot to tell you . . .'

With the rooms sorted out, the corpse billeted, and the Vietnamese engineers under a sort of open-air house arrest until someone could formally investigate the death of Madame Peung, Civilai and Mr Geung took a stroll to the temple which was the centre of the evening's activities. The old politburo man still couldn't quite get it. People were dancing and singing and joking without even the vaguest hint of alcohol. It didn't seem natural. The crew on the boat had glowed with that same generic joy. The buzz of being together with friends. Freedom from an endless war. Freedom to work the land and earn enough to feed the family and put a little aside for these three days off a year when their village could drag its boat to the river, laugh, capsize, collide, win a prize for the slowest time or the fattest rower, throw the winners into the water, launch all the boats to pay homage to a great serpent. That's what they were *on*: the euphoria of simplicity.

'Geung,' Civilai asked, 'when do you suppose I first entered that state that convinced me I had to be drunk before I could enjoy life?'

'You're an ad . . . dict,' said Geung.

'Yes, indeed. Should I give it up, do you think?'

'No.'

'You were supposed to say "yes".'

'It's too late. The drunk Comrade Civ . . . Civilai is the real Comrade Civilai now.'

Geung saw a dart stall with bright balloons on a board. He was a hot shot with a dart so he abandoned Civilai and jogged over to it. The old man, his mouth open just a fraction, watched him go. He wanted to defend himself somehow but had no idea how to do so. He wondered exactly when it was that the drunk Civilai had taken the alpha role in his personality. It was troubling. He decided he could really use a drink.

Dr Siri had supervised the overnight stowage of Madame Peung. Tobacco leaves were the wrapping of choice for a dead body but Pak Lai had none. Instead she was laid in a half section of concrete piping and garnished with hay and marijuana. After dinner, with Daeng's blessing, he had returned to check on the body. He was a little disappointed to find her lying there still. He wondered whether reincarnation was a buy-one-get-one-free deal, that we were all allowed one return. He pulled over a ten-litre paint tin and sat beside the woman who twice used to be.

'How is everything?' he asked.

The gentle smile was still on her lips as if she were keeping a secret. There had been no contact at all since her death. Siri had been hoping she would come to him somehow – offer herself up as his spirit mentor. He needed her to continue the tutorials that had brought him to the edge of two-way communication. He'd been the thickness of a TV screen away from a conversation with a dead king. And now she was gone. Her eyes were closed but all the while he pictured the *Wolf Man* scene when everyone knew Lon Chaney was dead but his eyes had sprung open and given Siri a near-bowel-evacuation in the front row of the picture house.

He edged his paint tin a little closer.

'So, you have nothing to say to me?' said Siri.

He waited for an answer. Looked around for subliminal messages. Closed his eyes in search of a vision. The chickens clucked in the next room. He wondered if that were a sign. He clucked back. He waited. No. They were just chickens. He was alone again. His two guides were lost, Auntie Bpoo, the cantankerous transvestite fortune-teller, to her going away party in a week, and Madame Peung, silent as the grave. Why was this all so difficult? He just wanted to talk to ghosts. That was all.

*

Inspector Phosy had little use for a clock. He worked

until the work was done or until he fell face down on to his desk from fatigue. As his office was only twenty minutes on foot from the police dormitory, he used the walk to clear his head of all the legal clutter. Apart from the passing curfew patrols there was nobody on the street after ten. He could admire the stars and take lungfuls of air that weren't seasoned with smog or smoke. He could filter out the news he would not tell his wife, like a description of the crushed face of the Lane Xang Hotel gardener they'd pulled from the pool. He could organize the unavoidable, like his imminent dispatch to Vieng Xai to train another batch of reluctant soldiers in the art of policing.

The voice came from a bank of hedges he'd just passed.

'I have a gun pointed at the back of your head,' it said. 'I never miss. Don't turn around.'

The accent was Vietnamese. Phosy stopped and held up his palms in front of him. He was unarmed.

'Good boy,' said the voice.

'What do you want?' Phosy asked.

'Facts.'

'The Ministry of Information has a whole department full.'

'Don't get cute, cop. The last patrol passed three minutes ago. It'll be an hour before the next one finds your body. Nobody around to hear the shot. Keep that in mind next time you get the urge for stand-up comedy.'

'You're right. I'm sorry.'

'That's better,' said the voice.

Phosy had a suspicion the man was speaking from the back of his throat to sound more threatening. The gunman stepped out of the vegetation and came up close behind Phosy. So close that the policeman felt the mouth of the gun in the small of his back. It was a stupid move. Amateurish. It told Phosy three things: exactly where the weapon was, exactly where his adversary was, and the fact that the fellow didn't have a lot of experience in this hoodlum game.

Phosy spun to one side, swept the gun away with his right hand and thumped his left fist into the side of the gunman's face. He was out of practice but he still heard the satisfying click of a cheekbone fracturing. The rest of the punches had probably been unnecessary but Inspector Phosy was very touchy about having guns pointed at him.

Madame Daeng had headed away from the riverbank foolishness and the noise of revellers and found that old wooden swing in the garden of the administrator's office. She lowered herself slowly on to the seat and listened to the cries of the cicadas. She admired the panorama of stars, the trails of lightning bugs joining the celestial dots. She considered her good fortune and sighed with every memory that came to her. To have succeeded and survived. To have known great people. To have been reunited with the love of her life. And what a good life it had been.

*

I was pregnant when I met him. A Frenchman's child, I told him. A general. It was more than enough to keep a junior officer at arm's length. But still I smiled at him and he came to the noodle shop for his lunch. I was in my early forties by then but I was blessed with good skin and a youthful face. I often claimed to be in my late twenties. The French had no idea how old we were. We were a different species.

Our head of clandestine operations had pointed him out to me. The Frenchman was tall, good looking. But, more importantly, he was a courier. He had his pouch with him all the time and, in the daytime, an armed aide. We spoke, me with my poor French. My bashfulness. I knew how to flirt by then. Knew what effect I had on a man. And then, one day just before he left for Saigon, I took his hand and put it on my belly.

'What the . . . ?' he said.

'It's a pillow,' I told him. 'I'm sorry I lied to you. I wear it to keep away the soldiers. A terrible thing happened to me once. So this is what I do to stay safe. Nobody else knows. Only you. I really want you to know. I hope you don't mind.'

It always worked. It was a big ego boost to the men who had little success with women. And I could tell he was new at this romance game. In no time at all we were together. Of a night, my round pregnancy pillow sat comically on the chair beside the bed. We laughed about the fact that I'd been pregnant to that scoundrel of a general for three years without a break. He thought it was a lovely story. That I was lovely. He was wild for me. I told him that he was the first man I had volunteered myself to. Such a confession tends to make a man stupid and careless.

He'd returned from Paris that particularly important night. He came straight to my room. He was still in uniform. He was carrying a briefcase. I'd been through his pouches before but I had the feeling this was something much more important. I produced a bottle of champagne and told him a West African member of the French legion had given it to me one day as he was about to board the ferry. I thought he must have stolen it so I didn't feel guilty to have brought it home. I'd saved it for a special day. I honestly believed this was it. We drank. The excitement of the day. The heat. The exhaustion of love. He fell asleep. I knew it was a sleep deeper than any he'd ever known.

By the time he woke, the briefcase was locked and the papers seemingly untouched, and I was still naked beside him. But he was late. An Aéronavale *was waiting to take him to Vietnam. Everything rested on the contents of that briefcase. Everything.*

'Mademoiselle. Mademoiselle.'

Daeng was stirred from her reverie. A dark shape loomed in front of her, a silhouette against the lights at the riverside and a rising moon.

'*Mon capitaine*,' she replied.

'One of thousands, I don't doubt,' he said.

'I'm impressed that you found me,' said Daeng.

'When the wolf scents blood . . .'

'I'm not bleeding, *monsieur*.'

'Oh, yes you are. You may not admit it. Not yet. But you have been bleeding for many decades. You are still bleeding for all my brothers you led to their deaths.'

'And who's bleeding for all my brothers and sisters?' she asked.

The Frenchman took two paces towards her. She could make out the outline of a stick or a bar in his hand. He lifted it and rested it on his shoulder. It seemed heavy. Iron, perhaps. Madame Daeng had no doubt whatsoever what he intended to do with it.

'Two hundred of your kind are not worth one Frenchman,' he said.

Daeng laughed.

'That's the attitude that made you so popular in the colonies, my captain. The attitude that lost you Dien Bien Phu. Or is that a touchy subject?'

'We did not lose that battle.'

'No?'

'No.'

'The history books would have it otherwise.'

'It was the Americans and the British who lost it.'

'No it wasn't. It was arrogance. You assumed you'd have air support from the Allies so your generals dug in to a non-defendable position. They knew for sure their old friends would get them out of yet another mess.'

'I'm not here to have this conversation with you.'

'Yes you are. This is one of those "get it all out in the open" murders my husband hates so much. If you'd wanted me dead without any exchanges you'd have crept up behind me and cracked my skull in two. You have things to say. Perhaps you want to hear my confession before you dispatch me. You want to justify my death with some sort of righteousness. Well, you're in the wrong place.'

He took another pace forward. He had it in mind to strike her. She distracted him.

'How many others know?' she asked.

He stopped.

'Know what?'

'That it was you who lost them the battle.'

'I . . . what are you talking about?'

'Oh, do stop it. Surely you aren't still denying it after all these years? Do you want me to remind you? You'd attended the meeting in London. Winston Churchill had categorically refused to give your troops any aerial support in Vietnam. You were the harbinger of that bad news. You carried the documents. You were flown directly to Bangkok and from there the shuttle to Pakse. You should have taken a night flight to Saigon but you refused. You said it was too dangerous to fly at night relying on instruments. You said your cargo was too valuable to lose. But all that was a lie. Your real reason was that you wanted to come to me. To spend the night with your little native girl.'

'I never did such a thing.'

He shifted uneasily. It was the first indication that he wasn't completely in control of his emotions.

'You were head over heels in love with me,' she said. 'You told me so many times. You—'

'Silence!'

'You'd arranged travel documents. You'd bought me a little cottage in Provence.'

'You . . .'

He was one metre from her, the bar raised. He was close enough for her to see the blood vessels in his eyes, to hear the rasp of his breath. But she leaned back on the swing, her feet firmly on the ground and she smiled. And whether it was the memory of that smile or merely a desire to prolong this execution – dreamed of for a lifetime – he hesitated.

'When did you realize it was me?' she asked, her voice still calm, her smile still held out in front of her like a shield.

Tears appeared in the old man's eyes. He lowered the metal bar.

'I fought it,' he said. 'I considered every other possibility. There were others at that meeting in London. There could have been a spy. It wasn't necessarily me. It wasn't necessarily you. And so, with this colossal doubt inside me, I set out to find who else could have leaked the information. Nobody suspected me. My name never came up in the endless debates. I was trusted. I was even promoted after it all. I was given more and more responsibility. But still I doubted myself. And, one by one, I eliminated every other possibility until there was only you.'

'You poor man.'

'The weight of the secret became a tumour and it is ready to kill me. That's why I'm here. You are the reason

I had a miserable life. You are the reason I shall die without a family. But all I ask in return for this wretchedness is that you answer one question.'

'And I know what that is.'

'Are you so clever? What is the question, my little whore?'

She pushed back with her feet a little more and leaned forward.

'What it all basically comes down to,' she said. 'What every major decision, every career move, every stupid mistake made since the beginning of time comes down to. *L'amour*. You need to know whether it was real. Whether your role in the destruction of your national pride had an acceptable foundation. Was it really love we had?'

Neither spoke. Daeng looked up at the old man and wondered whether the last words she spoke on this earth would be true or false. She didn't really know. Could she have loved him despite their polarity? Could she have followed him to France and entertained him at weekends in their love cottage? Would her life have been happier? She stared up at him.

'Look at you,' she said. 'You are a hateful person. And, you're mad. You have to admit that. Do you think I wouldn't have recognized these faults back then? You fell so easily in love with me because nobody else had made the effort to love you before. My *amour* was the best, perhaps the only, love you'd ever had and you so desperately wanted it to be real that you closed your eyes to the illogic of it all. A daughter of the oppressed kneeling before the oppressor. Every minute spent with you was a minute in hell. I detested you and your kind. No, my captain. I never–'

The metal bar rose and fell in a split second. It came crashing down with a sickening crack. Blood gushed from the wound. It was a marvellous moment. Barnard smiled, gave a deep sigh that gurgled in his throat, dropped the metal bar and headed towards the jungle. It was all over.

Siri returned to their room in the administrator's building only to find his wife missing. He washed his hands in the attached bathroom and wondered what had become of the small mirror above the sink. He returned to the guest room. In Daeng's place on the bed was a notebook. He sat and turned up the bedside oil lamp. He flipped to the last page of writing and there in large print were the words *THE END*. He smiled. Madame Daeng, once given a challenge, was not one to back down. She had set about documenting her life with relish. She had included chapters that would most certainly never clear the censors at the Ministry of Information, but would take Hollywood by storm. She'd asked him from time to time whether this or that passage was appropriate. He'd told her that suitability was irrelevant. This was a life and a life was not to be reworked. In many ways, the book that he held in his hands was worth every bit as much as his lost library because this one had a pulse. It had been marvellous to read the wisdom of the philosophers but what purpose did they have with no warm body to apply their theories to? This book was Daeng. He knew he would read it time and time again with as much joy as he had derived from Sartre and Camus.

He glanced at the final paragraph above *THE END* and read her hurried note there.

I feel his presence. He is here to kill me and he has arrived with a lifetime of hatred as his weapon.

Until that moment, Siri had felt secure in his decision to bring Madame Daeng to Pak Lai. But something in those words sent a chill across his shoulder blades. The words 'The End' suddenly took on a more ominous note. He left the room and ran across the lawn to the guest house with Ugly at his heels. He climbed the outside staircase to his old room and looked around. The space was crowded with partygoers but neither Civilai nor Daeng was there. He went back down a floor and banged on Mr Geung's door. The guest house had no locks but something was wedged against the door handle from the inside.

'I . . . I . . . I've gotta gun,' came Geung's voice from inside.

'Geung,' called Siri. 'It's me.'

Mr Geung freed the door.

'Have you seen Madame Daeng?' Siri asked.

Geung turned the colour of a Mekhong sunset. He stepped back.

'You can ... can ... can search,' he said.

'It's not an accusation, Geung. Just a question. Have you seen Madame Daeng?'

'Come in and look,' said Geung.

There was no time to repair Geung's feelings this time. Something had happened to his wife. Of that he was certain. Siri hurried back down the stairs and walked double time around the guest house. Ugly fell in beside him with the same urgency. A full moon was rising gently beyond the river. It picked out the smiling faces of the boat crews walking aimlessly, just as they had rowed. Siri and the dog completed a circuit of the guest house grounds and were met by Mr Geung who had put his trousers on back to front in his hurry to follow the doctor.

'Comrade Civilai is at the te ... mmmple,' he said.

'Of course, that's where Daeng will be,' said Siri.

Siri's lungs no longer filled completely and he had to stop several times on his way to the temple. But he felt that every missed second was condemning his wife to some unavoidable disaster. The last night of the races had produced a desperate surge of fun before normal life resumed the following day. Siri, Geung and Ugly waded through the thick crowd, blocked here and there by villagers who'd stopped to look at the sideshows or try their hands at throwing hoops and shying at coconuts. Siri could no longer hear the music nor sense the gaiety. It wasn't a vast temple, but one complete circuit took fifteen minutes. At the end of it he sat on the stupa steps, his chest wheezing, his eyes red with tears.

'Where is she, Geung?' he asked. 'What's he done with her?'

Mr Geung sat on the step beside the doctor.

'Com ... Comrade Daeng won't come to a party without her doctor,' he said.

'You're right,' Siri agreed. 'This would be too much for her. She'd look for somewhere quiet. Somewhere she could ...'

Siri got to his feet and stumbled down the old stone steps.

'I know,' he said as they exited the temple grounds. 'I know where she'll be.'

He stole one of the lighted torches that stood beside the gate and broke into a trot across the green, back in the direction from which he'd first come. He ignored the pain in his old lungs. There was a buzz now that ran through his nerves. This was more than concern. This was fear. His body was on alert. He ran along the side of the French residence building and into the garden at the rear. He could see the wooden swing by the grey light of the moon. It still rocked slightly as if caught in a strong breeze, of which there was none. Ugly reached it first but braked suddenly as if he'd run into a wall. His ears tucked back. His tail drooped. He turned and slouched behind Dr Siri. The moon passed behind a cloud and the only light now came from Siri's torch.

'Oh, no,' he said. 'No, please.'

He held the torch forward and approached the swing. At night, lit by fire, blood tended to stand out like oil. The swing and its supports and the sand beneath it were as black as charcoal. As black as murder. There were shards of broken glass all around. Siri couldn't find enough oxygen to fill his chest. He felt faint. He knew someone had died in this place not a few minutes before. At any second he expected the spirit of his wife to come to him, caress his cheek before heading to the waiting room. Perhaps she would speak to him. He was empty of hope.

Ugly, whose sense of smell was deficient in many ways, had picked up a scent. He stood at the point where the lawned garden abutted the jungle and he barked. It was the first time Siri had heard him do so. The doctor had no strength to follow him. No will.

'Geung, go and look,' he said.

Without questioning, Mr Geung took the torch from the doctor and followed the dog into the bushes. Siri lowered himself to the ground where he sat cross-legged, eyes closed, searching desperately through the lost souls for one he might recognize. He could not continue in the world without Daeng. She had become everything to him. She was his *raison d'être*.

'Com . . . Comrade Doctor,' came Geung's voice. 'Not dead yet.'

Siri was across in a blur. He ignored the branches that thrashed at his face as he made his way to the flame.

'Still alive,' he thought. 'A chance. A pinch of hope. I can save—'

But just then a cold damp wind blew into him. It was like a wet raincoat wrapping itself around him in search of a warm body. He recognized it as a brand new spirit, lost, as they usually were. Disoriented. If it was Daeng he didn't want to remember her like this, because in a second it was gone and he was left with nothing more than a shudder.

He trudged the last few metres to where the body lay and the cloud pulled back for the moon to illuminate the scene like the opening of a theatre curtain. He sighed and looked down at the body. It was . . . wrong. Gory but wonderful. It was a long body. Siri's heart clanged inside him like a pachinko ball. One rarely used the word tall when describing a man face down. The intestines trailed away from the body like the string of a downed kite. They seemed endless. One might have imagined him out here in the jungle attempting to gather together his wayward insides. The doctor had never been so delighted to see a dead body. Not even the corpses of his enemy on the battlefield had given him any joy. He wanted to fall to his knees and kiss both cheeks but first he had to see the victim. With Geung's assistance he knelt beside the body and flipped him on to his back. He was surprisingly light, padded with several layers of clothing for the appearance of bulk. In reality he was little more than a skeleton. His face was white. Above his right eye was the starred scar of early smallpox.

It was a knife wound. The blade had sliced through four layers of cloth before slitting a neat gash across his stomach. It was a classic hara-kiri insert. Across and up. You would live to see your stomach spill out, perhaps even walk away with your insides cradled in your arms. But the loss of blood would defeat you soon enough. It was the expertise of a professional assassin and he only knew one. The souvenir that Madame Daeng had taken from Frenchy's Elbow had not been a Buddha image. Of course not. She had returned for the Vietnamese man's knife. The rock she'd coveted at the dock had been used to sharpen it to a razor's edge. She'd known even then that her killer would come for her this night. But had she survived the battle? There had been a vast amount of blood at the murder scene. Was it too much for one person? Was she now lying wounded somewhere in this thick jungle? Once more, Geung's logic overcame Siri's fears.

'When I worked in . . . in . . . in . . . the red tag bbbag room,' he said, 'the first thing I did after ehhhvery load was I washed off the blood.'

'The river,' said Siri.

They headed in the direction of the slow-moving Mekhong. The moon had turned the night into a grey afternoon. Everything was clear. The revellers had abandoned the riverside and gone to the temple to listen to the closing concert. Geung and Siri stood on the bank. They could hear first the generator roar, then the microphone screech, then the singer miss three notes on her way into a popular Thai song before being belatedly joined by a guitar.

'See anything?' asked Siri.

Geung and Ugly scanned the surface of the river. There was nobody.

'Daeng!' Siri shouted. 'Daeng!'

He noticed that Ugly was focused on something upriver. The dog's tail signalled that it wasn't an unpleasant sighting. They heard a cheer from the drinkers on the guest house balcony. And there, some fifty metres away, was a tractor inner-tube rotating slowly as it followed the river. And at its centre was a grinning Madame Daeng. She waved as she passed them on the current. Mr Geung blushed and looked away because, by the light of the full moon, he had clearly seen Comrade Madame Daeng's naked breasts.

15

The French Letter That Leaked

'No, I mean, not the result,' said Civilai. 'I saw the result. In fact I helped scoop the result into a plastic bag. What I'm after is the details. Exactly how did you avoid getting brained?'

The ferry was twenty minutes from Vientiane. Civilai had been hounding Madame Daeng the whole journey. They sat on their deckchairs with the last of the beers they'd confiscated as evidence from Governor Siri's supply.

'You might as well tell him,' said Dr Siri. 'You know he'll never let up.'

'I really don't like to dwell over things like that,' said Daeng.

'Not dwelling, Daeng,' said Civilai. 'Debriefing is what it is. A necessary military tactic to bring a conflict to a satisfactory end. Look, I promise this is the last time. When next you slice somebody open with a fish knife, I swear I won't even ask.'

'I want to . . . to know too,' said Mr Geung.

'Oh, very well.'

'Excellent,' said Civilai.

He left his chair and sat at her feet like a handmaiden.

'First of all, how did you know he was there?' he asked.

'They were all talking about him,' said Daeng. 'I heard them as we walked back to the administration building. Only a few people had actually seen him but word spread like foot rot. They called him "the tall Soviet". Russians are the only Westerners they've seen here for the past three years so that was their guess. But I didn't see any foreigners at the races or at the festivities and there was precious little point in being in Pak Lai if he didn't want to enjoy the party. So I knew it was my Frenchman.'

'Marvellous,' said Civilai. 'And how did you gut him?'

Siri laughed.

'Be subtle, why don't you, brother?'

'I was on the swing,' said Daeng. 'I had our bathroom mirror tied to the swinging post in case he might come at me from behind. It was broken later. But I had a feeling he'd want to talk. When he first arrived in front of me I was leaning forward. My head was a clear target. I let him digest that fact. As we spoke I walked the swing backwards. The headrest was a few centimetres above the seat. With every step backwards I was reducing the angle of his first stroke. He didn't notice because I continued to lean forward. A clear target. Of course he could have hit me from the side and then it would have been all over. But you men tend to cosh vertically. It's a fallback to your days in the caves with your wooden clubs.'

'Fascinating,' said Siri. 'And they run courses on this at the Women's Union?'

'Observation, my husband,' said Daeng. 'And the predictability of the male.'

'Continue, my teacher,' Civilai urged.

'He could have finished me a lot quicker with a gun,' said Daeng. 'But the fact that he'd brought a chunk of iron told me he wanted that personal touch. And I was certain after all those years of bottled-up hatred he'd want to tell me what a cow I'd been. He'd betrayed his country because of a tryst with me and he hadn't been able to tell anyone. This was his confessional. I was sure he'd want to stretch it out.'

'Meanwhile, back at the disembowelling?' said Civilai.

'I had to be ready, Civilai. Ready for that split second when he decided there was nothing more to be said. And I had to be the one who pushed that button. I had to rile him enough to force his hand. But I needed to be ready for it. A younger man's reflexes would have beaten me. But I saw Barnard's shoulders dip before the bar rose and I pushed back on the swing with all my might. He was a tall man with long arms so the bar was coming at me in a wide arc. I leaned back. The metal crashed into the seat rest above my head. Smashed the wood. He was off balance but he brought the bar up for a second blow. That was my moment. I had the fish knife in the fold of my *phasin*. I'd honed it to a razor's edge. I didn't have the leeway for the blade to be blocked by his clothing. It passed through him as if he were butter. A thrust. A twist. A swipe. A spray of blood. It was over. I expected him to fall at my feet but he dropped the bar and stood there. It was an eerie moment. He had that look on his face. One I'd seen many times before. Amazement that the Lao could be trained to do anything right. Then he walked away. He didn't stagger, which surprised me. He walked upright, quite naturally, into the jungle with his hand on his stomach. I knew he would soon die there.

'I was covered in his blood but once the adrenalin wore off I couldn't get my legs to walk or my hands to stop shaking. I was crying, of course. I felt nothing in my heart but tears came to my eyes every time I killed a man. I never learned how to stop them. I'm not heartless, you see. Some subconscious part of me wanted to grieve for all the victims. When, at last, I had my limbs under control, I took the knife to the river and threw it as far as I could. I stripped off my bloody clothes and I bathed. That combination, naked and victorious, was just too seductive. The celebrants had left inner tubes and paddles on the bank so I went upstream on one. I felt I could paddle all the way to China. I went until I really had no more breath in me and that was when the calm draped itself around me. I threw away the paddle just as the moonlight illuminated the river. I lay back on the tube and let old Mother Khong take me where she wanted.'

Mr Geung was looking away.

'You. You must not. Not . . .' he began.

'Be stark naked in public?' Daeng asked.

'Yes.'

'I probably won't do it again,' she said. 'It was a one-off.'

'Well, I'm sorry I missed it,' said Civilai. 'I was embroiled in a serious game of rummy with the abbot. If I'd known . . .'

Siri leaned across and flicked his friend's lobeless left ear with his finger.

'Ouch,' said Civilai. 'So tell me. I consider myself something of an authority on the region, but I fail to see what difference the London document made to events in Dien Bien Phu?'

'As long as there was a possibility of Allied airstrikes,' said Daeng, 'the Viet Minh was reluctant to place field guns in strategic positions for fear they'd be wiped out by an air attack. With that threat in mind, the Vietnamese had to keep their objectives modest; just to hold the French. It would have been a long campaign with a lot of casualties on both sides, but with no resolution. But once they knew there would be no additional support, that the French had to go it alone, it gave the Viet Minh the green light to go on the attack. They went all out for victory. The leaking of that document lost the French their war.'

16

The Phasing Away Party

Nurse Dtui had an hour before her Intermediate Russian class. An hour seemed barely enough time to thank someone for two lives. Barely enough time to explain how everything from that moment in the morgue had been a gift. How long would it take to say that every second until those two lives met a more natural end would be dedicated to that good Samaritan?

But what a revelation it had been. Not until her conversation with Dr Siri the previous evening had the possibility crossed her mind. Of all the men in Vientiane, he would have been the least likely. She'd never heard him speak and, although Inspector Phosy and the others claimed to have heard him utter a few words on one occasion, she doubted he had the ability to conduct a conversation. But Dr Siri was adamant. On the day he deposited Ugly the dog at the Happy Dine Restaurant, he'd taken Crazy Rajid to one side and entrusted him with a task. The Indian was a young man who spent his life wandering the streets of Vientiane. He walked endless circles around the Nam Poo fountain and slept beneath the stars.

Siri had told him, 'If you see a tall Westerner, an old man with a star over his right eye – don't let him out of your sight. Don't let him see you but don't lose him. He's up to no good and you could be the only person around to stop him doing harm.'

When he had spoken those words, the doctor hadn't been certain the young man had heard him. Nor had he realized how true the prophesy would be. At some point, Crazy Rajid had found the Frenchman, probably too late to prevent the fire. He'd followed him to the morgue. He'd heard the threat and he had acted. The young man was no mute. His was a psychological silence caused by a family disaster. Inside his troubled head was a poet, a linguist, a mathematician, and a hero. The gun? Perhaps a result of his fascination with fireworks. A Chinese cracker or two? Again, who would know? But Siri had been certain of one thing. It was Crazy Rajid who'd saved the lives of Dtui and her daughter.

The nurse parked her bicycle in front of the Happy Dine Indian Restaurant and removed Malee from the sizeable shopping basket. The restaurant owner was gushingly polite until he realized she wasn't there to eat. But the restaurant was empty so he had no excuse not to point her to the kitchen. Mr Bhiku, large and shirtless, sat on an upturned bucket reading an ancient copy of *Bangkok World*. When he saw Dtui he dropped the paper and crumpled into a deep *nop*. He was a man who considered himself to be every other man's inferior. Dtui returned the *nop* and pulled the old chef to his feet. Malee reached out to him and he wrapped his dark fat fingers around her light, tiny ones. His smile lit up her face.

'Hello, Mr B,' said Dtui. 'I'm looking for Jogendranath.' Crazy Rajid's actual name.

'Oh, goodness. What has he done now?' asked Mr Bhiku.

'Well, I believe he might have saved the life of me and my daughter here.'

Mr B's face gave off a glow like a two-bar electric heater.

'If that is so, I would be most delighted,' he said. 'Most delighted indeed.'

'Have you seen him lately?' she asked.

'Sadly, not for four days. He was given to sleeping here in my open-air kitchen but I have seen neither hide nor hair of him since Sunday.'

Crazy Rajid's walkabouts were legendary so this was not a matter of concern to either of them.

'When he gets back, could you tell him that Malee and I would really like to see him.'

'I most certainly will,' he said. 'And how is your handsome and hardworking police husband?'

'He's fine. He's off training the untrainable in the north-east. Should be back in a day or two.'

'Give him my regards.'

*

It wasn't until she was almost back at the nursing school that a thought entered Dtui's head. One that she couldn't shake away. Nobody had seen Crazy Rajid since Sunday. Sunday was probably the day that Hervé Barnard had crossed into Thailand in order to enter Sanyaburi from the rear.

Could Rajid really have followed the Frenchman across the border? And if so, what chance of survival would a mentally disturbed Indian have on the Thai side?

Siri and Daeng were actually living in Siri's allotted house at That Luang. Daeng's restaurant was a shell but it was a tough shell and somehow the block had held up. There was no roof, of course, and they had no money to begin refurbishing, but there was promise. Of Siri's splendid library there was no trace. In Phnom Penh, he had shed tears at the sight of all the tomes from the national library ruined by rain and smoke. But that had been a premeditated act by the Khmer Rouge. The books had been the enemy. His own library was an innocent bystander shot with a stray bullet. It wasn't the same. His books died loved. There would be more.

The house refugees had started to filter back. Pao and Lia were already in their room. Comrade Noo, the Thai forest monk, had reclaimed his wooden cot on the back balcony. With the position of Head of Housing Allocation currently unfilled, and the file of Dr Siri temporarily sequestered by the police investing Comrade Koomki's death, there was every hope that the Siri residence would soon dance to the tune of companionship once again. But, this night, it was just Siri and Daeng sitting alone on the front step.

'So?' said Daeng.

'So what?' said Siri.

'Why haven't you said anything about my book?'

'I said it was good.'

'You said it was good that I'd finished it. I'm still waiting for the review.'

Siri looked at the stars that dotted the tarpaulin of night above his head.

'It's history, Daeng. A personal historical document. I'm not about to make fun of your spelling and grammar.'

'I don't want you to. I want to . . . to know how it made you feel.'

'As in . . . ?'

'As in . . . Damn it, Siri. I've confessed to . . . to using intimacy to extract information. I've slept with men I didn't love. Men I hated.'

'A lot of women sleep with men they hate. But they're usually related.'

'Siri!'

'What?'

'How can you be . . . be near somebody like me after you've read all that?'

'You know? I've been thinking about it.'

'And?'

'Did you always hate it?'

'What?'

'Was it always really awful or did the thrill become a drug?'

Daeng lowered her face from the freckled night sky and stared at her husband.

'Siri . . .'

'You're a passionate woman, Daeng. My goodness, do I know that. Once you realized you held that weapon, and that you could use it on any one of those *faux empereurs* and destroy them any time you liked, that's an awful lot of power to hold in your gut. Oh, you must have been full of that power. Bursting. I wouldn't be surprised if the adrenalin channelled itself right to your pleasure nodes.'

'I didn't . . .'

'And, as a result of that, I wonder if in subsequent years you didn't sit on your noodle stool after the lunchtime rush and start to feel guilty about it all. Not the lies. Not the subterfuge. Not even the killing. That was all unavoidable. But the fact that you enjoyed it. The fact that there were times you took pleasure from those men. That your work had given you an excuse to break out of your culture and be promiscuous. There was even something about the awful times that made you happy, because you could always see the final scene played out in front of you. You knew your victims would suffer one way or another. And, Daeng, I tell you, if the French army had been all female, I would have been at the front of the queue of volunteers.'

She laughed.

'I doubt you would have been recruited,' she smiled.

He leaned away from her.

'Madam, are you casting aspersions as to my prowess on the mattress?'

'Not at all. You're a veritable gymnast. But women like to look up at their men. French military Amazons would tower over you, my husband. You'd need stilts just to dance with them.'

'I'd win them over with my boyish charm. We're all the same height lying down, you know. And, no matter how ugly they were, I would engage them boldly for the nation.'

'Now you're making fun of me.'

'No I'm not. I'm just telling you I admire you for what you did. That, if roles had been reversed . . .'

'It's not the same.'

'Why not?'

'Because you're a man, and men are lauded in our society for the number of times their pestle hits the mortar. I'm a Lao woman. Do you honestly believe if that document were published, there wouldn't be an outcry about my morality? That mothers wouldn't tell their daughters, "If you continue with your loose ways you'll end up a Madame Daeng"?'

They were silent for a long time. They both knew she was right. He took her hand and massaged her palm with his thumb.

'So you wrote it for me,' said Siri.

'Of course.'

'Thank you.'

'You're welcome. Siri?'

'Yes?'

'What was so funny about my spelling and grammar?'

It was the night of Auntie Bpoo's Phasing Away party. Siri and Daeng had debated not going. It seemed . . . weird. Were it a wake, at least you'd know what to wear. Everybody had a white or black wardrobe for such occasions. But to arrive at a party knowing that the host-cum-hostess would be kicking the bucket sometime in the middle of it all, made you want to take your funeral clothing in a plastic bag and change when the time was ripe. But Siri was concerned that nobody would show up at all. That Auntie Bpoo would die alone and friendless – a lonely, wandering spirit for eternity. And so Siri and Daeng spruced themselves up and decided to make the best of it. And there was one more reason for attending. Inspector Phosy had been off in Vieng Xai since before their return and would have arrived back in Vientiane late that afternoon. They'd all bullied Nurse Dtui to drag him along. There were numerous questions about his investigation of Madame Peung that still had no answers.

Auntie Bpoo had told them to meet her at the Russian Club at six. The Russian Club was neither Russian, nor a club. It was one of the few surviving nightlife venues in Vientiane still standing on the bank of the Mekhong.

It was a large wooden restaurant whose only walls surrounded the kitchen. The rest was open to the elements. It held on to its licence and its profits by catering to the large Eastern European expat community. It had an endless supply of beer and other more expensive tipples such as vodka, leading one to believe that the owner had friends in high places. The restaurant was always full and it often stayed open after curfew. Siri had bemoaned the choice of venue.

'I doubt she'll even be able to book a table,' he'd told Daeng.

It was therefore not a total surprise when they arrived at the club fashionably late to be met by military guards in full uniform including holstered weapons. They were standing out front checking invitations. There were large placards in Russian and English apologizing to esteemed regular guests for the fact that the restaurant would be closed this evening as it had been booked for a private function.

'See? What did I tell you?' said Siri. 'That really stuffs up Auntie Bpoo's plans. I bet she didn't know about this. You'd think a fortune-teller would have predicted it.'

'Don't you be so hasty,' said Daeng. 'Who's that sitting over by the railing?'

Siri looked up to see a table of friends waving; Phosy, Dtui, Mr Geung and his fiancée Tukda, Civilai and his wife, Noy.

'How the hell did they get in?' Siri asked.

'I'd say this is Auntie Bpoo's party,' said Daeng.

'Don't be . . . How could she?'

Siri walked up the steps where he found a large hand on his chest. He looked up into the face of a middle-aged man in uniform.

'Invitation,' said the soldier.

Daeng followed demurely behind her husband.

'Take your hand off my chest, son,' said Siri. 'Do you honestly believe I'd be here without an invitation?'

'No. But if I don't see it, I don't believe it,' said the military bouncer.

'You obviously don't know who I am,' said Siri.

'You're Dr Siri,' said the soldier. 'You took a chunk of shrapnel out of my knee once.'

'Well then.'

'No invitation, no entry. Sorry.'

'If I ran past you, do you think you could catch me?'

'Yes.'

'Then the operation was a success.'

'Yes.'

'Then?'

Madame Daeng laughed and produced her invitation from her sequinned soirée bag. The soldier looked at it and nodded for her to pass.

'Where's mine?' called Siri.

'You threw it in the bin, remember?' Daeng told him. 'Said it was ridiculous to take an invitation to a funeral.'

She walked to the top of the steps, turned around to see the sad sight of her husband behind the barrier, then relented. She returned to the guard and produced a second invitation.

'I rescued it,' she laughed.

The place was crowded. The tables were full and others stood around. In 1978 Laos, it was rarely necessary to raise one's voice. There were the late insect choruses and monsoons on tin roofs and thousand-amp speakers at large gatherings but being heard at social events had hardly been a problem before this. There was no music in the Russian Club that night but everyone was shouting. There was a selection of beverages on each table and an open bar for those who had nowhere to sit. There were spirits and, to Daeng's delight, red or white wine. They had asked a passing waitress whether she might open a bottle of Cabernet Sauvignon for them. She produced a beer bottle opener and left it on the table for them. Fortunately, Civilai remembered that his Swiss Army knife had a corkscrew attachment.

'What on earth is going on here?' Siri asked.

'Auntie Bpoo's last stand,' shouted Civilai.

'Has anyone actually seen the party girl yet?' Daeng asked.

'Not a sign,' they shouted.

'I don't understand it,' said Inspector Phosy. 'She's a street fortune-teller. She reads the cards at five hundred *kip* a pot. Where did the money come from for all this?'

'She obviously has other resources,' said Dtui.

Daeng stood up.

'Look,' she shouted. 'How about we wander down to the river's edge with our respective bottles so we can actually hear ourselves speak?'

'We . . . we might lose our table,' said Geung.

'Look at us,' said Civilai. 'Do you think anyone would dare take the table of such a scary group?'

Mr Geung laughed and they upped and followed the narrow dirt path to the water. There was a concrete foundation down there for what was once a boat landing. It made a perfect seat.

'That's better,' said Civilai. 'Who are all those people up there?'

'It would appear Bpoo has more friends than we thought,' said Daeng. 'And it's invitation only so they aren't all freeloaders.'

'And who would have expected all this anyway?' said Dtui.

'All right,' said Siri. 'While we have a few minutes of quiet, let's listen to what Phosy has to say about his investigation of the Vietnamese and Madame Peung. We've all been on the edge of our seats these past few days.'

In fact, the only person even vaguely likely to fall off his seat had been Siri. It had been a difficult few days for him. He'd done everything Madame Peung had suggested: the breathing exercises, the yoga, the cat's whisker grass tea. He'd been patient with the spirits he saw. He'd tried not to judge. Not to tell them to their faces that they were scientifically impossible. As the witch had told him time and time again, he had to be an empty house with a sign out front saying *VACANCY* in large letters. He'd done just that but nobody had knocked on his door. He'd constructed no end of mental devices to lure them inside. He'd even strewn mental nails across the road out front so that souls passing on motorcycles might have a flat tyre and come in to use the telephone. Nothing had worked. But most frustrating was the fact that the used-to-be woman had not made an appearance. He was beginning to have doubts, and Phosy's findings would help a great deal to maintain his faith.

Phosy had brought along his notebook but he rarely referred to it. He took a sip of his whisky and coughed.

'Madame Peung,' he began, and coughed again, 'was everything we'd heard about her. The wife of a general who got rich by diverting United States funding to his own projects. She was wiser than her husband it seems because she could see the direction this country was headed. Without his knowledge she contacted the Pathet Lao and provided them with donations to fund their underground operations. As a widow, once the PL took over the country, she was on their list of wealthy sympathizers. She made numerous trips to Hanoi and was responsible for a number of profitable deals. Everything seemed to be running as regular as clockwork until this past July when she went missing for eighteen days. I patiently awaited my turn at our central post office and talked to the manager at the hotel she always stayed at in Vietnam. We have a Vietnamese translator at HQ.

'When she turned up after her mysterious disappearance, she'd told the manager that she had no idea where she'd been. She said she'd woken up in a small clinic somewhere and they told her she'd suffered a brain aneurysm and had been in a coma. The doctor had been very pleased with her recovery and released her. She paid her hotel bill in full and returned to Laos. That night, she was killed.'

'Sounds like just a little too much of a coincidence to me,' said Daeng.

'I talked to her live-in girl about that night,' said Phosy. 'She said that Madame Peung had arrived late that afternoon with a truck and a driver. The driver had his hat pulled down over his eyes. There was a crate on the back of the truck. The girl came out to help carry it but Madame Peung called to her from the passenger window and told her to go down to the village and bring ten litres of petrol for the truck. She didn't know why the truck driver couldn't go down there himself but she wasn't one to question orders. By the time she'd lugged the container back up the hill, the truck was gone. Either the crate went with it or it was in the widow's room, because the girl didn't see it again. The door to Madame Peung's room was shut and when the girl asked if she wanted dinner the old lady declined. But it appears that Madame Peung often went to sleep early after a long journey so the girl thought nothing more of it. She went to bed at about nine and, the next thing she knew, she was woken by a shot. She'd been in a deep sleep so she wasn't sure she hadn't dreamed it. But the second gunshot most certainly came from inside the house. She wasn't particularly fond of the job or the widow but she heard footsteps running away so she took a look at the widow's room. That's when she saw the body. She ran out the back door and hid in the bushes until she heard the villagers arrive.

'There were a couple of things she mentioned to the young officer but that he didn't consider important enough to add into his report. One was the fact that, when she came back to the house with the petrol, one of the piglets was gone. The sow had given birth three days before and had stopped giving the babies milk. The girl had been weaning them by hand. They were penned up so it couldn't just run off. She wondered whether a crow had snatched it. Then there was the fact that when she was hiding in the bushes she thought she'd heard a truck starting up down on the main road. Sound carries at night in the countryside and road transport is so rare you tend to notice. She admitted she didn't know if it was the engine of the truck Madame Peung had arrived in.'

'So, do we know who the driver was?' Civilai asked.

'Now I do, but that was a breakthrough that came as a result of the photographs of Tang and Madame Peung that you sent me, Madame Daeng,' said Phosy.

'You sent photos?' Siri asked.

'I thought it might help,' she smiled.

'I'd sent them to the Vietnamese Intelligence Unit with my request to speak to the Hanoi cops,' Phosy continued. 'When I received their official response, there had been no mention of the photographs. I assumed nobody had recognized them. But then I was cornered one night by a shadowy character who'd been watching too many spy movies.'

'Nothing wrong with that,' said Civilai.

'To cut a long story short, he had a gun and I beat him up.'

'My brave policeman husband,' said Dtui.

'I don't like guns,' he said. 'So I had this fellow at police HQ and he insisted on making a phone call to his Vietnamese buddies. I reminded him whose country he was in and how unlikely it was he'd ever see his homeland or his family again.'

'You bully,' said Civilai.

'He was an arrogant little runt,' said Phosy, by way of explanation. 'But once he believed I was out of control he became very chatty. It turned out that he was a minor official at the Vietnamese Intelligence Unit. They'd sent him to extract the location of the character in the photograph from me. They must have thought I'd see the gun and blurt out where he was. They had every reason not to do all this through official channels, you see. Although it took me a while to get the whole story out of him. Your widow's supposed brother, Tang, had been an agent at the Vietnamese Intelligence

Unit. A very senior agent, in fact, and, by all accounts, a genius. He went AWOL. Hadn't reported for duty for six months. Nobody knew where he was. His superiors were anxious to trace him. He'd been the head of Data Analysis. Name of Tang Cam. Before his disappearance he'd been working on French and American aerial photographs of the Mekhong River. But he had maximum security clearance to all the top secret files both in Vientiane and Hanoi.'

'I'm certain they'd have files on all of us tucked away in Hanoi,' said Civilai.

'Together with witness reports and family history and psychological examinations,' said Daeng. 'I was one of their agents towards the end. They'd know more about me than I do. And with the recent agreement they'd have a share of all the files on our side too. They'd know about the minister's background and his brother.'

'All the things Madame Peung plucked out of the air,' said Civilai.

'I . . . I have a fffile?' said Geung.

'You're technically a government worker, Geung,' said Civilai. 'They'd know everything about you.'

'That's . . . rude,' said Geung.

Siri had remained quiet throughout this exchange. He was a stubborn man but he never ignored the facts. And they were stacking up against Madame Peung.

'And the woman?' he asked.

'He wasn't so certain about her,' said Phosy. 'But some

of the operatives suggested there were similarities to a female officer who had once been Tang Cam's mistress. Her name was Nguyen Hong Be. Vietnamese father; Lao mother. She had retired from the propaganda division after reaching the rank of colonel. But she'd spent most of her career directing entertainments for troops. They staged dramas for the villagers. She was–'

'An actress,' said Siri.

Madame Daeng squeezed his hand.

'A very competent one too,' said Phosy. 'If things had been different she might have become famous. But the wars and . . .'

'No, wait,' said Civilai. 'This is ridiculous. They find a Lao businesswoman and he gets this actress to impersonate her? Who's going to be stupid enough to fall for that?'

'No. I think it was the other way round,' said Phosy. 'Tang Cam had the actress already. All they had to do was wait until a Lao of similar appearance turned up. She didn't have to be rich at all, or a businesswoman. A government official would have worked just as well. A visitor. A maid. Anyone single or widowed. Tang Cam would have access to the files to know who was unattached. Who lived in a remote area. All the spirit mumbo-jumbo would play into the hands of we ignorant Lao country folk.'

'Am I the only one who doesn't see the point of all this?' said Nurse Dtui.

'It's complicated,' Phosy told her.

'Could I try to explain it?' asked Daeng.

'Be my guest.'

'This is how I see it,' she began. 'A senior official at the Vietnamese Intelligence Unit with an interest in Lao history hears the legend of the French pillaging the treasure from the Royal Palace in 1910. He has an ancient mandarin concept of what treasure is: riches beyond dreams. He studies the French and American aerial photographs of the Mekhong and he sees it: the shape of the gunship that went down. With instruments he can measure it categorically to prove that it can only be that boat. There he is, a senior clerk earning twenty dollars a month and he knows his future would be assured by salvaging that vessel. But how? There are no Vietnamese projects in Sanyaburi. He doesn't have clearance to travel in Laos. But he is a clever man and he comes up with a complicated but brilliant plan. He contacts his old lover who's living in a dingy one-bedroom retiree's apartment in Hanoi and together they hatch a plan. If it all works out they won't need to recruit any other people. All the work will be done for them.'

Ugly growled and licked his balls.

They all laughed.

Daeng continued.

'Somehow, they drug and kidnap Madame Peung and set up a hospital room to keep her in,' Daeng continued. 'She believes she's had an aneurysm. Tang Cam is her doctor, Hong Be, her nurse. I would imagine they used a combination of drugs and hypnosis to learn about her village and the people who lived there – a way to recognize them. Under hypnosis it's difficult to extract secrets but remarkably easy to draw out gossip and anecdotes. They would have kept her half-in, half-out of consciousness, Colonel Hong Be, her best friend, joking with her, learning her mannerisms and speech patterns.'

'Does any of this have a factual base?' Civilai asked.

'None,' said Phosy, 'but circumstantially I'd say we're heading in the right direction. We found the booking on Lao Aviation. Madame Peung was in a seat beside someone called Nguyen Be, a Vietnamese nursing sister whose paperwork said she was headed to hospital forty-nine. They'd never heard of her.'

'Then, lead on, madam,' said Civilai.

'I wouldn't be surprised if one other seat on that flight was occupied by our friend Tang Cam,' said Daeng. 'The Vietnamese secret service produce their own passports.'

'I'm seeing the how,' said Dtui, 'but I'm still missing the why.'

'The why is that the Vietnamese secret service knew all about the Minister of Agriculture and his relationship with his nutty wife,' said Daeng. 'The upper class Vietnamese community in Laos is very close. They would have known she was concerned about her brother-in-law and was looking for a medium. If they could convince her that the brother was in a boat, submerged in the Mekhong, he would have the resources to dig it out. And because it was a spiritual matter, he wouldn't have told too many people. But they had to establish Madame Peung's reputation in a hurry. News of a reincarnation would spread like a forest fire. The fact that the widow had been reborn with the gift of finding the dead was exactly what the minister's wife was looking for.

'And with all that success, the minister's wife hears of the witch in Ban Elee and seeks her out,' said Daeng. 'And the actress uses the knowledge accumulated by Tang Cam to convince her to dig up the river. She was a very convincing liar.'

She looked into her husband's green eyes.

'So how . . . how did they achieve this miracle?' Siri asked.

'Well, from the fragmented parts, I've put together a scenario. If I'm correct the whole thing was a remarkable example of sleight of hand. You see? Madame Peung was already dead when she arrived back in the village. Her body was in the trunk on the back of the truck. The driver, Tang Cam, had been forced to stop at a checkpoint on the outskirts of Vientiane. The officer there noted it down in his ledger. It appears it's easier to travel in this country if you're dead. I have no idea when they killed the poor woman. She was listed under cargo. Hong Be used Madame Peung's laissez-passer. Tang Cam must have used whatever ID was in the truck they stole and played mute.

'While the maid was in the village getting the petrol, the Vietnamese set up the killing in the widow's room using blood from one of the piglets. Hong Be waited in the room and Tang drove the truck down and parked it in the forest off the main road. When it was dark he came back. The first of the two shots was not into the widow's head but into the veranda post outside. I saw gunpowder burns on the wood which indicated that it was fired at point-blank range. That first shot would have woken the live-in girl. If she'd come to investigate straight away she would have caught Tang Cam firing the second shot into Madame Peung's head. But it didn't matter that she took her time. Tang and Hong Be had fled to the truck by the time the villagers came to investigate.

'I'm guessing that Tang Cam and Hong Be camped rough in the truck for three days to let the natural process of the cremation and the investigation run its course. When the widow was good and burned, Madame Peung, aka Madame Keui, aka Hong Be, made her astounding reappearance. This was where the acting experience kicked in. She had the mannerisms and the voice down. The right make-up and a knowledge of everyone in the village. Who would ever doubt that this was Madame Peung reincarnated?

'The second shooting had already been set up. One of the languages Tang Cam spoke was Hmong. His Lao wasn't fluent but it was easy enough to convince the villagers he was an addict from one of the district's

Hmong communities. He did the crazed assassin thing in front of the villagers and ran up to the house to have a second shot at the widow. Once the villagers had built up the courage to follow, he dragged Hong Be out to the veranda, and pretended to fire at her head. The gun he used wasn't loaded and the bullet was already embedded in the post. He knew he couldn't use a blank because at point-blank range the wadding would be as lethal as a real bullet. So, he had two weapons. The sound they all heard was Tang Cam firing a second gun into the porch steps unseen from behind his legs.'

'What about the wound?' Dtui asked.

'There would have been some paint or something on the barrel of the unloaded gun to leave the trace of a wound when it was pulled away. That pretty much convinced everyone that Madame Peung had joined the ranks of the living dead. Evidence and twenty witnesses. The live-in girl had run off and nobody was bold enough to visit the house, leaving Tang Cam free to move in. Word spread and the visitors started appearing. I located some of the families who went to consult with Madame Peung,' said Phosy. 'There's a police registry of people who have reported family members missing in action. By working down that list it wasn't long before I came across families who had contacted Madam Peung. They had all received anonymous notes telling them the story of the medium in Ban Elee and that she had been visited by their deceased relatives. She knew where the bodies were buried. In fact these were ex-servicemen whose remains had been discovered by local headmen in remote provinces. The details were on a government list that had not yet been released to the relatives. The VIU would have had access to that list. Madame Peung directed the relatives to the grave sites just as she directed the minister to his brother.'

'And, the engineers being Vietnamese . . . ?' Siri asked.

'I asked my new friend from Vietnamese Intelligence,' said Phosy. 'That unit had orders to be in Vientiane. Nobody seemed to know the origin of those orders. So it looks like Tang Cam had worked some more magic there too. The VIU had the power to relocate Vietnamese personnel. When the minister returned to the city he was looking for a unit of army engineers. It just so happened that this group was sitting around doing nothing. So they were immediately dispatched west. No time was lost at all.'

'My word,' said Civilai. 'Incredible. And it worked.'

'It would have if he hadn't been so blindly led by his lust for wealth,' said Daeng. 'What kind of a man can convince his mistress to join in such a venture then toss her off the back of a boat without any conscience? She'd served her purpose and he didn't need her to share in the spoils. Two dead women and nothing to show for it. With a mind like that he could have done some good in the world. Brilliance is wasted on men.'

Nobody disagreed. They hated the pair for killing the old widow but, deep down, there wasn't one of them who didn't have a touch of admiration for them. It was an incredible achievement that so nearly paid off. Tang Cam could hardly have figured the malevolent spirits into his plans. It was something they didn't teach at spy school.

A loud cheer echoed down from the Russian Club. It could only mean one thing. Siri and his friends scurried back up the bank and entered the restaurant from the rear. A few dozen people were sitting at their table but it didn't take much to shoo them off. Siri played the 'Don't you know who I am?' card. More full bottles had appeared at its centre since their departure, along with various food plates. The Russian Club always did a remarkable job of turning empty markets into tasty food. But there was some commotion near the kitchen and none of the other guests seemed in the mood to eat. As they couldn't see over the sea of heads, Siri and his team sat and tucked into the food. It was a feast that wouldn't have been out of place in a good hotel in Bangkok. They were on the third course when the noisy commotion finally reached their table.

Auntie Bpoo burst from the crowd like a brassy lion through a paper-covered hoop. She wore a silver cocktail dress with a train, shoes that Imelda Marcus would have died for and a gold scarf that covered her bald head. Mr Geung stood for her. She caressed his cheek and dropped on to his seat. She looked around at the guests and sighed. Nobody knew what to say.

'So, you all came, then,' said Bpoo.

'We're all naturally attracted to death,' said Siri by way of an ice-breaker. His relationship with the transvestite had never been that relaxed or natural. She'd saved his life perhaps but she hadn't made it easy to thank her.

'So, this is it,' said Dtui.

'Looks like it,' said Auntie Bpoo.

'I'll miss you,' said Dtui.

'We all wwwill,' said Geung.

'We all will,' said Tukda, who had taken to repeating her fiancé's words.

'What about you, Siri?' Bpoo asked. 'Will you miss me?'

'I'll miss beating my head against your front door,' said Siri.

'You don't know where I live,' she reminded him.

'I was speaking metaphorically.'

'Now, sweetheart. You know I'm too dense for metaphors.'

She called over a waitress and said something into her ear. The tones around them had become more hushed since Bpoo's arrival. It was possible to talk now without yelling. The waitress returned a few minutes later with a bottle of champagne and a dozen fresh glasses. Bpoo popped the cork and poured.

'Are you sure you should be drinking while you're transcending?' Civilai asked her.

'What can they do to me?' Bpoo laughed. 'Revoke my dying licence?'

'How long have you got?' Daeng asked.

Bpoo looked up at the large clock over the kitchen hatch.

'Half an hour,' she said.

'Are you afraid?' Dtui asked her.

'No more than I was about being born,' Bpoo replied. 'It's all part of the natural equation. Ashes to ashes. It's just that when you leave, you have some say in your wardrobe.'

'You know, I wouldn't be surprised if this was some elaborate hoax to confirm how popular you are,' said Siri.

'There,' said Bpoo.

She stood and raised her drink.

'That's the cynicism I've been waiting for,' she continued. 'Let's all drink to that. The elaborate hoax.'

They all downed their champagne. Even Geung and Tukda, who usually didn't, but thought, under these circumstances, they should.

'Ahh,' said Bpoo, smacking her lips. 'Seven thousand *kip* a bubble but worth every pop.'

'Did you win the Thai lottery?' Dtui asked.

'Yes,' Bpoo replied matter-of-factly. 'Three times, in fact. You'd be surprised how many trips I had to make to Udon Thani before I could find the winning tickets.'

They all glared at her.

'You really . . . ?' said Dtui.

'Of course,' said Bpoo. 'I see the future. How else do you think I could have funded all this debauchery? The

Thai lottery sellers have their tickets laid out so, if you have a little good luck, you can select the winning numbers. A platoon of uniformed soldiers doesn't come cheap, you know?'

'I thought you weren't allowed to use your gift for personal gain,' said Siri.

'I didn't,' Bpoo smiled. 'This is all for you lot. It's a thank you for not being cruel to me. You see gathered around you all the people I met in my life who treated me fairly – showed me some kindness. It wasn't a common occurrence, let me tell you. But I don't forget integrity. This is my present to them – to you.'

She walked around the table doing one unsteady pirouette as she went. It allowed everyone the first sight of the porthole at the back of her dress exactly the size of her naked buttocks. Mr Geung covered Tukda's eyes with a napkin as she passed. Nobody else appeared to be shocked. This was Auntie Bpoo who flashed habitually. Anything less would have been a disappointment. She stood behind Dr Siri and put her hands on his shoulders.

'And, for you, doctor,' she said. 'I have an even bigger surprise.'

'Why?' he asked. 'I've never been kind to you.'

'No. You never talked down to me, either. Never treated me like an idiot. Admittedly you were never that polite but you inadvertently showed kindness from time to time. And, to be honest, there's nobody else I can give this gift to. It wouldn't fit anybody else.'

'It's pyjamas,' guessed Mr Geung.

'It's pyjamas,' said Tukda.

'No, my little nincompoops, nothing like that,' said Bpoo. 'But, first things first. I have other people to toast. More champagne bubbles to inhale. So, goodbye my friends and good fortune. And here, at last. A poem.'

Siri groaned.

And we are dead
Fed to worms Underground
Then we're found
And we can speak
Not with groans
Our history revealed In our bones
Initially
Squishily
Doctors Never Appreciate

And, with that, she melted back into the crowd.

'Did that mean anything?' Civilai asked.

'Not to me,' said Phosy.

'Her poems never have meant anything,' said Siri. 'She just wants us all to go insane trying to work it out. Like this gift idea. She thinks I'll lose sleep over what it is she's going to give me. I'm used to her little tortures.'

They drank some more and picked at the food but they couldn't ignore the purpose of the evening, which had permeated their moods. They tried to have fun but

mind and was surfing for a channel. The screech made his teeth tremble. The talisman around his neck burned his skin. His missing earlobe tingled. Then, words filled his head.

'TESTING.

'ONE, TWO, ONE TWO.

'TESTING.'

'Bpoo? Is that you?' Siri asked, causing Daeng to look around.

'Well, that was much easier than I'd expected,' came Bpoo's voice as resonant in Siri's head as his own thoughts.

'Are you my . . . ?' he began.

'It's dusty in here.'

Unseen by the guests, a length of bamboo floated towards the bank. Its pilot – naked as the day he was born – smiled to be home. Crazy Rajid had returned.